LONDON UNDER MIDNIGHT

Recent Titles by Simon Clark

BLOOD CRAZY
HOTEL MIDNIGHT
THE NIGHT OF THE TRIFFIDS
VAMPYRRHIC
VAMPYRRHIC RITES

LONDON UNDER MIDNIGHT

Simon Clark

This first world edition published in Great Britain 2006 by
SEVERN HOUSE PUBLISHERS LTD of
9–15 High Street, Sutton, Surrey SM1 1DF.
This first world edition published in the USA 2006 by
SEVERN HOUSE PUBLISHERS INC of
595 Madison Avenue, New York, N.Y. 10022.

British Library Cataloguing in Publication Data

Clark, Simon
    London under midnight
    1.   Vampires - Fiction
    2.   Horror tales
    I.   Title
    823.9'14 [F]

    ISBN-13: 978-0-7278-6398-0 (cased)
    ISBN-10: 0-7278-6398-3   (cased)
    ISBN-13: 978-0-7278-9173-0 (paper)
    ISBN-10: 0-7278-9173-0   (paper)

All Severn House titles are printed on acid-free paper.

Typeset by Palimpsest Book Production Ltd.,
Polmont, Stirlingshire, Scotland.
Printed and bound in Great Britain by
MPG Books Ltd., Bodmin, Cornwall.

For Janet

First Blood

VAMPIRE SHARKZ
☺ They're coming to get you ☺

Just as spores drift in the atmosphere, the ones that are New-Life are carried from the mountains in fast-flowing rivers to infect the waterways of England. They advance through this myriad of arteries to reach deep into the heart of its capital city.

Here, the ancient Thames still runs its cold, dark waters between shining office blocks. Once, where there was barely any life in the river, little more than eels and rats, now there is New-Life. And it's to this place that New-Life brings the Gift . . .

'Madam! You have ten minutes to save your life. *Quickly!* How are you going to do it?'

The girl merely waved at him as she jogged along the riverside path in the direction of Tower Bridge, London's iconic landmark of lattice steelwork and Cornish granite.

'Don't stay out too long,' he called after her. 'The sun is setting!'

So far, Elmo 'Diogenes' Kigoma had spent ten days in the mock sailing boat on top of the pole. He asked the same question of everyone who passed by.

A pair of youths roller-bladed along the path.

'Gentlemen! You have ten minutes to save your life,' he told them. 'Quickly! How are you going to do it?'

'You daft bollocks!'

'Drop dead!'

Elmo had heard worse. 'I'll tell you how to save your lives. Abstain. *Abstain.*' He continued even though he knew they were out of earshot. 'Abstain. That, my friends, is the secret

1

to longevity. I came from the Congo when I was twenty. I'm now eighty-six years of age. Abstain, my friends.'

The sun slipped behind the city's horizon. After the fierce heat of the day it would soon drop cool enough to drive him into his sleeping bag in the little airborne vessel, one that could only be accessed by the rope ladder that he'd pulled up after himself. The council promised they would come back again in the morning to take down the boat, which he'd fixed up here on top of the pole in the dead of night. His two sons had helped him. Both were as embarrassed as hell to do what their father asked of them. But they're good sons, Elmo told himself. They are loyal. He always knew they'd help him on his final mission. One that would end tomorrow; if the Mayor of London got her way.

He peered in the direction of Tower Bridge that spanned the Thames. It was one of the quirks of the river that its currents nearly always deposited the bodies of those it claimed at the foot of one of its baroque towers that soared almost two hundred and forty feet above the water. The bridge even boasted its own morgue for the drowned. One of the party boats glided downstream. Strings of coloured lights blazed along its flanks and festooned the superstructure. He could hear music from a band. On deck, sleek men and women in beautiful clothes drank champagne.

Elmo shouted, 'You've got ten minutes to save your life. Quickly! How are you going to do it?'

From the boat he heard a PA announcement. The captain was pointing Elmo out – London's latest landmark: an old black man in a plywood dinghy fixed ten feet above the ground on top of a telegraph pole.

'Save your lives. Abstain!'

The floating revellers cheered, then toasted him with their effervescent wine.

'If you desire longevity – abstain.' He sighed, then said to himself, 'Oh, they can't hear you, Elmo.' Nevertheless, he still had faith. Taking a deep breath, he tried to reach out to them with his voice. 'People ask of me, "Elmo? Why sit in the boat?" I reply: "I sail in search of the new man and new woman who have the ears to listen to my words."'

Lights had appeared in the neighbouring hotels and apartment blocks by the time he'd finished calling out to the occu-

2

pants of the pleasure boat, although they'd long since lost interest in him.

'Maybe I should debate with the fish in the river and the birds in the air,' he told himself. 'Will they have a better understanding of my message?' He allowed his gaze to settle on the bank of the river where bushes swayed in the breeze. For a moment his sharp eyes regarded the movement of leaves without realizing what he was seeing.

Elmo stood up in the boat; it swayed a little on the pole. It was safe . . . even though the council claimed it wasn't. Elmo had built boats that had run rapids and navigated rivers full of crocodiles. So why should a boat that would never ever touch water be *un*safe? He angled his head to one side to identify what he saw.

'Don't be afraid.' He spoke gently. 'Child, come out where I can see you.'

He was certain he could see a young woman standing in the bushes, as if fearful of being seen. 'Please don't be afraid, child. I can't hurt you. Look, I'm up here in the air in my little sail boat.' The girl stayed in the bushes, though he could see the glint of her eyes. 'My name is Elmo Kigoma. I have a mission. I'm here to save these people's lives, but no one will listen. Sometimes they shout out bad names. Yesterday, a boy threw bottles at me. Look at that on my arm. I had to use my scarf as a bandage.' The old African preacher tilted his head to one side. 'Why is it you won't come out here and speak to me? If you're in trouble I might be able to help.'

The gloom deepened the shadows, yet he could still see the pair of eyes. They shone like twin splinters of glass. 'Are you hungry?' he asked. 'Alas, I don't have money. There are sandwiches. And cake. A lovely ginger cake my neighbour baked for me.' A pause. 'Child, are you hungry?'

From the direction of Tower Bridge, a cyclist casually pedalled his machine, while listening to music on headphones. He was oblivious to the world around him as day decayed into night. Elmo watched the girl as she stepped out of the bushes. The movements were rapid, almost feline. He glanced from the girl, who stared at the approaching cyclist, to the area around the riverbank. It was as deserted as a graveyard at midnight.

His heart thudded as he stood up in the plywood boat.

'You!' he cried at the girl. 'I know what you are. Edshu the trickster made you. You're a Dead-bone Woman! Is your hair sticky to the touch? Can you feel the beat of your heart? Or does it lie still in your breast? Do you know it yet, girl? Do you know the truth?' He witnessed the cyclist's lazy approach. Elmo yelled at him, 'Go back! Don't come any closer! She will hurt you!'

The man simply stared vacantly forward as he pedalled. Even from here Elmo could hear the music pounding through the man's headphones. Dear heaven, the man wouldn't hear the thunder of Armageddon above that.

'Hey!' Elmo screamed. 'Watch her!' Then he turned to the young woman. She was incredibly gaunt. Her fingernails were the same deathly blue as her lips and the rings beneath those feral eyes that blazed so hungrily at the man on the bike. Her jeans and T-shirt were nothing more than worn bands of fabric through which he could see her pallid skin.

With a panther-like grace she leapt on the man. For a moment he continued to pedal as he fought to maintain the balance of his machine. But the girl clung to his back. As he twisted round to look at his attacker Elmo saw that she clamped her mouth over the man's face. She chewed with such an expression of bliss that Elmo had to turn away.

The metallic crash of the bike falling on to the path forced the old preacher to look once again. The man lay on his back. His fists were clenched in agony by his side. The girl sat astride his chest. After she slammed her mouth on to his bulging eye the head of tousled hair twisted from side-to-side as yet again her jaws crunched shut, like a starving man would bite into a ripe, juice-filled apple.

Elmo gulped. He could hardly breathe. Yet he couldn't turn away. Even when she moved from her victim's face to another part of his body, Elmo couldn't close his eyes. The horror of what the creature did next would remain seared on Elmo Kigoma's heart until his dying day.

One

VAMPIRE SHARKZ
☺ They're coming to get you ☺

The graffiti spread across London that long, over-heated summer in a great, blazing rash. The big blood-red lettering was everywhere: bridges, walls, subways, statues, gravestones – you name it. This time, some joker had sprayed it in crimson along the aluminum flanks of the train that squealed to a stop in the tube station at Piccadilly Circus.

The subterranean station lay deep under the London streets. On this humid July night it made the atmosphere more stifling than a tropical nightclub. The comparison wasn't a wild one. The platform swarmed with men and women who'd already spent hours in the pounding clubs and pubs. On the hot midnight air, perfume and alcohol odours clashed amid the sound of laughter and party beasts singing the night away.

'Vampire Sharkz! Vampire Sharkz!' A drunk male dressed as a nun used both his fists to pound the VAMPIRE SHARKZ graffiti on the side of the train. 'Vampire Sharkz! They're coming for you!' His foot caught in his wimple and he staggered backward ranting, 'Vampire Sharkz! They're coming to get you!' The drunken man-nun whirled across the platform swinging a fist. Mascara smeared the man's face. His lip-glossed mouth was a vermilion slash.

Ben Ashton stepped in front of the girl to shield her with his own body until the man went windmilling away.

The girl smiled up at Ben; it was so warm it made the sultry air chill in comparison. 'Thank you,' she breathed. 'Nobody's ever saved me before.'

Ben smiled back. 'Don't mention it.'

The man-nun punched wildly into the air.

'Just who is he fighting anyway?' the girl asked.

'His own personal demons, if you ask me.'

'Ben.' Her expression took on a certain quality that made Ben Ashton's spine tingle. 'We don't have to go to the club. You could come home with me . . .' The shrug she gave with a bare shoulder managed to be both shy and suggestive at the same time. 'I like you.' The smile was like a flood of warm plasma in his veins. 'Do you want to?'

The surge of people for the train carried them into the carriage. A moment later they sat side-by-side. Ben had only met the girl a couple of hours ago. He'd been to collect a cheque from an editor who insisted on paying contributors in person, just so he could have that pleasure-thru-power buzz of watching them sign a contract that waived all their creative rights away. Later, Ben had wound up at a party at Soho House, the club for film industry young-bloods. It had been hotter than hell. He'd manoeuvred his way through the packed bodies to the only open window in the upstairs bar where a girl, with blonde hair cascading down her back, watched the clientele.

'Is this the coolest part of the room?' was Ben's best opening line, after he had endeavoured to make himself heard in this raucous hot-house of ambition. The beautiful woman conceded that it was. Then she invited him to share the breeze from the window. They hit it off like magic. Everything they discussed they agreed on. They loved the same food; the same music, and concurred that London was slowly going mad. Then he suggested a quieter club that he knew so they'd caught the tube even though it was only a couple of stops away.

Just a moment ago she'd made that tantalizing suggestion: *'You could come home with me.'*

As the train surged along the tunnel he said softly, 'I'd like that.' Then, as his mouth broadened into a grin, he added, 'A lot.'

'That's great.' Her eyes twinkled as she scrunched her bare shoulders with pleasure.

Ben said, 'What line do we need?'

'We'll stay on this one. We can get off at Holborn then get a taxi from there. It's not far.'

This was a theme-park ride of erotic proportions; that headlong rush downward where gravity takes hold. There's no going back. In his mind's eye he saw himself making love to

6

this beautiful blonde-haired goddess. He glanced down at her bare ankles. A gold chain glittered there. On her feet were sandals that displayed toe-nails that had been painted a vivid purple. She scrunched her shoulders again. Ben found it so sexy – a suggestion of shyness and, in the words of the song, sweet surrender.

Her eyes twinkled as she gazed into his face. 'I'm glad you said yes.' Her hand found his.

'I'm glad I said yes,' he replied with feeling.

Then she shared an intimate secret with him. 'You'll be able to watch me have sex.'

The train sounded loud again. Ben Ashton found he was noticing the clamour of revellers sat around him.

'Watch you?' he echoed.

'Yes.' Her face shone with excitement.

'Damn,' he groaned.

'What's the matter?'

'I've just remembered. I've got to work tonight.' He grimaced. 'Deadline tomorrow. I clean forgot.'

'Oh no. I was so looking forward to you being there tonight,' she told him. 'I can just picture you in my favourite costume.' She squeezed his hand even more tightly as if its pressure would be enough to change his mind.

'Sorry. I'll lose my contract if I'm late.'

'What is it you do again?'

'I'm a writer.' He slid forward on the seat, ready to stand as the train roared into the station.

'A writer! That's amazing. I've always wanted to do that.' Through the glass behind her, the graffiti sprayed there made it appear as if her blonde head was haloed by a blood-red mist. 'What do you write about?'

'Vampires.'

Before he knew it he was standing on the platform watching the train pull out, carrying the beautiful woman away. She waved to him but what he noticed most was the graffiti:

VAMPIRE SHARKZ
☺ They're coming to get you ☺

Two

From a wonderful night to crap had taken seconds. Ben Ashton now walked along the embankment. The night still burned hotter than a Bangkok knocking-shop. The chimes of Big Ben sounded a shimmering two across a town that seemed hell-bent on enjoying itself until the doomsday. Lights blazed from buildings. Taxis hurtled along the road to the right of him. To the left, the wide stretch of the River Thames was an expanse of liquid darkness. From this angle it didn't even reflect the lights on the opposite bank. It was as black as the pupil in the centre of your eye.

There were no other pedestrians nearby. Only a couple approaching arm-in-arm in the distance. Now was a great time to vent his frustration.

'If it wasn't for bad luck I wouldn't have any luck at all,' he fumed. 'I thought I'd struck gold . . . and what is it she wanted? Me, to watch her performance with her boyfriend . . . that's just . . . just bollocks . . .'

Ben paused to lean forward against the wall so he could look down into the river. The full tide had swollen it. Its surface now lay just a few feet below street-level so he could see his forlorn reflection gazing right back at him. 'And you know something else, Ben Ashton? You shouldn't be talking to yourself. You know what happens to people who do?'

His own reflection held his gaze. A broad face framed by unruly black hair. There I am, he told himself. A thirty-something writer that feels as if Christmas has just been cancelled. Stupid bugger . . . Now you're feeling sorry for yourself.

A shape floated by in the water. Even though it was the dead of night he could see enough in the street lights to identify it as a jacket, perhaps chucked into the river by a reveller. Come to think of it, he disliked looking into the river. It was more than dislike, it made him shiver. To look at the Thames creeping blackly along like that seemed to divert some of its cold currents through his own bloodstream; chilling a vein or two. Ben took a step back but the water exerted an uncanny grip on him. When he was as close as this to the river it always snatched him back to the week he'd moved to London, and left his mother's home for good. He'd been high on the exhilaration of living footloose and fancy free in one of the biggest cities in the world – all those thrills and possibilities: they were lying waiting for him to come along and scoop them up in his two hands. That's when he'd walked down here, just like tonight. Full of the joys of freedom, he'd come to this very spot, near Cleopatra's Needle, to gaze happily over the wall into the water.

A corpse had been floating there. It had been naked with the arms and legs stretched out so it formed a white X mark there in the oily, black water. He remembered alerting a group of men nearby, 'There's someone in the water.' Then it all happened so fast. More people appeared from nowhere. A police car arrived. Within moments of Ben shouting 'There's someone in the water', the body had been dragged out on to one of the pleasure-boat jetties.

Ben had stared down at the sopping remnant of human flesh in the street light. Someone had said, 'It's the body of a young woman.' He'd seen the butterfly tattoo on her waxy arm. The tattooed image had pink wings fixed to a green body. He'd seen a pattern of freckles on her thigh in the shape of a palm print. There was a bizarre detail he still remembered clearly. These days he couldn't figure out whether it was some product of the shock; a detail burned into his brain by imagination, as he tried to deal with the horror of this dripping corpse that two hours ago might have been a living, breathing woman, laughing and talking with friends in a bar. But in one of the cadaver's hands that had bunched into a tight fist was a child's plastic doll. Strangely the doll – also naked – and the woman appeared similar. But the woman must have been struck by the propeller of a passing boat because that's where the similarity ended. The plastic doll still had her head.

'Hey!'

Ben's bones nearly jumped free of his skin.

'Ben! Where on earth have you been? I haven't seen you in months.'

Ben whirled round to find a familiar face. 'April?'

'Why the hesitation? Don't tell me I've changed that much ... but you haven't seen this.' She touched her short dark hair. 'I had the old mop cut off just after you left.'

April's familiar face was a welcome one. Even though he'd been back in London six months he'd convinced himself that he'd never see her again. Now, here she was: April Connor. The same sparkling eyes, the same light-up-the-room smile. Her body-language now exuded a supple confidence that she lacked before. Meeting April Connor by chance at two in the morning would have made his night. What tore the pleasant surprise apart was that she stood arm-in-arm with a tanned man, sporting close-cropped blond hair and gold neck chains. The man appeared every inch a millionaire success story.

'April, it's lovely to see you.' Immediately Ben's words sounded awkwardly formal. He tried to be more easy-going. 'How's life treating you?'

'Great. Oh, I haven't seen you in ages. I can't believe it. Come here, you lunatic.' She slipped a bare arm around his neck. For a second he occupied her air-space, and breathed in her perfume. She kissed him firmly on the cheek. The sincerity of it made his heart beat hard.

'You're looking well.' Hell, that sounds lame, he thought. 'Are you still flogging the mag?'

'No, I'm doing PR for an agency now. So it's Hollywood movies one day, sewer pipes the next.'

April gave him a playful punch on the arm. 'But what happened to you? All I got was a text saying you were going to New York and you'd be back after the weekend. Then you vanished.'

'The magazine liked the article I did for them so much they asked me to stay.' The blond man's wide-eyed stare was beginning to irritate him. 'What was supposed to be a five-day assignment became a six-month posting.'

April laughed, marvelling at it all. 'Congratulations. You must have loved being in New York. All those beautiful women.'

'It had its moments.'

'I don't know whether to hug you or strangle you. Why didn't you call me?'

'Someone stole my case with my computer and—'

'Oh, I'm sorry. I'm being so rude,' she broke in, still smiling in an outrageously pretty way. 'I haven't introduced you. You'll have to excuse me, we've been celebrating. We just signed for an apartment today.'

Ben's heart sank. 'That's great. Congratulations.'

'And this is Trajan.'

The blond man held out his hand. A handshake every bit as businesslike as Ben expected it to be. 'Trajan.' Ben nodded.

April continued. 'Trajan, this is Ben Ashton. One of the best feature writers in the world – and craziest man in London. Only he'll never admit to either.'

'April, you should be my agent.'

'Then I could have been rich, not a poor little PR girl.' Her eyes twinkled even more brightly as she said, 'Trajan's in shipping.'

'Container logistics.' Trajan's voice was oddly flat as if reluctant to say any more than the minimum.

'Trajan, everyone used to think that Ben and I were an item . . . or even married. Imagine that, Ben.'

Ben forced a laugh. 'Imagine.'

'For over a year we were best friends. People couldn't believe there was never anything more to it than that.' She squeezed Ben's arm as if to reassure herself he was really there. 'Ben, what have you been doing with yourself?'

'Freelancing mainly. There's a new magazine that needs—'

'April.' Trajan checked his watch. 'It's getting late.'

'Oh, of course.' She hugged Trajan's arm. 'We're going up to Aberdeen tomorrow for Suka's wedding. Do you remember Suka? She told everyone that she was going on this odyssey to India . . . overland by car, would you believe? She got as far as Folkestone, met a schoolteacher in a café, and fell in love with him.'

Ben smiled. *Is it as wistful as it feels?* he wonders.

'Ah, there's fairy-tale romance for you,' Ben said. 'Like a bolt from the blue.'

'I'll say,' she said with feeling.

Trajan awarded his wristwatch another of his wide-eyed stares. 'April?'

'Sorry. Gotta go. Lovely to see you again, Ben. Keep in touch!' She kissed him and for a second he was swimming

11

in a warm ocean of her body heat and perfume. Then she'd gone as abruptly as she arrived.

He murmured to himself, 'Keep in touch? How? I don't have your number anymore.' More important than the *how?* was the *why?* For as long as he could bear it he watched April walk away, her arm linked with Trajan's.

'Damn,' he hissed, then trudged in the direction of home.

April Connor had to walk briskly to keep up with Trajan. They hadn't intended to stay in the restaurant for so long, but the hunt for a new apartment had been brutal, so when they signed the contracts today it hadn't been easy to stop celebrating. A light breeze rustled the trees along the embankment. The smooth surface of the river became rippled. She heard the slap of a wave against the embankment wall that channelled the river. At this time of night the road traffic had become lighter. There were no pedestrians in sight. No one, that is, other than the dwindling speck that was Ben Ashton.

'Damn, I forgot to ask Ben for his telephone number.'

'April!'

Trajan's fierce grip on her forearm made her cry out. 'Trajan – oh, Trajan . . . stop it . . .'

'April . . . *look.*'

Sex games. A late-night fuck in a public place. Those thoughts skated through her head. A woman lay back on the wall that separated the river from the road. A large, male shape leaned over her. The masculine image oozed a predatory power.

April stared. Sights of what appeared to be an erotic encounter whirled out of the darkness at her. The woman was aged about thirty. Her curled red hair gleamed with copper glints in the street light. She was moaning, her head rolled from side to side on the wall. Her hands were raised as if she squeezed at something invisible in the air above her.

Now April saw what Trajan had seen. And what had caused him to react by inadvertently hurting her arm. The man held the woman down on the wall. He'd yanked up her T-shirt then he'd pushed his face against her belly flesh. He wasn't kissing or licking. He was gnawing at her skin. With his teeth he'd torn open a gash. Blood streamed from the wound across her white flesh to dribble to the ground. And all the time the man sucked and groaned. It was like watching a starving wretch faced with food for the first time in weeks. And he was gorging. He drank so deeply he grunted as if it hurt him to force so vast a draught of blood down through his throat in one go.

There wasn't much life in the redhead now. She moaned. Her movements were weak. She stared bleakly upward into the night sky.

Then the woman's attacker did something that pushed April's sense of disgust beyond the limits of what she thought she could take. The man ripping at his victim's stomach with his bare teeth was bad enough. What he did next was worse.

'Oh, God, no.' April stopped dead. Even Trajan wavered now, not believing what he saw unfolding just feet away from them.

The brutal figure in front of them had raised his head. He was panting. The blood he drank gurgled wetly in his throat. His pale face had been violently smeared with crimson. He lifted his own face to the sky. He panted faster. His shoulders began to shake. Convulsions ran through his torso, stretching the fabric of his shirt across his back so much April thought it would rip at any second.

Then he snapped his head down at the woman's torn belly. His face struck it with an audible slap. His mouth clamped tight to the wounds, lips forming a seal, then the body convulsed again.

Dear God in heaven, April thought as she rocked back in horror. He's vomiting it back into her!

The pressure of the regurgitation was so violent that crimson fluid spurted from where his mouth met the woman's flesh. April heard the sound of liquid rushing through the man's mouth to surge back through the ripped skin of his victim's belly.

For a while she'd been comatose. A second later she jerked her torso up from the wall, her hands clasped her attacker's head, as her mouth opened into a huge O. The sound that tore from it was half scream, half bellow. A howl of pure agony.

Both April and Trajan had stared at the scene in shock. This shriek broke the spell.

'Leave her alone!' Trajan leapt on the man's back. With hardly any exertion on his part the figure shrugged him away. What happened next was incredibly fast. The blood-soaked attacker stood up straight, pushed his victim over the

13

wall into the river; the splash seemed a tiny sound in comparison to the woman's tortured cry. Trajan ran at the monster. He did not have a chance to land a blow before he was thrown to the ground. His head struck the pavement with such a loud crack that April froze. Meanwhile, cars passed by on the road just a dozen paces away. But nobody stopped. Maybe they thought it was just drunks fooling around. Or maybe they were afraid to become involved. Sometimes it's better to lock the vehicle doors and drive quickly out of harm's way.

Trajan lay flat. His eyes were closed. The brutal figure of a man approached her. There was something about him . . . The way he walked. Something wasn't right. But at that moment she couldn't identify what it was. Desperately, she looked behind her. In the distance she could still see Ben. She saw the whiteness of his shirt as he walked away.

'Ben!' she cried.

Then the stranger's hands were on her. She felt herself picked up, then slammed down on the wall. The force of striking the stonework knocked the air from her lungs. April felt his powerful fingers tear a hole in her dress at her waist.

As she waited for his teeth to crunch through the skin in her side she knew the same would happen to her as the redhead. And there was not one thing she could do to prevent it. April Connor didn't even have the luxury of one final, heart-rending scream.

Three

'Raj, don't! You'll regret it.' He grimaced as the understanding sank in. 'Never give me paranormal assignments. You might as well commission me to track down Elvis for a come-back special with Glenn Miller, Jimi Hendrix and the crew of the bloody *Titanic*. Besides, you promised me the

14

film festival.' Ben Ashton glared at Raj's boyish Asian face that always assumed an air of mature gravity when handing out editorial assignments.

'Jack Constantine can cover that. He's mad on Chaney anyway.'

'If Jack ever comes back. Last I heard he's locked away in some love shack with that singer from Cuspidor.'

Raj gestured away the objection as if he lazily waved away a fly in that sweltering office. From the street came the steady roar of traffic. Ben wished he'd stayed in the riverside pub to read up on Lon Chaney's films. Then he could have claimed he was already too deep into research to be shunted into some spook hunt.

All Ben could do was swing into a new strategy. 'Jo Suster loves the occult stuff. Send her.'

'No, Ben. You're the man for the job. You always get a fresh angle.'

'With ghosts?'

'Sure.'

'No way.'

'You can do it.'

'No.'

'You'll wish you had. This story will be big when the global news networks get it.'

'Then why are we bothering, Raj?'

'Because *Click This* is a brilliant magazine and you are a brilliant writer, Ben.'

Ben Ashton pushed a pile of photographs into the centre of the desk and sat on the corner.

'Make yourself at home, Ben. Be my guest.' Raj eased the photographs safely aside. 'But don't go crushing my cover girl.'

'So . . . film festival. Where are my tickets?'

'No, you're not going to the festival. Snowdance will have to muddle through without you this year.'

'Then I'll take myself round to *Screen*. They've offered a monthly column.'

'Ben, don't make me get down and beg. It's not a pretty sight. I get all jowly.'

'I don't write-up ghosts.'

'There aren't any ghosts.'

'Damn it, Raj. What have you dragged me in here for, then? I've still to finish your article for "Where The Hell Are They Now?"'

Raj picked up his phone from the desk. 'It's more visceral than phantoms, Ben. I want to show you something.'

'Tickets to Montreal would be nice.'

'Ben, I'm offering you the lead article for the next issue. Plus our premium fee, *plus* a name check on the front cover.'

'Seriously?'

'And expenses.'

'Hell, you must be serious. You've never given me expenses before.'

'I'm very serious. This is going to be a big story.' Raj's youthful face broke into a grin but Ben realized the boy-wonder editor meant business. And, despite his belly-aching about Snowdance, Ben respected Raj. The guy had a knack of sensing what would grab the public's imagination. He'd turned *Click This* from a cheesy pop culture magazine into a market leader that had the agencies clamouring to buy ad space.

Raj pressed a key on a mobile phone then turned it so Ben could view the screen.

'If you haven't seen this before,' Raj said, 'you should stop doing whatever's damaging your eye sight.'

Ben looked at the screen. Illuminated there was one of the stone lions that guarded the base of Nelson's Column. Someone had painted the words on the plinth:

VAMPIRE SHARKZ
☺ They're coming to get you ☺

Ben shrugged. 'Of course I've seen it. That graffiti's on hundreds of walls, trains, buses; it's everywhere.'

'When did you see Vampire Sharkz first?'

Ben's shrug grew more expressive. 'About three weeks since?'

'I'd say that. A month at the most.'

'So – it's just the latest fad among graffiti artists.'

Raj pressed another key on the phone. The next picture revealed the same graffiti violating the side of a Harrods' delivery van.

16

'So, who's doing this, Ben?'

'Kids.'

'Why?

'It's what kids do.'

Raj rubbed his jaw. 'Then you figure there's nothing behind it?'

'Raj, it's some graffiti artist who's just trying to work up five minutes of fame for themselves.'

'What if you dig deeper?'

'You're asking me to investigate this?'

Raj nodded.

Ben laughed. 'Then you can't handle the heat, old son. You've flipped. This is just some joker with a crate full of spray paint and a big ego.'

'I disagree. So, this is me, your editor, giving you, Ben Ashton, a valuable commission. Five thousand words by the end of next week. Premium word rate. Expenses. Front cover credit.'

Ben breathed in deeply. This was a good offer. No bones about it, the best assignment all year. His old sofa at home had become a pain in the backside – literally. The fee for writing the article would buy something smart in black. He shot Raj a glance.

'Vampire Sharkz,' Ben said as he rubbed his jaw. 'You've got word on this, haven't you?'

'I was hoping you'd uncover that for me when you take the assignment.'

'This . . . Vampire Sharkz? What is it? A film? A rock band? A new type of cocaine? And: "They're going to get you." Why are they going to get us?'

Raj shrugged.

Ben let out a low whistle as a more disturbing thought struck home. 'Or is it a new street gang? Or a drug franchise marking out their territory?'

'Find out for me, Ben. You've got eleven days.'

'Photography?'

'Jenny's got the graffiti covered with beautiful art shots. Anything else, you've got your camera, haven't you? Okay, what's so funny, Ben?'

'I met a girl in Soho House on Friday night.'

'Congratulations.'

'No, I had to . . . you know, make my excuses. Well, I told her I was a writer, and she asked what I wrote about. Because I needed to leave in a hurry I told her the first thing that came into my head.'

Raj invited Ben to continue with a lift of an eyebrow.

Ben laughed louder. 'I told her that I wrote about vampires.'

'Vampires? Then the gods must have heard you. Now they've made it your destiny. It's become your sacred quest.' He handed Ben a sheet of green paper. 'Expenses form. Receipts please. Now do it. Go vampire hunting.'

Four

That moment of waking . . . which sense comes alive first?

This time smell. Wet soil.

Second: Sound. A rustle. Paper? Leaves? A dry whisper.

Third: Touch. A pressure on the side of her jaw.

Another sound; this one liquid in motion. A bath?

Where is this? Am I in bed? Have I forgotten to empty the bath?

Look for yourself.

For a moment she willed her eyelids to slide back. She tried again. For some reason she couldn't open her eyes. Come to that, she couldn't move her arms. She sensed she was lying on her stomach with her head to one side.

Why can I hear water, and smell wet soil, if I'm in bed?

Then without planning to say it she asked out loud: 'What's your name?'

The question blazed through her like lightning. This time her eyelids flew back. A light of such brilliance shone into her face she gasped. Even though she couldn't move her head her eyes darted in panic trying to see her surroundings, but all they did tell her was that a retina-searing light filled her

18

world. Only now she couldn't close her eyes again. All she could do was stare into what seemed the heart of the sun.

'What's your name?' she whispered. Vertigo tugged at her because the only fact she was certain of was this: *I don't know my own name . . .*

Noises, sensations, smells jostled for attention. There were more of them. The pungent tang of oil. A subtler odour of pond water. She heard her own breathing. It suddenly seemed over-loud; its rhythm all wrong. Abrupt intakes of breath followed by a long exhale. What's more she realized that she whispered as she breathed out, yet she couldn't make sense of what she was saying. With an effort she managed to move her tongue. Particles of grit scratched against her teeth. Her mouth tasted bitter, as if she'd taken a mouthful of mouldy bread.

'What's happened to me?'

Reaching deep inside of herself, she clutched at the strength to close her eyes. They slid shut blocking out the awful intensity of daylight. For ten seconds she kept them closed. Her lungs sounded like some weird pneumatic apparatus. Spasmodic inhalations followed by a long whispering release. Overlying that, a persistent rustling alongside liquid notes. Strange music . . .

The next time she opened her eyes it was easier. The violent blaze of light had gone. It had been replaced with a flood of tungsten brilliance. Okay, still very bright but no longer painfully so.

'What happened to me . . . what's my name?'

The only reply was the dry rustling close by. She found she could blink easily now. As she did so, what she gazed at swiftly resolved itself into sharp focus. There, in front of her, just inches away, was a ruffled expanse of little stones. The area had been formed into ridges, each one no more than an inch high at the most. Beyond those, moving in an eerie dance, were slender green limbs.

'I know what you are,' she murmured at the green dancers. 'Just need the right word.' She licked her lips. They tasted bitter, too. 'You are . . .' The effort of remembering ran through her with all the force of a painful cramp. '*Reeds* . . . you are reeds.' She sighed with relief at recalling the word. The relief was brutally short-lived.

19

Reeds? Stones? With another supreme effort she moved her head so she could look down along her body. She was wearing her black dress. The bottom half of her body lay in water. In this light the water resembled liquid platinum. What had been a numb sense of bewilderment backed off before savage jabs of panic hit her.

'Oh, please, God . . . what's happened to me?'

Panic threatened to become a deluge of horror. Her mind swam with vertigo once more. At that moment it seemed preferable to retreat back into unconsciousness in the hope that when she awoke again all this would turn out to be a dream. But anxiety nagged her. *Why can't I remember? Something terrible happened? Why don't I know my own name?*

Her breathing grew more erratic. Crimson sparks flew out from the reeds at her. She knew she was starting to disintegrate mentally.

'You've got to keep it together . . . you're in danger . . . you've got to save yourself.' She took a deep breath; when she asked that question again her voice exploded weirdly from her lips. 'What is . . . your name?' She tried so hard to remember her body convulsed. 'Something else,' she gasped. 'Something easier.' Her lips pressed together as she made the effort to control her growing sense of terror. 'Listen. What's your favourite colour?' This time the answer came straight away. 'Green.' Another question: 'Chocolate or chips?' The answer came as part cry, part laughter. 'Chocolate!' Keep going. 'What are you afraid of?' This time it came as full-blooded cry. 'This . . . I'm afraid of *this*. I don't know my own name.' She took a deep breath. 'I'm also afraid of loneliness . . . and going into a room at night without switching the light on first . . .' More: 'What's your earliest memory? Don't know . . . come on, think . . . think!' She gasped. 'Bakku . . . the white kitten. Christmas in the house with red gates.' It was if a mechanism was freeing itself in her mind. Wheels turned. Gears made connections. She blinked at the reeds. They were so green they appeared to be luminous. On the gravel near her face were bits of flotsam – a gum wrapper, a triangle of green glass, probably a fragment from a beer bottle. 'Tell me about a happy memory,' she demanded. 'Tell me about a time you were happy.' On the shingle just inches from her eye was a silver coin. It looked like a star against a dark sky it shone so brightly.

'Come on, tell me a good memory.' She swallowed a lungful of air. Her skin began to tingle. 'I'm little. There's a boy wading in the river. He calls to me, "Don't come too close. It's dangerous. But you can watch me if you sit on the bank. Did you hear me . . .?" Then he speaks my name. But what is it?' She swallowed. 'Keep going. What happened next? The boy smiles at me . . . he's my brother . . . the sun's shining. We're staying at Grandma's. My brother's annoyed that Dad won't buy him a metal detector so he can find coins, but he's found another way . . . what's the other way?' She closed her eyes. She pictured the twelve-year-old boy with his mass of frizzy hair. He's standing on a bank of shingle midstream. The sun shines. Not far away a horse drinks from the river. Her cousin flies a blue kite in the field. Then she saw the boy in her mind's eye again. He says a word that must be a name. But what name? 'Then Leo says . . . that's my brother's name: Leo . . . and Leo says: "I've been reading about treasure hunting. The book says just use your eyes. It's all about teaching your mind to see the right shape. You see this patch of shingle? The river sorts stones into certain shapes and weights; it's all to do with current flows. See here? It's left stones that are the shape of coins. That means if coins fall into the water when the bank is eroded they'll be deposited in places like this. Treasure hunters call them Glory Holes." So . . . if I bend down and picture a coin in my mind . . .

'Leo crouches to stare at the stones. I see the concentration on his face. Then he yells out, "I've found one . . . I'm sure it's Roman!" I was so excited for him. He came splashing through the water to me, and he's shouting . . . "It *is* Roman. Look . . . April!"'

In one convulsive moment she sat up. 'April. My name is April.'

Recalling her name, and the sudden ability to move again, left her dazed. April looked round. She was sitting on a shingle beach with her legs still in the water. At either side of her were patches of reeds, their tips were higher than her head. In front of her appeared to be a limitless tract of water. Behind her, the ground rose in a slight incline to a stand of willows. She touched her hair. Even though it was dry there was a slight sticky sensation. When she examined her fingers she could see no trace of liquid or matter. But the stickiness remained. Puzzled, she looked up at the sun. But the light blazing in the sky wasn't the sun.

April squinted against its brightness, even raising her hand to protect her eyes. 'The moon?' She shook her head. What had happened to her? How did she get here? Why is the moon so impossibly bright? She didn't recollect being on a boat . . . or even wandering here across dry land. After a wobbly false start she managed to climb to her feet. She looked back down at the coin lying in the shingle. It blazed there with a silvery light. That's the key that unlocked your memory, she told herself. It's your lucky charm. Take it. Still shaky on her feet, she managed to pick it up. In the process she noticed one foot was clad in a sandal, while the other was bare.

Unsteadily, she moved along the shingle beach. If the stones pricked her feet she didn't notice them. After walking through that weirdly bright moonlight for barely more than a minute she found another beach run in from her right to meet her stretch of stones. Seconds later she stood on a spit of shingle that jutted out into gleaming water. The moon was duplicated there so it appeared as if a vast chrome disk floated on the sea. From this vantage point she could look back at both sides of the land on which she found herself.

She explained to herself, 'This is an island.' To her ears her strange respiration sounded louder. 'April Connor, you know what's happened to you, don't you?' The reeds rustled their own cryptic reply. April, however, furnished an intelligible answer: 'You've been shipwrecked. You're marooned here.'

Now that she could move her limbs and remember her name she at least remained calm. Even when she noticed that her dress had been torn open at the hip it didn't seem so bad. For some reason seeing the wounds in her bare skin through the torn material didn't form connections in her mind, so there was a sense of unreality. As if the breaks in her flesh that exposed the red, raw lips of a wound didn't relate to the process of washing up here on the island.

The reeds rustled; a dry sound like whispers from the mouths of ancient Egyptian mummies. She stared at the head on the coin in the moonlight and confessed, 'I'm lucky to be alive, aren't I?' The moment she uttered the words she shuddered as other possibilities rose in her mind. What if she hadn't survived? What if this was heaven? Or hell? Or some eternal state of limbo? With an effort she repressed those disturbing thoughts. What she must do is explore this place, then – and only then – draw her conclusions.

April walked slowly toward the other end of the island. The reeds waved at one side of her, while a light breeze sent shivers through the branches of the willow trees. An animal scuttled away under her feet. A rat? She couldn't tell. What if it returned with more of its kind? Further along the beach she came across the ribs of a small boat. The timber had been gnawed away by the elements, until it resembled the skeleton of a dinosaur. She couldn't have arrived on that, it must have lain here for years. Besides, she had no recollection of being on board any kind of ship.

If I'm marooned here, what's going to happen to me? This question provoked a sense of unease. She found herself touching her hair on the side of her head. The strands were sticky. Once more she realized her respiration was arrhythmic. Two or three sharp intakes of breath followed by a long exhale. When she breathed out she whispered words. But what was she whispering? She couldn't understand them. But there was an urgency there; some unconscious element inside of her hissed a warning.

All of a sudden she was aware of the wound in her side. It didn't hurt. Instead a prickling sensation circled the open wound as if ants ran round and round it, searching for a way into her body. When she checked she saw nothing in the moonlight but the hole torn in her dress and the rips in her skin. Nevertheless, it seemed as if the injury was undergoing some kind of change.

Again, she found herself asking the question, 'Dear God. What happened to me?'

The breeze tugged the willows. The whispering became a dark muttering. In a moment of paranoia she found herself believing the trees were talking about her. As if April Connor disgusted them. With a sense of rising panic she walked faster. Ahead of her, the beach turned back on itself behind a clump of bushes. When April at last reached the corner and turned she knew she was no longer alone.

Five

Bodies. Dead bodies. All lying stretched out at the high-tide mark on that little shingle beach. The hard light of the moon blazed down on the motionless figures. A breeze drew sinister whispers from the willows. They might have been hissing, 'Welcome to the Isle of the Dead, April. These will be your companions forever and ever. Amen . . .'

April couldn't take her eyes off them. Here she was, in her black dress with one foot bare, the other clad in a sandal. Her dress was ripped. The wound in her side itched, and she wanted to scream out to the world that she'd gone insane. April walked along the beach, and even though she tried not to, her eyes locked on each dead face in turn. And the trees whispered, 'Welcome to the Isle of the Dead . . . Welcome to the Isle of the Dead . . . Welcome to—'

'No, they're not saying that,' she snarled. It's in your mind.'

'Welcome to the Isle of the Dead . . .'

'Shut up!' The shout exploded from her lips. The moment it did so, the prone figures on the beach came back to life. One moment they lay there with their eyes open, their arms stretched out, where the receding tide had left them in those weird after-death poses, then they were suddenly awake. It was as if the process left them traumatized. Men and women sobbed.

'Mother, where am I?'

'Kerry, he hurt me . . . I didn't do anything. Why did he hurt me?'

They sat up on the beach. A couple scrambled to their feet as if they'd been knocked down just a second ago and were still in the heat of a fist-fight.

'I won't let you – I won't let you!'

'Bastard!'

24

'I'll get you for this. You won't get away. I know people . . . they'll rip you in two for what you've done.'

'Mother? What did he do to me . . . ?'

'Bastard!'

'Oh God, look what she did. Look what she did! She bit me . . . look at my stomach!' The guy in a yellow shirt that was ripped open to the waist stared in horror at the wounds around his navel. 'Hey, look what she did!' The man locked eye contact with April as he framed the wound with his hands. 'Did you see where she went?' As he advanced on April, his fear turned to rage. 'Hey, I asked you! Did you see where she went?'

April shook her head.

'Are you stupid? She was right here a minute ago. A kid with ragged clothes. Jeans that were all torn open. You must have seen her attack me?' The look in his eyes suggested he'd beat a response from her if she didn't reply.

'I didn't see anyone.'

'Bloody liar!' That's when he paused. 'But I wasn't here. I was on Waterloo Bridge . . . so how come I'm here now?' He advanced again. 'Have you got anything to do with it?'

She shook her head. 'Please. I don't know how I got here, either.'

'Stupid girl. You must do.' The rage fled to be replaced by an expression of pleading. 'You know something, don't you?'

'No . . . I'm sorry. I woke up to find—'

'Hey, you've been bitten, too. Look at your side.'

'Don't let him near me again!' A woman with short blonde hair blundered past. She looked around as if she expected terrifying creatures to attack her at any moment. 'Don't let him near me!'

A youth scrambled from the shallows, a dripping whirl-wind of terror. He didn't use words; instead he screamed in mindless panic as he ran up the beach, cannoned off April, then sped away into the bushes. April recovered her balance only to find the man in the yellow shirt had grasped her wrist and then lifted her arm so he could examine the wound in her side.

'What's happened to us? Look, we've all been bitten.' He roughly squeezed her flesh to open the wound. 'See? Teeth marks! They've gone right through the skin.'

25

Now, that hurt. With a gasp April pulled away. Even so, she asked, 'Do you remember your name?'

'Of course, I do. Do you think I'm crazy? It's . . .' His face muscles slackened as the shock hit. 'My name is . . .' He clenched his fist. 'It's . . . oh, God. Wait. I'll remember in a minute . . .' He backed away with his eyes down on the beach as if he would find his identity there.

'You were there, weren't you?' This came from a woman with copper-coloured hair. 'Did you see what he did to me?'

The image flashed back of this woman being held down on the wall at the edge of the river as the brutish figure sucked blood from her stomach.

'Yes.' April stared into the woman's face. The expression of pure horror had the power to hold her. 'I was there. We—'

'For God's sake, why didn't you stop him?'

'We tried. My boyfriend—'

'You bitch, you just watched, didn't you? You probably thought it was funny!' The woman backed away with her arms folded. She panted as if her lungs couldn't draw enough air into her body. 'Bitch,' the red-haired woman gasped. 'Someone should do the same to you.'

'He did, look!' April pointed at her own side with the raw flaps of the wound raised above the skin. 'See? Everyone else has the same kind of wound.'

The man in the yellow shirt appeared in a daze now. 'How did we get here? Why is the sun so bright?'

'That's not the sun, it's the moon.'

'You're lying,' he told her. 'Bitch. You must be in on this. Did you put something in our drinks?'

Alongside panic a sense of violence crackled in the air as if that bunch of terrified victims on the beach were desperate to find someone to blame.

'Listen.' The man pointed at April. 'She knows what's happening.'

'I don't. I'm the same as—'

The redhead glared at her. 'That woman stood and watched me being mauled.'

'I didn't. My boyfriend tried to stop it. He was knocked down.'

Fear drove these people now. They were desperate for

26

answers. Approximately twenty men and women formed a circle around her.

The man in the yellow shirt snarled, 'She said that was the moon. Look how bright it is? It's got to be the sun, so why's she telling us it's the moon? This is a trick. She probably drugged our drinks, then followed us outside.'

April felt close to weeping. 'Listen to me. I'm just like you. I was attacked. I was thrown in the water. I woke up here on the island. Yes, that's the moon. I don't know why it's so bright.'

'See, she knows all about it.' This was a kid in his teens. The denim jacket he wore had chains stitched to it so they clinked as he pointed at her. His bite mark disfigured his face. 'How does she know about an island?'

The man in the shirt rubbed his stomach. The wound must have started its maddening itch. 'She knew I wouldn't be able to remember my name. There's a drug that does that to you.'

'You were washed up here, like me,' April insisted. 'This is a Glory Hole for bodies. My brother said that the tides and currents gather objects—'

'What the hell is the bitch talking about?'

'Listen to me. Like coins, and stones of a certain size, the river currents grade them naturally and then deposit them on beaches. If you look down here all the stones are as big as coins.'

'Watch her,' the youth warned, 'she's trying something.'

'She's playing for time.' This was the redhead. 'Whoever brought us here is coming back so she's trying to distract us.'

'I can make her talk.' The youth reached into his pocket and drew out a clasp knife. He took pleasure in easing the blade from its recess.

'Please. You've got to believe me.' Nausea surged through April. For a moment she thought she'd vomit there and then. She took a deep breath. 'Listen. We were all attacked. We ended up in the water. The river washed us up here . . . this island.' She swallowed to push down that ball of heat rising in her throat. 'Washed up here. That happened to all of us.'

The guy in the shirt screamed at her. 'Washed up here! We're not stupid! If we floated here, how come we didn't drown?'

'I don't know . . . sorry . . . don't know.' Inside, she went from searing heat to ice. 'Something's happening to me.'

'Wrong, sister,' spat the redhead. 'Something *will* happen to you.' She took a step toward her. 'I'm going to rip every hair out of your damn head until you tell us what's happened.'

'Please . . .'

The man in the shirt kneaded his stomach rather than rubbing it. Something was working on him, too. 'And if she doesn't talk then I'm going to break her neck.'

A flush of heat ran through April's face as her stomach was hit by cramp. 'Doesn't anyone here remember their name?' She looked at the twenty faces. But now those faces blazed hostility at her. They could beat their fear by *beating* her. That was their solution. 'And aren't the colours too bright? They blaze at you, don't they?'

'That'll be the effect of the drug you put in our drinks.'

'I didn't spike any stupid drinks.' April couldn't stand straight now, the stomach pains were so intense. 'Don't any of you feel a sense of confusion? Like you've been spun around and around so much you . . .' A bitter taste flooded her mouth.

The redhead lunged at her and grabbed her hair. 'Confusion? That'll be the drug. It's all adding up now. You drugged us, then you and your friends brought us here, didn't you?'

'What about the bite marks?'

'Fucking sadists, that's what you are.'

The man in the shirt grinned manically. 'That's right. You were going to fuck us round and do something perverted but we woke up too soon. Now we're going to fuck around with you until you wish you'd never been born.'

'But I'm the same as you! I'm a victim!' Overwhelming spasms ran through her. With them came searing heat and an urge to vomit.

Only . . . the sensation was mutating inside of her. Mutating . . . that can't be the right word, she told herself. Only it was *mutating*. That's exactly the right word. This wasn't merely change in her stomach; this was mutant transformation. Her very guts seemed to writhe inside her. She clutched her belly as she cried out.

The redhead who gripped her hair must have thought it was the pain in her scalp that did it. She nodded with satisfaction. 'See how you like being hurt. How about a bit more? Hmm?'

She dragged April back by her hair. Only it wasn't her scalp that hurt.

'Something's happening to me,' April gasped.

'I'm going to make her tell us,' the man said. 'Before her friends come back . . . uh . . .' He pressed the heel of his hand into his midriff.

'You feel it, too, don't you?' April felt the woman release her hair. The redhead backed away as she massaged her own belly with her two hands. 'What is it you feel?'

The kid in the denim jacket muttered, 'It's the crap she gave us. I've got to eat something. Christ, I'm hungry.' He tried to laugh but there was fear in his eyes. Whatever affected April had started on him, too. The kid's throat muscles twitched.

Instead of the people directing their anger at April Connor they moved about the beach in a restless way. Their expressions suggested they were preoccupied with what was happening to their own bodies. They were no longer interested in her, or their paranoid accusations. No, they were gripped by another obsession now . . . April licked her lips. The pain in her stomach morphed into another sensation entirely. Hunger. A desperate need to eat. A burning, screaming, shouting, overwhelming need: food, hunger, eat, satisfy. The craving to stuff food in her mouth was suddenly everything. It was the whole universe. What matters now? Damn it! Nothing matters now. If news arrived of the deaths of her mother, father, Trajan: it wouldn't matter. The necessity now was food.

From the expressions on the faces of that bedraggled group on the beach that's what mattered to them. Can hunger be infectious? How can they all be hungry simultaneously? These thoughts still flitted through April's mind but the supernova of all sensation now was the incandescent hunger that raged inside of her. It didn't seem confined to her stomach. That lust to gorge blazed through her veins. And it was more than hunger; that need to wolf down food hurt. It became a living pain inside of her. Nothing mattered but food. Wildly, she looked round as if expecting to find mounds of roast beef on the beach. There had to be something to eat. If there wasn't she'd go out of her mind.

Out of her mind? God, she'd left rational thought behind.

Eating, eating, eating . . . that's all that mattered now. The others were the same. They ran along the shingle like a pack of hungry dogs. They even sniffed the air as if a hot meal waited for them close by. The kid with the denim jacket sped into the bushes to lift up branches; no doubt he hoped that he'd find a sizzling T-bone steak dripping its beautiful juices on the grass.

The man in the yellow shirt shuffled on all fours across the beach; his hands picked amongst the stones with a fevered speed. She knew the overriding impulse that drove him; that if there was the slightest chance he'd find something edible there he'd search until doomsday. With a strange cry he snatched up a large stone. His expression was the same as an alcoholic knowing that next whisky might kill him, but his will power had collapsed. For a second he held the pebble that was the size of a peach in front of him. He stared at it in horror. His hands shook; tears streamed down his face. Then he opened his loose, pink mouth as wide as he could, stuffed the rock between his jaws, then bit down as hard as he could. The sound of his snapping teeth made April Connor flinch.

Madness . . .

And yet . . . and yet . . . the incandescent hunger that seared her entire body drove her to search the beach, too. It made sense. There had to be food here, too. The waves washed all kinds of things on to the shore. Why not food? Container ships full of meat lose their cargos from time to time. Images of dead fish being carried in amid the scum of high tide filled her head. Fat fish, bursting with moist, pink flesh.

All around her, those men and women searched for food in the bushes, the reeds, the flotsam on the beach. The man still broke his teeth on the rock, screaming in frustration as he did so at his inability to devour it as if it were a hunk of chocolate. April scrambled to where waves lapped the shore. There she saw a little bank of dirt emerge from the falling tide. All of a sudden this struck her as an amazing sight. The moonlight made the dirt glisten; its silky texture captivated her. She approached it at a crouch as if terrified she'd somehow frighten it away, so it would be beyond reach. Gently, gently, gently she squatted beside it. Its smooth purity was unearthly. Instead of pebbles this was a velvety accumulation of tiny particles that had the texture and appearance of black sugar. 'Oh . . .' Just to look at it made her sigh with pleasure. The thought of sinking her fingers into the moist confection sent a dizzying whirl of anticipation through her. Nothing else mattered now but that juicy up-swelling of luscious black sweetness. *I'm so lucky,* she told herself, *all this is mine. Those idiots haven't noticed what's lying here under their noses.*

As she dipped her hands into it she couldn't stop the tiny kitten-like cries escape her lips. It was all she could do to stop herself screaming with joy at capturing this luxurious mound of candied blackness from the water. Every cell of her being glowed with pleasure. Her mouth was wet with anticipation at the first mouthful. April dug her hand deep into the mud then crammed it into her mouth. Munching those moist particles was sheer bliss. Her teeth crunched against the larger fragments. Swallowing was something else! It was pain and ecstasy all at the same time. The ball of cold matter squeezed down her throat, stretching the gullet until it almost split. But this is what she wanted . . . this is *everything* she wanted . . . Even the tiny voice in her head that told her she squatted in the water devouring silt was nothing to her. A gnat on the periphery of reality; nothing more. She prepared to savour the next handful of the glistening delicacy, which was deliciously speckled with fragments of crisp, white sea shell, when a hand grabbed her arm.

'Let go!' she screamed. 'This is mine! Find your own!'

A man's voice hissed urgently, 'Get away from here!'

'You're not having any. I found it!' Using both hands she scooped mounds of the black sugary treat to her mouth where she sucked at it with a ferocity that was nothing less than gluttonous. Its flavors were chocolate, roast beef, red wine and a vivid honeyed nougat. She couldn't get enough.

'Get away from here! Any minute now they're going to go crazy!'

Something about that note of warning pierced the insane lust to eat. April looked down at the black stuff on her hands. Puzzled, she uttered, 'That's mud.' She wiped her lips. 'I'm eating mud?'

'If you don't come now, I'm leaving you, and I don't fancy your chances once that thing comes down on them.'

31

'Uh?' She peered up at the man who helped her to her feet. 'What?'

'It's going to hit them any second now. The feeding frenzy.'

April peered at the beach where the bunch of men and women had been searching for food. They'd stopped now. Instead, they stared with a peculiar, fixed intensity at the redheaded woman as she knelt at the high tide mark. There she stuffed green seaweed into her mouth – slimy strands hung down from her lips as she fought to cram in more. The woman never noticed that she was the object of such scrutiny.

'See?' the man told April. 'They're realizing they need something more than dirt to stop the craving.'

Dazed, April asked, 'Why was I eating that stuff?' Even though she knew that glistening mound was mud she had the same reluctance leaving it as saying goodbye to a loved one. The sense of loss didn't seem bizarre; she even found herself rationalizing the idea of taking a handful with her, just in case the hunger returned.

'First, it's a good idea to get away from here.' He tugged her to her feet. 'You're not like the rest. There's a different look in your eye. Your mind hasn't gone yet. Understand?'

She didn't understand. All she could manage was to stand up straight. There, in moonlight that was bright as the noonday sun, was a man with curly black hair. He was perhaps mid-twenties and wore an expression of such concern she could have been his child that he was rescuing. When he spoke she noticed that the tips of his front teeth had been covered with gold. He had the air of someone who loved the luxuries life offered but wasn't troubled how he acquired them.

'Yeah, I can see you've still got some human left in you,' he said. A mysterious statement that troubled her. 'You're looking at me, right? And you're telling yourself you see a gangster.'

'I don't know you.'

'No, you don't. Okay, I got stupid as a kid. I did time inside. But now I straighten out other kids with bad habits. Theft, drugs, self-destructing. And I read Charles Dickens because he knew poverty. But all that's for later, yeah? Because if you don't come now they're likely to start ripping you apart once they've finished with her.' Something of his alarm communicated itself to her. *Get out of here! Now!* his expression hollered loud and clear, so she followed him.

The twenty people – people? People! – were beast-like now. They appeared to slink toward the woman who fed on green river slime as if they were panthers. Their feet made faint crunching sounds on the shingle. When one grunted, clearly feeling a ravenous hunger, the redhead looked up to see the pack closing in on her.

The youth in the denim jacket chewed the air as if in his imagination he already chewed on firm meat. When the attack came it wasn't what April expected. The movement was a blur as the redhead launched herself to her feet, then hurled herself on the man in the yellow shirt. Sheer bloodlust made her howl at the top of her voice as she slammed her mouth against his head to bite into his skin. As if frightened to be denied their share of food the pack pounced on the man. After that, April Connor only saw the man's face two more times as the mass of people buried him. First, she saw his agonized expression as his eyes turned skyward as if to ask: *God, why me?* His mouth opened wide to reveal the teeth he'd broken when he tried to eat the pebble. Then the squirming, swarming mass of bodies covered him as they clamored to bite. The second time she saw his face was when his head broke the surface of that scrum. His attackers' teeth had ripped his face. Both his cheeks hung down at either side of his neck; they swung there; two crimson flaps.

The mob buried the man from April's sight again as they devoured him.

'That isn't what they need,' her rescuer panted. 'They think they want to munch down every shred of his skin, but that's because they don't really know what they want yet.' He nodded toward them. 'Once they realize that he hasn't satisfied their hunger then that's when they'll start on you. Come on.'

Together they loped away into the trees, leaving the feeding-frenzy to rage on the moonlit beach.

Six

Home for Ben Ashton is an apartment in a converted warehouse by the Thames. It came recommended to him by a fellow writer by the name of Jack Constantine. Jack occupied a ritzier loft dwelling on the top floor. Ben's trio of rooms – lounge/kitchen, bedroom, bathroom – occupied part of the third floor. For a century the building had swallowed spices from the East Indies by the ton; lifting them directly from the ship, which moored alongside the wharf, then swinging them on derricks into the cavernous interior. Well, what *was* the cavernous interior of the building. Fifteen years ago it had been subdivided into individual dwellings. Even so, when nights were warm, just like this one, Ben would wake in the early hours to catch the exotic aromas of nutmeg and capsicum overlaid with those spikier scents of peppercorns.

Ben lay flat on his bed that right at that moment seemed as big and as desolate and as lonely as the Gobi desert. He stared into the shadows as his clock-radio burned a forlorn 2:47 a.m. at him. Usually he slept well but meeting April Connor had unsettled him. He murmured to himself, 'They do say you only regret the things you didn't do; not what you did.' He clicked his tongue. 'You're feeling sorry for yourself again, mush.' He closed his eyes and told himself, sleep, soon you can get up and start hunting for Raj's phantom graffiti artist. His eyes flicked open again. The assignment of the century, he thought. Ben Ashton, investigative journalist, finds kid who sprays funny slogan on walls. He groaned. Crap assignment, good money, stop complaining. He ran his fingers through his hair. Five seconds later he sat upright in bed. 'Okay, Ben, my old china, what's keeping you awake?' he asked himself. He knew the answer. April Connor. When he saw her arm-in-arm with the fabulously blond Trajan it hurt like having a red-hot poker rammed into a place that had never seen the light of day before. He took a deep breath. That piquant aroma of spices reached into his nostrils from where it had seeped into the brickwork long ago. 'Right, Ben. Shall we take it from the top?' He groaned. 'Not this again. Not a list of my failings. Why do you do this to yourself?' He climbed out of bed and began to pace while he recited his old litany. 'First off, you talk to yourself too much. Why do you do that, Ben? Because you are lonely. And why are you lonely? I'm lonely because I let April Connor slip through my fingers. We were best friends; only when I lost touch with her did I realize, first class, gold-plated idiot that I am, that I loved her. Satisfied?' He folded his arms as he gazed out of the window. The lights from the far bank painted luminous streaks on the surface of the river. 'You loved her; lost her; and she never even knew. There, that's my confession.' He found it hard to leave the litany at that. He tried to be flippant, but bitter currents crept into it. He stared up at the full moon as it floated there above London. It could have been the vast orb of a godlike eye, gazing coldly down at one Ben Ashton, magazine writer, lonely soul. *You blew it, Ben, didn't you? For the first time in your life you find the woman that suited you . . . You let her go without finding out how she felt about you.*

'Shut up, Moon.' He smiled, although he recognized the sadness. 'What do planetary bodies know about human feelings?' He leaned forward until his head touched the glass. Below him the street light illuminated a stretch of the river. Its surface dimpled, while a small whirlpool that formed around a mooring post seemed to be busily in the process of drowning the reflection of the moon. A branch drifted by. After that, an assortment of fast-food packaging: fragments of polystyrene, plastic bags, newspapers. The tide was ebbing so it quickened the flow of the river. For the next few hours the current would rush its flotsam downstream, away from London and toward the sea.

After a moment staring at this aquatic convoy heading eastward Ben said to himself, 'You've got two choices. Either forget April. Or find her. Tell her exactly how you feel. The thing is, if it's the latter option you've got to move fast.' A sense that he stood at a crossroads in his life stole over him. 'Remember what they say, you only regret the things you *don't* do . . .'

35

As he stared out at a night-time London illuminated by the full moon, a barge surged along the waterway. Some prankster had decided that vast steel flank too much like a blank canvas to be resisted. Painted there were these words and symbols:

VAMPIRE SHARKZ
☺ They're coming to get you ☺

Seven

'Why don't you answer me?'
        'You're not asking the right questions.'
    'What's your name? Why are we here?' She caught the man by the elbow. 'They seem good enough questions to me.'
    'Keep moving,' came his reply. 'If you want to live, you'll follow me and you'll shut up.'
    'Why?'
    'Because if they hear you they'll catch you, then they'll tear you up like they tore up the guy in the yellow shirt. Understand?'
    His words took some of the heat out of April Connor's anger, so she followed this man with the gold-tipped teeth along a path that wove through clumps of willow. Above her, the unnatural moon still burned down as brilliantly as any sun.
    'Why is the moon so bright, then?'
    He put his fingers to his lips and kept walking: a rapid, purposeful walk. Although she didn't know where they were going exactly she realized they'd cut across the island, and even though it couldn't have been more than a hundred yards wide by a couple of hundred long – nothing but a sandbank with a few clumps of trees and bushes – April could no longer see the water. Or that mob on the beach.
    After a few moments the stranger asked, 'Hungry?'
    'I thought talking was forbidden?'

36

'We're as far away as we're going to get from your friends, but keep it low, okay?'

'They're not my friends.'

'They're nobody's friends now.'

'That's cryptic.'

'I asked if you were hungry?'

'Ravenous. Have you got any food?'

'Nothing *you'd* like to eat,' he snapped.

'I don't always eat mud.'

'I'm not talking about mud.'

'Look, what's your name?'

He paused. 'My name?'

'Can't you remember it, either?'

'I've got it back now, but it doesn't feel as if it belongs to me.' He gave a grim smile. Those gold-tipped incisors glinted. 'For the record, I'm called Carter.'

'Why the record?'

'Names don't mean anything round here.'

'They do to me. I'm April Connor.' She held out her hand. 'Mr Carter.'

He stared at her hand. 'Carter Vaughn. No mister. Still hungry?'

She nodded. 'To the point of nausea.'

'They all get like that, April.' He shook her hand. 'That's why you ate dirt, and the others ate stones, then they decided that the big guy should become dinner.'

'Why did they choose him?'

'Juiciest. Start walking.'

She walked in silence for a moment until they reached another shoreline. This one was deserted; the falling tide revealed a stretch of sand that ran out a hundred yards or so. The pains in her stomach flared up again. A sickening spasm that fluidly transformed itself into raging hunger that attacked her veins as much as her stomach.

April talked to distract herself from the hunger. 'What's this place called?'

'As far as I know it doesn't have a name.' When he saw the anxiety in her face he smiled. 'Okay, I know you want answers. I call it Willow Island. On account of . . .' He pulled at the fronds of a willow. 'And Rat Island would do. There's hundreds of the little buggers.'

'I've been calling it the Isle of the Dead.' She rubbed her stomach. 'It seemed apt.'

'Yeah, that's a good one, too.'

'But how did I end up out here in the ocean?'

'Ocean? This is the River Thames. When it's daylight you can make out Gravesend upstream.'

The vastness of the twinkling water astounded her. 'But it's huge. I can't see the bank.'

'That's because it's low-lying. Also we're down near the end of the estuary. Is it getting bad?'

'Uh?'

'The hunger?'

She pressed her lips together as she nodded. Images of cooked meats seared through her – chops, steaks, rib roast, hams, hamburgers, you name it.

'This is when mud starts looking like Sunday dinner, doesn't it?'

Again she could only nod as painful cramps snapped her stomach muscles tight. In another effort to distract her she spat out another question. 'How did we get here, Carter?'

'You know how, April. You know exactly how.'

'I was attacked. Thrown in the river . . . from the embankment near Westminster.' She found it hard to speak, the pain was so intense. 'You?'

'You were bitten on the waist. See the bite mark on my wrist? I thought I was helping some homeless kid in a park. He nearly chewed my hand off, then dumped me in the water at Woolwich. I drifted down with the tide like the rest.'

'I don't understand . . .' The pain grew worse.

'What is there to understand? It's the way it is. All we can do is keep away from the headcases, they get so hungry they'll eat anything. See those teeth marks in the tree trunk?'

April eyed the trunk of the willow. The bark resembled bacon – or at least it did right then. She saw how satisfying it would be to sink her teeth into the flesh of the tree.

'Don't try it.' Carter guessed what she was thinking. 'You'll only break your teeth.'

'But I've got to eat,' she said. 'I can't think properly. I need to bite down on . . .' She rubbed her forehead as nothing less than starvation ripped through her. 'Just to bite. That would be enough for now.' Even as she spoke she eyed the sand at her feet. Its sugary whiteness shining in the moonlight was so alluring she longed to gorge.

'Look at me, April. No, look into my face. Eating that crap only makes you sick or snaps your teeth. I'll show you how to stop the worst of the hunger. It won't make it go away but it'll be tolerable. Understand?'

Reluctantly, she forced herself to stop ogling the crisp sand that offered nothing less than a whole feast beneath her feet.

'Listen,' Carter told her. 'First we'll deal with the hunger pains, then I'll tell you everything I know. Okay?'

'Okay. Tell me what I have to do.' By now, she found she couldn't take her eyes off the firm roundness of his Adam's apple.

Carter pointed at the pool of water left by the high tide. 'There,' he told her. 'Don't eat the mud or the sand, just drink as much as you can.'

'That puddle?' April Connor clutched her stomach. 'I need *food*!'

'You won't get what you want here. Drink that, it'll stop the pains.'

'Bloody moron,' she hissed. 'That's river water . . . are you trying to poison me?'

'Your choice, April. Drink, or go back to those lunatics and eat each other; I've seen it all before.'

'There's been more of us?'

'Lots more. Usually they go so crazy they end up back in the water.'

They made their way down on to the shore that glinted with a series of tidal pools. The one that Carter had indicated was clear enough to reveal bits of broken glass in the bottom. There was a latex glove, too, with a finger and thumb missing. She fancied she could see some worm-like creatures squirming amongst the sludge.

'You want me to drink that!'

'It's the only way, April.'

'I can't.'

'You're different from the rest. You haven't gone crazy like them.'

'Maybe . . . better . . . uh, if I had.' Wild lusts blazed through

39

her. A rat scampered up the banking. *Catch it! Don't bother killing it first. Devour it alive . . .*

'Start drinking. If you don't it'll be too late. You lose self-control.'

'No. I'm not drinking out of a filthy puddle!'

'Your choice.' He backed away along the path, his hands held out at either side. 'Don't say I never tried to save you.'

The instant her will power collapsed she didn't so much get down on to her knees as attack the puddle. She hurled herself at it and began drinking. When the palms of her hands couldn't contain enough water she buried her face in it and sucked it straight into her mouth. What she thought would have been cold and bitter turned out to be warm and satisfying. As long as she drank, that is. The moment she stopped the hunger pangs slammed through her with so much force she gasped. So she relentlessly gulped down the water. This came from the estuary; it wasn't freshwater but partly saline. It was that saltiness that made the flavour so irresistible. The minerals in that blend of river and ocean had a pleasing tang. In her mind's eye she saw that solution of saltwater spread through her veins to damp down those fires of rapacious hunger.

Carter crouched beside her. 'It's working, isn't it?' Quickly, he scooped handfuls of water to his own mouth. 'Every few hours you'll need to come back here and drink.'

Panting from the exertion of devouring pint after pint of water, she gasped, 'Why this stuff? Why does it work when eating mud doesn't?'

'If you fill your belly with water it tricks the mind into believing you've eaten. Mud only makes you sick.'

April sucked each finger in turn where the water had soaked them. 'It's the salt.' Her eyes fixed on those pools of estuary water left by the tide. 'If you drink straight from the river it doesn't have the same effect, does it?'

'No. Always stick with the tidal pools.'

'The liquid begins to evaporate leaving the salt behind. These are more intensely saline . . .' She paused. 'But why do we have a craving for salt?'

'We crave something that contains salt,' he told her.

'What's that?'

'It'll come to you.' As he stood up he continued licking his fingers. 'Come on.'

40

'Where now?'

'I want to show you something.'

'A boat would be nice . . . and food.'

'I've got neither. We're marooned here.'

'Mr and Mrs Robinson Crusoe.'

'Hey, you made a joke.' He smiled revealing the gold-tipped teeth. 'That proves you must be feeling better, yeah?'

'I'm wandering round a desert island in a torn dress, wearing one sandal; I've eaten mud and watched a man torn to pieces. I feel downright tickety-boo.'

He stopped and looked her in the eye. 'In my book that's feeling better. You're a million times better than those animals back there on the beach. They'll be sat chewing on that guy's face. Not that it'll help them. By morning they'll have gone mad with hunger and thrown themselves back into the river.'

'Why not show them your magic cure?'

'The tidal pools? They wouldn't listen. They've all disintegrated up here.' He tapped his head. 'I call them Berserkers. We're the only ones who are still functioning mentally.'

She became wary. 'So there'll just be me and you on the island?'

'Not quite. I'll introduce you to the rest of our family.'

'Family? I've no plans to stay here.'

'Okay.' He shrugged. 'But how are you going to leave?'

Once more April Connor found herself following this man, Carter Vaughn, through the clumps of willows.

'Best make it quick,' he told her. 'The sun will be rising soon.'

'Thank God. This has to be the longest night of my life.'

'Trust me, you won't like sunshine anymore.'

'Why?'

'Feel your hair,' Carter said.

'Uh. Yuk.'

'Sticky, isn't it?'

'It feels . . . disgusting. I must have got something on it. Oil or tar.'

He shook his head. 'Mine's sticky too. We all have sticky hair.'

'I'll wash it in the river.'

'It won't do any good. It stays sticky, like you've rubbed syrup into it.'

41

'Why?'

'Because we've changed. I'm not the same Carter Vaughn anymore. You're not the same April Connor.'

'Oh, I'll be me again, once I get away from this island.'

'Okay, just you wait and see. Then you'll believe me.'

Carter made his way up a slight incline into a clump of thick bushes; he was hurrying as if time was running out.

April called after him, 'So, what's all this about sticky hair and not liking sunlight anymore? What's it all mean?'

He didn't look back. 'Hurry up. Before it starts to get light.'

So, what could she do? The man knew enough to stop her going crazy when the hunger pangs started. Maybe he had other information that would be useful. She plunged into the bushes after him. A bird screeched at being disturbed. Dark shapes flitted by her feet as rats fled . . . or were they circling behind her, ready to sink their incisors into her bare heels?

'Carter? Where are you?'

The bushes concealed him now. In fact they were so dense she had to push her way through the lush green branches. The air was heavy with musk-odors as if animals curled up here to sleep in the vegetation. When she reached out to push a creeper back so she could scramble through she encountered a horizontal mass of hard material. For a moment she thought her way had been blocked by a sandstone cliff, but then she saw the remains of a window that was nearly obliterated by ivy.

A house? With a surge of optimism she pictured herself knocking on a door that would be opened by some boatman who'd say, 'Of course, you can use the telephone.' Then she'd leave this hump of dirt in the river. Only that image of a smiling face fizzled into disappointment when she put her face to a pane of grubby glass. The place was clearly derelict . . . and derelict for years at that. In the gloomy interior she could make out what appeared to be abandoned furniture. Peeling wallpaper hung down, like the room was some weird reptile that was in the process of shedding its skin.

A hand gripped her wrist. April recoiled in shock.

'This way.' Carter leaned through a mass of trailing willow. 'Hurry. You need to see them before the sun starts to rise.' He beckoned her into a green tunnel formed by the vegetation that led to the front door. The paint had cracked on the timbers. The only window she could see on this side of the property had old cupboard doors nailed across it. As he pulled her through that green tunnel to the derelict, unloved house she suddenly stopped.

'I don't want to go in there.' That strange arrhythmic breathing began its stuttering gasps again. For some reason the house terrified her. He wanted to show her someone in there – the 'family' – only she didn't want to go. It seemed wrong. There was something rotten inside. She didn't want to see it . . .

Terror ran through her in a dark, pulsating stream. The sense of dread was every bit as powerful as the hunger that had gripped her earlier. If she stepped into the house nothing would be the same again. This is where the April Connor she knew would be no more. It wouldn't be her death because death is the end of everything. No, this would be a transition from her old way of life – of planning a new home with her fiancé, Trajan – to something new, but something so alien, and so shocking she didn't know whether her mind could handle it. At that moment it really did seem preferable to flee back to the beach where those maniacs tore at one another.

'April. Hurry. Before it's too late.'

With a sudden furious strength he grabbed hold of her arm and dragged her along the leafy green tunnel toward the door of the derelict house. It had been partly open. Now it creaked back of its own accord as he dragged her toward it.

'Carter? What are you going to do to me?'

Inside. Gloom. Silence. Stillness. A sense of the very air being imprisoned for decades. On the wall a framed photograph of a man and woman standing in front of the house when it still functioned as a dwelling. On the lawn in front of the cottage the photo revealed a rowing boat. Wicker cages of the kind used to catch crabs were stacked against a wall. The faces of the man and woman had vanished. The creeping damp had erased them from the photograph long ago.

Carter guided her across the hallway to a room. Sheets of wallpaper hung from yellowed plaster. A solitary armchair faced a fireplace that contained dead leaves. Either standing or sitting in the room were six figures. Their clothes were little more than scraps of material that hung from their bodies. They were men and women of different ages. Their skin held bluish tints, their hair glistened . . . Sticky, April told herself. Sticky hair. She touched her own. It was sticky, too. Like her, they'd either lost their footwear or still retained one shoe. And what struck her the most was their stillness. Their expressionless faces could have been cast from solid plastic. Although their eyes were part open they appeared to focus on nothing. They could have been a group of eccentrics pretending they were recreating a still photograph.

'Misfires,' Carter whispered. 'At least that's what I call them.'

'Misfires?'

'See? They're a lot like us. They were washed up on the shore but they never came back to life properly. They wandered around the island aimlessly until they ended up here. I guess there's some ghost of a memory in their heads that tells them to take shelter in a house. So in they come. They stay. They don't do anything else.'

'Like they're waiting?'

'Waiting for doomsday, more like. They don't talk, don't move. Nothing.'

April shivered. 'They are alive, aren't they?'

Carter's gold teeth gleamed as he smiled. 'Alive? As much as you and me.'

She stepped up to a man of around forty who still wore the remains of a business suit. Before this transformation he could have been an executive working in some prestigious office building. Now he gazed bleakly through slitted eyes. Yes, the name Misfire was appropriate. They failed to function properly.

'These Misfires,' she began, 'why have you shown them to me?'

'Because you're not exactly like them and you're not exactly like the Berserkers on the beach. These Misfires don't feel hungry like we do. Then again that hunger hasn't pushed us over the edge like the others.'

She turned to a woman of around twenty. The woman stood by the fireplace, her arms hung loosely down by her side. Her brown hair stood out in sticky tufts. The eyelids were half closed revealing dull splinters of white. Slowly, April reached out to touch the woman's cheek. Cold as a pane of glass. The woman didn't know April was there, or that she'd touched

44

her. These weren't men and women. They were things that were nine tenths dead. Only for some reason the last shred of life hadn't deserted them. It clung to their body tissues, feeding just enough vitality into their flesh to prevent them rotting where they stood.

April stepped back. These things made her nauseous. 'I want to leave now.'

'Leave?' Carter shook his head. 'We can't go outside now, the sun's rising.'

'I can't bear it in here.'

'Compared to out there this is going to be paradise.'

'I feel sick.' She blundered past him as a bright light began to shine into the hallway. He grabbed hold of her to stop her leaving.

'Let go of me!' April wrenched free of him; the movement so explosive that she reeled back into one of the figures. It toppled to the floorboards with a thump, then lay there to stare upward. Not a flicker of expression. No surprise, no shock, no hurt.

'April, stay here!'

She knew he pursued her through the doorway into the hall.

He keeps these people here. They were normal when they arrived at the house. He's done something to them. Now he wants to do the same to me! Those thoughts snapped through her head as she ran. He'd tricked her to come to this miserable hovel hidden in the bushes. His feet pounded the boards as he raced after her. In front of her the door was part open. Beyond it was the green tunnel of vegetation that led back into the island.

'April! You can't go out there!'

'Don't you touch me!'

'April, it's too late!'

She hurtled down the hallway to the door, then ran outside. At that moment she longed to see the sun again after a night that had seemed eternal. Instead of following the tunnel of foliage, she ripped aside the branches to find a new way through. She had to escape the monster that pursued her at all costs. Yet the moment she pushed aside the branch she found she was facing the dawn. Only it was a dawn she'd never encountered before. The sky was white. That's when a wall of incandescence surged across the island, bleaching out all the trees, the bushes, the bare expanses of dirt into whiteness. Nothing but whiteness. A dazzling, ubiquitous universe of blistering light. She screamed as the sun's rays seared her face. The wound in her side felt as if it shriveled to pucker her flesh. The light itself could have been the hand of a god pressing her down toward the ground. As she toppled a pair of hands seized her then dragged her inside the house. She heard the door bang shut but still the light shone with the intensity of laser beams. They blasted through the keyhole and gaps between the door and frame.

'I warned you,' Carter panted as he hauled her deeper into the house. 'I told you that you wouldn't like the sunlight anymore.' He half carried her into a back room. The windows were boarded but still rods of searing, white light pierced chinks to drill holes through the darkness. 'Lay down against the wall.'

Dazed, she did as he told her. Exposure to the sunlight had half-blinded her. The wound in her side itched. All she could make out was that the room was bare. A scrap of carpet covered part of the boards that in turn were scattered with dead leaves and clumps of ancient cobweb. Sitting on the floor, with their backs to the wall, were three of those Misfires. Two men and a woman. Their eyelids were such a burden to them they could barely keep them open. Without moving, without any sign of them noticing April, they maintained that dull, unfocussed stare into nothingness.

April Connor had barely any strength in her to move. So there was nothing she could do when Carter lay down beside her. She expected him to reach out and grasp her. But all he did was seize the piece of carpet that was the size of a bed sheet then drag it over their two bodies so it covered them completely. Then he lay there as if his ability to move had all of a sudden ceased.

Outside came the dawn chorus as bird-life welcomed the arrival of the sun. Beneath the carpet in their little world of gloom and stillness April Connor listened for the beat of her own heart. The hours passed. She strained to hear that familiar pulse in her chest. And it was a long time before she could finally admit to herself that there was nothing there.

Eight

Ben Ashton left his apartment before seven. The morning sun blazed down on to the River Thames as he walked along the path and past his car parked at the side of the road. London's population was bursting through the seven million mark so driving wasn't the quickest way of negotiating the metropolis at the best of times. He decided to nose around, seeing what facts he could dig up in the neighborhood. His editor was convinced that there was more to that rash of graffiti than met the eye. Ben wasn't persuaded but he'd been paid to investigate this to the best of his journalistic ability so that's what he'd do. As always, when he received an article assignment, he began to map out how he'd write up the story. Of course this was a voyage into the unknown.

The identity of the Vampire Sharkz graffiti writer – or should that be dauber? – was a mystery. He didn't know who. He didn't know why. Again, Raj was certain there was some motive for the graffiti beyond the fun of spraying the words in big red letters on buses, trains, walls, gravestones, you name it. So the *who* and the *why* were still intangibles; it was only the *when* that he had a reasonable handle on. The graffiti had just appeared in the last month or so. It seemed to arrive on the first breath of the heat wave that they were enjoying right now. Although from the marked increase in humidity Ben guessed it wouldn't last. A British hot spell tends to end in a thunderstorm. As well as uncovering information about the graffiti artist's ID he ran through the presentation of the story. It made sense to put the graffiti into historical context. He could mention the kind of comments and pictures the ancient Romans and Egyptians violated their walls with – or should it be expressed their creativity with?

Graffiti serves all kinds of purposes. Some is political comment, religious or social matters. Some of it is downright rude. And most simply mundane: 'Joe was here', that kind of thing. Then there were proclamations of love: 'Tiz and Bex forever'. That thought nearly diverted him to his late night brooding over April Connor. Instead, he turned his mind back to the article. The magazine had won an international readership, so, as well as his investigation into the Vampire Sharkz street art, plus some history about graffiti, he should also describe the graffiti artist's canvas: London itself.

Just how many facts to include is crucial. Use too many and the article becomes a tourism commercial rather than a penetrating investigation into a singular message that infects every street in London . . . yeah, he was getting that tingle now as the words started to flow. How about this? A brief description of Britain's capital city of seven million souls, standing on the river that is quaintly known as Father Thames. If anything, most of the graffiti seemed be clustered around the river itself so he could draw this geographical feature into the article. How's this for a description? The river is tidal and stretches from the wide estuary with its tiny forgotten islands to its source in the Cotswolds. It became a favourite port of the ancient Romans because the tidal surge was so strong their boats rode the influx of water fifty miles inland without even having to dip an oar or raise so much as a sail. Too much? Yeah, too much history. Focus more on the phantom nature of the graffiti artist. They're never seen but their work appears magically overnight. So how does the phantom artist move around? Probably on the London Underground tube – more than two hundred and fifty miles of subterranean track that allows them to flit undetected about the city.

Ben paused on the corner of the street. On one side was a billboard that advertised suntan lotion. In turn that bore the now well-known warning: Vampire Sharkz. They're coming to get you. Directly opposite that was a café, which boasted it opened at five in the morning and closed at midnight.

Okay, he told himself. This is where you turn detective. Time to start asking questions.

At that time of the morning the café catered for just two customers who wore suits despite the heat. They must have been early for an appointment in one of the office blocks that towered over the river and were killing time by discussing the strategy of their forthcoming meeting. The smell of coffee was a fine one and Ben breathed it in. Even though the décor was homely the range of coffees was an exotic one: mocha, espresso, cappuccino, latte; it seemed almost an insult to ask for his regular filter, no cream. The proprietor, a balding man in his fifties, chalked today's specials on a board above the counter. This eastern swathe of London used to be the place to dine on jellied eels, or pie and mash doused in something called liquor (Ben still wasn't sure what this savoury liquor was other than it was a cream-coloured sauce speckled with parsley), but the traditional eateries were being pushed to the margins by more cosmopolitan cafés. The specials board boasted an array of salads with mullet, freshly grilled sardine, calamari, crayfish, Thai shrimp, Scottish salmon . . . the list went on . . . not an eel in sight, though. Years ago the eel would have been devoured by the ton in this neighbourhood. Although Ben had tasted those snake-like fish he couldn't admit to liking them. That first mouthful had been a combination of cold slime and what seemed to be around a hundred little bones that he'd grimly chewed before swallowing with all the pleasure of someone forced to drink chilled poison. He thought about those eels worming their way along the Thames and told himself they were safe from his jaws at least.

The proprietor finished chalking 'bouillabaisse' in pink then turned to Ben.

'Hot enough for you?'

'Plenty,' Ben replied. He wondered why most conversations in England begin with the weather. 'Looks as if we're heading for a thunderstorm.'

'The dog's hiding in the cellar. He can't stand thunder and he always knows when it's coming. Right, what can I do you for?'

'A cappuccino please.' Journalists know that to order a coffee that takes longer to prepare than other varieties gives them more chance to pump their target for facts. 'Quiet today?' Begin conversationally, that's the way.

'You should see it in an hour when the offices e-mail orders for sandwiches. That salmon's going to walk right out the door.'

'Not much call for jellied eels these days?'

'My grandfather ran a stall at Spitalfields that sold nothing but. Thirty years ago he was making a fortune. Today you can't give eels away. Same goes for whale meat. The first man I met who owned a Rolls Royce earned his money boiling up whale. Even with all his money he couldn't find a girl that would marry him. It was that stink of boiled blubber. It stuck to him like glue. Pastry with your coffee, sir?

'A Danish, please.'

The man operated the steam machine to froth the coffee.

Ben took a paper napkin from the dispenser. 'Any call for shark?'

'Oh? We used to do a shark's fin soup but tastes change. Why do you ask?'

'Shark seems to be all the rage these days.' Ben nodded back through the window at the graffiti.

'Ah, the infamous Vampire Sharkz.' He chuckled as he set down the frothed beverage. 'It's everywhere.'

A woman wearing chef whites emerged from the back to set a dish of chopped tomatoes into a chill cabinet.

The man turned to her. 'Vampire Sharkz, Julie. I was just saying to the gentleman that the graffiti is everywhere.'

She wasn't amused. 'The so-and-so got us the other night. It's painted all over our gate.'

Ben nodded in sympathy. 'Makes you wonder who's doing it?'

'Kids,' the man said firmly.

'It's more than that.' The woman closed the chill cabinet door. 'Whoever's painting it is on a mission.'

'They'll be on a police charge if they don't watch out,' the man joked. Then he held up a silver shaker. 'Sprinkles?' When Ben nodded the man dusted the cappuccino with chocolate dust.

'So what's your theory?' Ben asked the woman.

She gave him an appraising look. 'Why are you interested?'

He decided to be upfront. 'I'm a writer. I've been commissioned by a magazine to investigate the great Vampire Sharkz mystery.'

The man chuckled. 'It sounds as if you don't think there's much of a story in it.'

Ben shrugged. 'Probably not. But you never know. Last year I worked on the green bottle mystery. You might—'

'Oh, the drug smuggling.' The woman smoothed down her chef's whites. 'I remember that one.'

The man looked bemused. 'The green bottle mystery. What's that?'

'You should spend some time reading instead of watching the telly. Shall I tell him?'

Ben nodded. 'Be my guest.' The couple were chatting freely now. If he indulged them then he might be able to tease out some clues about the phantom graffiti artist. People who work in pubs and cafés are great sources of information. It's just a question of filtering fact from gossip.

'The green bottle mystery,' she began. 'Correct me if I'm wrong, sir.'

'Call me Ben.'

'Ben,' she said. 'Let's see, a gang of drug smugglers filled green bottles with marijuana then dropped them over the side of the boat down at the river mouth. That way they avoided sneaking the stuff through customs.'

'Doesn't seem very clever to me.' The man sniffed. 'How did they find it again?'

Ben said, 'The bottles were a distinctive green. They had a gang collect them off the beach right under the noses of the police.'

'But they must have lost most of their stash.' The man began slicing bread in readiness for the office orders. 'The bottles would've floated anywhere and everywhere.'

'Ah, that was the clever bit.' Ben sipped his coffee. 'When the tide rises a mass of water surges up the Thames. If you drop a bottle way downstream, where the river empties into the sea, providing your timing is right, the bottle will be carried by the tide right into the middle of London.'

'But you've still the problem of fishing the bottles out.'

'It's all down to the mechanics of tidal flows but all rivers will methodically sort out all material thrown into the water. If you go along the banks you'll find distinct areas where the shore consists of sand, go a bit further then you'll find a stretch of stones that are the same size and shape. Go a bit further and that's where all the driftwood will congregate. It's a known fact that anyone drowning in the river will, likely as not, wind up on the shore at Tower Bridge.'

'So all these green bottles filled with drugs ended up on a particular beach?'

'Exactly.'

The man squirted steam into a jug. 'Now that's what I call cunning.'

'Did you catch the smugglers?' the woman asked.

'No. My job was to write about the river and its tides and currents.'

'And now you're investigating the Vampire Sharkz. Good luck, mate.' The man stacked the sliced bread. 'My opinion, for what it's worth, is that it's kids.'

'You're wrong,' the woman countered. 'This graffiti's different. Vampire Sharkz. They're coming to get you. Don't you see? It's either a threat or a warning.'

The man caught Ben's eye. 'Who am I to argue? The oracle has spoken.'

She bustled into the back with the words, 'There's a storm coming; I want you to get the dog out of the cellar or he'll howl the place down.'

Ben Ashton moved through the East End of London into the maze of streets around Spitalfields Market. This is the place that movies portrayed as being the fogbound haunt of Jack the Ripper. Where hansom cabs clattered along, and cries of 'Murder! Murder!' in a Cockney accent would be followed by the piercing note of the constable's whistle. The infamous London smog had gone now. Today, Ben strolled through the summer sunshine where the rows of Victorian townhouses were punctuated by modern buildings. A redbrick house with an ancient front door and extravagant cast-iron knocker that would be perfect as Scrooge's residence in *A Christmas Carol* might sit next to a glass-sided photographic studio. The reason for the mixture of architecture was apparent from the gouge marks in the old walls where they'd been scarred by Hitler's bombs. During the blitz of World War Two many properties had been literally blown off the map. Yet the street names were still there: Brick Lane, Chicksand Street, Fashion Street, Petticoat Lane, Whitechapel Road. Now Cockney sparrows lived side-by-side with middle-eastern families. Brick Lane exuded the mystique and aromas of a Damascus street market. Arabic music ran helter-skelter from café doorways. A heady mix of different nationalities thronged the streets. When Ben Ashton visited this neighbourhood it sent tingles down his spine. He loved how Eastern exoticism found a unique fusion with Cockney London. Although he noticed, regretfully, that it was only just mid-morning otherwise he'd be tempted to slip into one of the restaurants where he could enjoy the Moroccan flavors of lamb slowly cooked with almonds and honey.

But everywhere he went he was haunted by that graffiti rendered in blazing red paint:

VAMPIRE SHARKZ
☺ They're coming to get you ☺

Even though examples of the graffiti were easy to find in that distinctive script, the identity of its creator was going to be more difficult to uncover. Dangerous, too, if it was a criminal gang marking their territory. He passed offices built on the site of Miller's Court where Jack the Ripper's last victim, Mary Kelly, had been butchered. Even a rear wall of that building wore the blood-red lettering.

So exactly what are Vampire Sharkz? A bunch of drug dealers? An R&B band? But why are they going to get us? How will they get us? What do they intend to do with us? Why the smiling face motif? Was the lettering the work of one artist? Or were there teams of them?

Ben did what he was paid to do. He asked around. Had anyone seen the graffiti artist? Mostly, the responses were smiles, shakes of the head. Some people were annoyed by the vandalism of property. One kid declared it 'Cool', and gazed at the five-foot-high letters in admiration. A man with a shaved head told him he'd heard a Vampire Shark was the new narcotic that would replace cocaine. A stony-faced woman with bags full of oranges insisted that the Arts Council had paid some millionaire conceptual artist to violate her beloved city. So the rumor mill had begun to turn out fanciful stories. The graffiti was already acquiring its own mythology.

The people he needed to speak with were the ones that watched the streets night and day. The security guards, the police, the paparazzi who lay siege to celebrities' houses at ungodly hours. He retraced his steps along Brick Lane in the direction of Whitechapel High Street. The sun blazed down on him; it made his back itch. The minutes were ticking away to the deadline next week. If he didn't deliver this high-profile assignment it was likely he'd be relegated to filler articles that the editor used when nothing newsworthy was happening.

'Come on,' he muttered to himself. 'Make this good. Make an impression.'

His eye caught a rack of newspapers outside a newsagent's. One headline ran with typical tabloid slickness: Boat Prophet Faces Boot. Then in smaller print: Mayor tells hermit his days are numbered.

Ben clicked his tongue. 'There's your man.'

Nine

'Ladies and gentlemen! You have ten minutes to save your lives. Quickly! How are you going to do it?'

Ben approached the plywood dinghy that sat on top of its ten-foot pole in the park beside the river, just a short distance from the distinctive landmark of Tower Bridge. The huge structure of the bridge with its latticework of steel, along which red double-decker buses flowed, rippled in the heat haze as if the sun melted it.

In the dinghy atop the pole sat a man with blue-black skin who called down to passers-by. He shaded himself beneath a black umbrella of the kind that used to be favored by London's office workers in the days of yore. A girl with bare, sunburnt shoulders walked by the boat-on-a-stick without looking up.

'Madam! You have ten minutes to save your life. Quickly! How are you going to do it?'

With her eyes down on the path she trudged through the hot air without responding.

Ben shielded his eyes against the glare and peered up at the man, sheltering from the blazing sun beneath his brolly. The man was elderly yet his unlined face appeared astonishingly youthful.

'Sir,' the man said. 'You have ten minutes to save your life. Quickly! How are you going to do it?'

'Mr Kigoma?'

The man moved his umbrella slightly as he leaned over the edge of the airborne vessel to look down. 'There's only one human being in the whole of London who lives in a boat on top of a pole; who the hell else could it be?'

'My apologies, Mr Kigoma. I wondered if you would like to talk to me.'

'Of course.'

'My name is Ben Ashton.'

'You from the Mayor's office?' There was a kind of wide-eyed innocence as the man gazed down.

'No, sir.'

'You're definitely not police.'

'That's right. I'm—'

'A reporter.'

'Well, a feature writer for a magazine.'

'That's not a reporter? Are you not writing for a publication?'

'Yes, sir, I am.'

'Writing a report about what you've been assigned to investigate?'

'Ye-ess . . .' Ben conceded. The man in the boat wasn't hostile. Oddly, his manner suggested a child-like curiosity. 'Can I ask you some questions?'

'Lord, yes!'

'Thank you, sir.'

'Call me Elmo.'

'Elmo.' Ben nodded. His neck was beginning to ache from looking upwards. The old man was neatly dressed in a shirt, buttoned at the neck with a neatly knotted tie. How the shirt could be such a pristine white and the tie so uncrumpled, Ben couldn't begin to guess. With an air of youth, the man seemed to glow with cleanliness despite residing in the boat. Short silver locks of hair hugged his scalp and Ben couldn't avoid picturing those statues of Greek philosophers in the British Museum with the same crisp hairstyles.

Elmo began to recite a speech that he must have given plenty of times before to TV crews and reporters. 'My name is Elmo Kigoma. Some dub me the modern Diogenes after the philosopher who lived in Athens four hundred years before Christ; there he resided in a wash tub, and reputedly he walked the streets in daylight with a lamp telling everyone he searched for an honest man. I was born in the Congo eighty-six years ago this very month. Two weeks ago my sons and I erected a pole in the park then set the boat on top. All this we did without the consent of the Mayor's office – she now wishes rid of me, and will send men to tear down my boat. But I have a mission. I am here to warn people that in order to save their lives they must abstain. To eat and drink frugally is the key to longevity.'

Ben jumped in when Elmo took a breath. 'I'm interested in what you see from your boat up there.'

'Oh?'

'Well, that's some vantage point, and you're here night and day.'

'I'll tell you what I see, Ben. I see humanity in danger. They are in peril. Death waits nearby.'

'From overindulgence?'

'Yes, Ben. But not only that.'

Ben took in the park. It was peaceful enough. A man in a red bandanna walked his dog. Children sat in the shade to eat ice creams they'd bought from a kiosk beside the river. And Old Father Thames flowed at an untroubled pace toward the sea. When Ben couldn't identify any source of danger whatsoever, he returned to the serene expression of the man who gazed down on him.

Elmo turned his head to scan the river. 'You won't see it now but the signs are there.'

Ben admired the man, and his fearless expression of his beliefs, not to say his devotion to helping humanity, though Ben guessed the threat Elmo identified might be difficult for most people to understand – Ben included. What Elmo uttered next bore this out.

'Ben. I've laboured to explain the danger, but people's minds are tuned to a different wave-length. Their minds are incapable of understanding when I tell them that Edshu has returned.'

'Edshu?' Ben echoed the unfamiliar name.

'Edshu the trickster god. Whose sole aim is to bring about conflict and disharmony. For Edshu, spreading strife is his eternal joy.'

'I'm sorry, Elmo, I've never heard of Edshu.'

'He's a deity from my homeland. When Edshu wishes it he can make all kinds of mischief. Listen, how can I explain it more clearly? When you drop a slice of bread. If it falls with the buttered side down on to your rug, that's the touch of Edshu. You know your dog has been touched by Edshu if your pet becomes lost and you spend hours searching for him. But when you find him, instead of the pleasure of being reunited the dog bites your hand. That's the touch of Edshu. The trickster god doesn't confront you with an enemy; he turns your friend into your enemy.'

'Just as food can change from a source of nourishment and pleasure into your enemy, too.'

'Ha!' Elmo threw down the umbrella and stood up in the boat. The post quivered alarmingly. 'Ha!' Elmo pointed down, his eyes wide. 'I like you, Ben. You are the first person to understand my message. Food and drink in moderation gives you life. Excess is death. I like you very much!'

Ben found himself grinning up at the man. While Elmo was in the process of thinking so highly of him it might be fruitful to ask that key question. 'Elmo, you've lived in this park for a while, so perhaps you can solve a mystery for me?'

'I like you, sir, so I will try my hardest.'

'My employer has instructed me to find out who is painting a message all over London. You can make out the lettering on that fence across there.'

Elmo nodded. 'I've seen it.'

'Vampire Sharkz. They're coming to get you.' Ben shielded his eyes against the sun's glare. 'Did you see who painted it?'

'The identity of the individual isn't important.'

'That's what I've been asked to discover.'

Elmo Kigoma's voice rang out with a sudden power. 'You must write about the warning. Soon Edshu will test the men and women of London. If they're strong enough to survive the enemy he has created then the gods will permit you all to live. If you are weak the gods will wipe out the city. I have seen the Dead-bone Woman kill a man on that very path. She's a creature of the sticky hair. When I was a child they would lash out at my people from the darkness of the jungle. Now the same creatures will lash out at people from the river that flows through this city. Write down the warning in your

57

magazine. Tell everyone that they must be on their guard because the battle they will soon fight will make all the battles of the past seem like nothing!'

'I'm sorry, Elmo, I don't understand the exact nature of this threat. You say there's something dangerous in the water?'

'You understood what I meant about abstinence and excess. Think about what I told you – you'll make sense of it!'

The sudden outburst of emotion exhausted the old man. He raised the umbrella over his head to shade him from the sun. In the distance clouds bubbled up on the horizon. Those thunderheads promised the arrival of a storm.

Ten

'Come back, you're going to get electrocuted.'
'The power goes through that third rail. The electricity goes nowhere near the bridge.'

'You're still too close, bro.'

'Stop your worrying, Mickey. Look, safe as houses.'

Ped proved the gantry that ran beneath the bridge was solid by jumping up and down. Not that it would reassure Mickey for long. Mickey dreaded electricity. When the tube train ran under the bridge the contacts brushed against the live rail, triggering blue-white flashes that were dazzling. Ped held a paint aerosol in one hand; the other arm he draped across his brother's shoulders.

'Listen, it can't hurt you, Mickey. The juice's down there. We're up here.'

Mickey's wide eyes tracked the train as it ran along the surface line. 'Look at them flashes, bro. All them sparks. The electric's getting out!'

'No. It isn't.' He hugged his brother so hard the kid's shoulder dug into his chest. 'Electricals are safe. They don't hurt no one.'

'Electric chair. Arc. Danger of death.' Mickey had begun to mutter his litany again. 'Voltage, volts, voltmeter. Amp, ampage. Power points, live terminals.'

'Mickey, look . . . hey, look at this. I'm painting your tag here.' He shook the aerosol; the bearings inside rattled. 'There . . . M for Mickey. Then I write mine. P-E-D. Then I put the wall around, keeping us safe inside. You see, Mickey?' He painted the initials in fluorescent green then circled it with a band. 'All safe inside, Mickey. No electric can touch us there. Nobody else, either.'

'The Electric Man?'

'We've been through that before, Mickey. There is no Electric Man.'

'He stood in the doorway watching me last night.'

'That was Ma's new bloke.' Ped shook the can. 'Mickey, I'm going to blast our tag on these bridge panels. We're going to be famous, bro. Tomorrow morning all those commuters are going to see your initials. Thousands and thousands of people. Keep watching me, Mickey. That's it; see how I form the letters – a big M; like I'm painting two mountains side-by-side.'

In the distance a church clock struck eleven. The lights of the city blazed all around them. Office blocks rose in shining pillars of light. From the kebab house on the high street the spicy odors of Levantine fast-food drifted on the sultry night air. Meanwhile, Ped talked to his brother; the tone always reassuring: they'd be safe; electricity couldn't reach Mickey up here. Ped glanced at his brother to make sure he was watching him aerosolling the steel bridge panels. Mickey turned twenty last week, and for the first time since he left school there was a chance he'd land paid work at the community farm. Ped had gone with him for the interview to make sure that he wouldn't get jerked around. Mickey had always been tormented at school, if not downright bullied. It's like this: once the kids found out that Mickey had this thing about electricity they'd use it to torture him. He'd get called names; sometimes kids would chase him with batteries. Just silly stuff to them but Mickey was really terrified. Once some thugs had held him down while they touched those metal nipples of a nine-volt battery against his lips. Okay, it only tingled, but Mickey had screamed the school down. So Ped did what he could to protect his younger brother.

'Electric Man,' Mickey said.

'No such thing, bro. Now let me work.'

'Electric Man!'

'You're stopping my arm, Mickey, I can't draw the circle.'

Mickey grunted with fear as he dropped to a crouch beside Ped; there he wrapped his arms around one of Ped's legs.

'Hey, Mickey,' he hissed. 'Do you want to throw me off this thing?'

'Electric Man!'

'Heck, bro, you nearly toppled me.'

His brother's frightened grasp felt close to snapping his knee.

'You're going to get your fingers burned doing that.' The stranger's voice made Ped look up from where he stood on the gantry, which in turn ran along the bottom of the bridge. A guy with a shaved head glared down at the pair of them. He was joined by three more men, each with shaved heads; as well as the shorn scalp they all shared an expression of hatred.

One said, 'Are you the bastard who's doing this Vampire Sharkz stuff?'

'No.'

'Because that bastard went and messed up our logo. And you don't slash our work round here.'

Ped kept his voice conversational to avoid antagonizing the men. 'I'm just doing tags. Nothing heavy.' Glaring down at him were fellow graffiti artists but there's no fraternity among wall daubers that over-paint another guy's work. Do that and you're in danger, pure and simple.

'This is our bridge.' The man angled his shaved head so he could see what Ped had inscribed. 'You've no friggin' right.'

Another of the guys peered over. 'Hey, who's there with you?'

'Just my brother.'

'What's he doing?'

'He gets scared sometimes.'

One of the shaved heads tilted to one side. 'Hey, I know him. It's Sparky.'

Ped shook his head. 'That was at school. His name's Mickey.'

60

'Sparky Lectric. That's what we called him. He's scared of batteries and plug sockets, anything to do with electricity.'

'I don't care what the fuck they call him.' The gang leader's eyes blazed with fury. 'They've messed our logo.'

'Look, I'm sorry. I didn't mean to slash your piece.'

The leader pointed. 'You? I'm going to break your arms. Your brother? We're taking him down to the track to fry his dick on the live rail.'

'We'll go home. We didn't—'

'Get them!'

The gang weren't listening. Ped knew that he and his brother were in for a kicking at least.

'Come on, Mickey. On your feet!'

'Electric Man.'

'If we don't get away they're going to hurt us, Mickey. Move!'

Ped noticed that the gang split into two. One pair to block the end of the gantry, while the others would trap them at the other side, then work into the middle. Ped bundled Mickey along the gantry as a train hummed beneath them. Electric contacts shot sparks from under the carriages. Mickey groaned with fear.

'Mickey, listen. We're going down the ladder. Then we cross the track. See the canal at the far side? There's a path we can use.'

As much as mapping out the route it was a way of distracting his brother from what would be the biggest obstacle. Mickey would have to step over the high-voltage rail. Just to see that gleaming band of steel was enough to scare the bejesus out of him. To get close would freak him out. 'It's either that or get pounded,' Ped grunted. 'I'll go down the ladder first. Follow me. But fast, okay?'

In the gloom he could see the gang members, who were going to seal one end of the gantry, had already climbed over the bridge wall, then they'd jump the last five feet on to the steel pathway. Down the ladder was the only exit.

'Keep following me, bro,' Ped called. His brother obeyed. The kid might be cursed with a phobia but he wasn't simple. He knew the gang wanted to hurt him, so the two brothers clanged their way down the ladder that was fixed to the wall. Soon they descended into a deep cutting where the trains clattered.

Ped glanced up. The gang had reached the top of the ladder. One of them was pointing down, so they'd spotted their prey. 'Keep moving, bro!' He climbed down another dozen rungs to where a light was fixed to the brickwork alongside the ladder. Ped zipped by it without a second thought, then he noticed his brother had stopped just a couple of feet above it.

'Come on, Mickey. You can't stop now.'

'I'm going back up.'

'No!'

The steel ladder convulsed under his hands as the gang swarmed on to it; they descended with their boots clumping against the rungs. In ten seconds they'd reach Mickey; then what? Stamp on his hands until they made him fall the twenty feet to the tracks below?

'Mickey,' Ped hissed. 'Hurry up.'

'Can't.'

'What's wrong?'

'Light.'

'It's just a light.'

'Red for danger. Danger of death. Electricity.'

'Damn.' Ped eyeballed the bloody light. It was nothing special; merely one of those signal lights that festoon the London Underground. Only to Mickey it represented danger. It *was* danger. Mickey saw it as a pulsating reservoir of electricity – a swarming hive of amps, volts and watts that were waiting to attack him. The kid probably imagined the light would fire a jet of crimson electricity at him that would blast through his body to make his bones pulse with that same blood-red light before burning the flesh from him. Mickey panted with sheer panic. Above him, the skinheads were descending fast. Soon the first boot would smash down on his brother's head.

'Mickey. It can't hurt you.'

'Red for danger. It'll burn.'

'No, it won't. Look.' Ped slapped the flat of his hand against the light. It wasn't even hot, but try telling his brother that. Mickey just moaned and closed his eyes.

One of the thugs shouted, 'Hey, Sparky? Sparky Lectric! We're gonna take you down to the live rail. You know something? A million volts go shooting through it. If you drop a rat on that it explodes. Boom!' The skinheads laughed. 'We're gonna pull your dick out of your underpants then stick it on the electric rail. Can't you just see what's going to happen to it? Just get that picture in your mind's eye. Your prick touching all that electricity. It'll go black. Shrivel up! Then your balls are going to get hotter and hotter . . . then *boom*!'

Mickey's scream echoed along the cutting.

Ped yelled up at the gang. 'Shut up! Can't you see he's scared?'

The gang could easily have reached Mickey now, but they were laughing so much at his terrified screams that they had to hang on to the ladder as they roared with hilarity. This gave Ped a chance. He pulled the aerosol from his jacket pocket.

'Mickey. Watch me. Please, open your eyes. See what I'm doing. I'm putting a circle around the light.' He sprayed a ring of florescent green round the red light. 'See, bro. I've closed it in. I've trapped it. Now it can't hurt you.' He reached up and yanked his brother's ankle. 'Now move!'

Mickey stared at the red light with the gleaming boundary of green. In his eyes the paint had become the protecting force field. The magic shield that stopped electrons streaming from the lamp to sear his face. Gulping repeatedly, he quickly descended; so fast, in fact, that he stepped on Ped's fingers.

'That's alright, bro. You can stand on my face if you want to. Just keep moving. That's beautiful. Yeah, beautiful, Mickey. You're doing the business.'

Seconds later they reached the gravel base of the cutting. Across the rails he could see the gleam of canal water. Nearly there. He glanced up. The skinheads' anger at being thwarted from simply booting Mickey off the ladder had killed their fit of laughter. Now they were hell-bent on catching their victims. The ladder shook as their boots clattered on the rungs. The clatter became a thunder. It was so loud it made the ground tremble. For a moment he believed it was the force of those feet crashing down the ladder. Then a flicker of light raced across the horizon. 'Great,' Ped muttered, 'all this and a thunderstorm, too.'

He grabbed Mickey by the elbow. After a train had passed, all lights as it clanked forward in the darkness, he urged his brother to move. Mickey's legs froze as he saw the dreaded live power rail in front of him. Running between the two rails that accommodated the wheels of the train, it was a thick continuous band of iron that even for Ped appeared to pulse with ominous energy.

'For God's sake, step over it when we cross. Don't touch it.'

But Mickey had clearly decided to go nowhere near it.

'C'mon, Mickey. We've got to cross over the rails. It's the only way we can escape those guys.'

Mickey shook his head.

'Don't worry. I can make it safe.' Ped leant over the track. He'd use the aerosol to spray two parallel lines. Then Mickey could walk through with the protecting lines on either side of him. Okay, its protective power only existed in Mickey's imagination, but it would be enough. He painted the first green line across the live power line. However, as he tried to spray the second, only a hiss of propellant emerged from the atomizer. Not so much as a drop of green. Behind him, the thugs reached the bottom of the ladder.

One shouted, 'We're going to fry your dick, too!'

A train roared down the track. Ped saw its lights in the distance. Another twenty seconds and this wouldn't be a healthy place for two very good reasons. The gang, or the train, was going to leave their mark, and Mickey had locked up tight with fear. His eyes bulged as he stared at the electrified metal bar that fed the motors of the approaching train.

Ped shook the aerosol and tried again. Just that fizzing sound. No paint. No way of creating a magical pathway for his brother.

'I'm going to have to drag you across.' He seized Mickey, but the kid seemed to have embedded himself in the gravel. No amount of wild horses, nor desperate siblings, were going to haul him across the line of living death. As Ped tried to wrestle the man forward he felt a hard cylinder in his brother's jacket pocket.

'Why didn't you tell me you had a can!'

Mickey merely stared at the electrified rail without uttering a word. Ped dragged the can from his pocket.

As he sprayed the green line across the track, he shouted, 'See what I'm doing? I've sprayed you a magic road. The electricity can't hurt you.' *As long as you don't touch the live rail*, was his unvoiced thought. 'Okay, Mickey. Run.'

Mickey leapt over the rail like a gazelle. Ped followed.

Behind him, those booted feet clattered over the gravel. To his right the train roared down at them. It was nothing less than a hell-storm of light and noise and movement. Twenty tons of electric-driven locomotive that would splatter any human standing in its way. Ped could swear that the carriage-work brushed a heel as he raced after his brother. Mickey didn't stop now. He leapt over the fence then ran down the slope to the canal towpath.

Five seconds later he stopped. In the light falling from buildings across the canal three figures stood in their way. To one side of them were the glistening waters, on the other side ran a high fence.

'Hell!' Ped screamed. 'There's more of them.' The gang must have sent some of its members down here. They had the foresight to appreciate that their victims might try to escape this way. The figures didn't move. They were purely silhouettes of ominous intent. Silently, they stood there, blocking the path as effectively as a brick wall.

Ped was running short of options. Nevertheless, he grabbed his brother and dragged him into the bushes that formed a green boundary ten feet deep between this section of path and fence. With luck there might be a gap that would allow their escape. A moment later he knew that there wasn't. The steel fence hemmed them in. All the pair could do was crouch there in the darkness. The gang would find them. That much was sure.

Then Mickey whispered, 'Those three . . .'

'I know. The gang sent them to cut us off.' He sighed. 'I'm sorry, bro.'

'They aren't skinheads.'

Ped groaned. 'Don't start this now. They're not electric men. Electric men don't exist.'

'No, they're not electric men.' Mickey spoke with conviction. 'They're not any kind of men.'

Ped risked a peek through the foliage. Only it wasn't the three figures he saw, it was the gang of four with their shaved heads. This is where thug collided with something altogether more monstrous. And when the end came it was fast, brutal, bloody.

Ped heard one of the gang snarl, 'Get out of our way.'

Then came weird grunts as if a pack of hungry carnivores

65

had found fresh meat. A second later Ped watched the thugs run back toward the track. They were howling in terror. The hunters now the hunted. It was too dark to see much but suddenly figures flashed by with the speed of panthers. They pounced on the skinheads in a furious maelstrom of movement. All Ped could make out was that the figures from the canal path were biting the men. He saw heads twisting from side to side as they bit through skin. Just for a second a blue-white face lifted itself from the frenzy of limbs. Ped had the impression that the owner of that uncanny face had raised their head so they could swallow a massive mouthful of food. But what kind of food?

The face was female. It was smeared with blood. Worse than the sight of blood was the expression of rapacious gluttony. Ped listened to excited grunts, then came a gulping as if thirsty people drank – no . . . more than thirsty – these were individuals maddened by thirst. They quenched their arid throats in an orgy of drinking. Meanwhile, the skinhead gang fell silent. After a moment of stillness came splashes from the canal as heavy objects dropped into the water.

When it had been silent for a time Ped emerged from the bushes with his brother beside him. The path was deserted. Briefly, ripples ran across the surface of the waterway. Mickey watched something gliding through the dark waters. Ped made a point of *not* watching. A sixth sense warned him that his sleep would be haunted by nightmares for years to come if he did see what manner of creature swam there.

Then came a scuffling sound from the bushes. One of the skinheads blundered by them; he wasn't interested in the brothers now. His blood-smeared face was furrowed with worry. He stared down at a heap of wet things in his hands. The thug carried his own intestines where they spilled out through a gash in his belly. As he walked he made gasping cries. Whether that was shock or pain Ped wasn't sure. All he could do was watch in stunned silence as that man cradled his own bloody entrails in his two hands.

The brothers saw the shaven-headed man stagger back toward the railway track. The intestines were slippery. It must have been like carrying a mound of soft, wet pasta. A length of it slipped through his fingers. Clearly, he was so deep in shock that he never noticed the five-foot strip of flesh dragging behind him.

'Electricity,' Mickey whispered. 'Danger of death.'

The skinhead limped on, trailing his flesh behind him.

'Voltage,' Mickey intoned. 'Amps.'

The intestine dragged through the dirt, then across the first track where it touched the live rail. Violet lightning blasted up the bloody ribbon into the man's body. As he convulsed a howl of agony burst from his lips.

Mickey stared as the man collapsed on the live rail that emitted searing flashes, which engulfed the body in an ocean of blue fire.

For the first time in his entire life Mickey was calm as he nodded. 'Electric Man,' he whispered. 'Electric Man dead.'

Eleven

At midnight Ben Ashton walked down to the river to look into the water. The hermit in his boat atop the pole had warned that London was under threat. Only was that a threat from an actual, touchable enemy? Or did Elmo Kigoma mean a spiritual threat? He'd talked about Edshu the trickster god testing the city's people. If they passed the test then they would live, if not, they'd be destroyed. Although the hermit hadn't been able to reveal the identity of the Vampire Sharkz graffiti writer it did lend a different dimension to the article now. The plot thickens, as they say. He could draw Elmo's warning into the investigation of the mysterious graffiti. After all, Elmo was a famous figure now. He'd been featured widely in the media. For a while there'd even been 'Elmo Watch', a live observation camera that could be accessed by 'pressing the red button' on digital news channels. The downside of using Elmo's words was that many considered him a nut. Ben didn't think so. That's why he'd left the comfort of his apartment for this midnight riverside stroll.

At the barrier between path and river Ben gazed down into the water. It reflected what appeared to be around a million city lights, so it was difficult to see past those shimmering glints on the surface to whatever might lurk beneath. Maybe Elmo's poetic use of language might have confused a simple explanation; maybe the old man had been talking about pollution in the river? After all, those exotic pronouncements about 'saving your life', and the touch of Edshu were Elmo's way of saying consume less; that the secret of longevity was a more Spartan diet. Yet Ben liked the man. He'd been impressed by the octogenarian's passion to save his fellow human beings.

Thunder grumbled over the capital. In the distance forked lightning sped from the sky. Humidity combined with the heat to make even breathing uncomfortable. The rain, when it finally arrived after this hot spell, would be a relief. Ben stared into the river for a while. Patches of oil made iridescent rainbow patterns for the city's lights to fool around with and make gorgeous, if fleeting, artworks. Beyond that there was nothing he could see. Certainly nothing to threaten a city of seven million people.

Okay, he told himself. Another ten minutes, then home to bed. Elmo's warning about a danger in the river was starting to look symbolic in some way that Ben failed to grasp. Not that the river appealed to him. To even glance at it usually brought back that old memory of the corpse in the water. Who needs ghosts when you have memory to haunt you?

As he varied the focus of his eyes in an attempt to peer past that glistening surface of the Thames, his phone sang out. When he answered he saw the caller's ID on screen.

'Raj,' he said before his caller could begin. 'You're more predator than editor. I'm on to it. I've another week before the deadline. I'll have your Vampire Sharkz artist in the next twenty-four hours.'

'I'm not calling about the article.' The editor's voice was chillingly grave. Immediately Ben tensed. 'Ben, are you alone?'

'I'm just outside my apartment.'

Raj paused for a moment. 'There's no easy way to say this, because I know you and April Connor were close friends.'

'April? What's happened?'

'I don't have all the facts but I've just heard from a colleague of April's that she and her boyfriend were attacked a couple of nights ago.'

'Are they hurt?'

'Well, that's just it. Her boyfriend is in hospital with head injuries. But there's no trace of April . . . Ben, she's vanished.'

As Ben stood there with the phone pressed to his ear the first drops of rain began to fall.

Twelve

First came hunger. She opened her eyes beneath that scrap of carpet. Lying beside her was Carter. He groaned. So he was hungry, too. After lying inert for hours, not moving, not talking, not anything, not even having the desire to move, suddenly she couldn't stay still. April fought at the carpet that covered her as if it was an attacker. The hunger pangs surged inside her. Once more they weren't confined to her stomach. That ravenous craving spread out from her belly along her nerves to her fingertips.

How can you feel hunger in your fingers? But she did. Her longing to eat pounded through every nerve ending. Eat, eat, eat. That's all that mattered.

'I know you're hungry,' Carter murmured, his gold-tipped teeth glinted in the gloom. 'But take it easy.'

'How can I take it easy? I'm going to die if I don't get something to eat.'

'Those Berserkers might be outside. Then you'll be breakfast.'

'Shut up, Carter. I want to get off this bloody island. I can't stand being like this. Feel my hair, why is it so sticky all the time?'

He was barely a silhouette as he climbed to his feet. A

grunt escaped his lips again as he pressed his palm to his stomach. 'I'm hungry, too, but you can't let it take control.'

'Oh, God,' she gasped as the emptiness gnawed her. 'What's happening to me?'

He put his arm around her. 'April. Trust me, sweetheart. I'll look after you.'

'I'm dying.'

'You're not. Remember what we did yesterday?'

'Uh . . . I'm not drinking puddles. I've got to eat proper food.'

'What is proper food?' His eyes were compassionate.

'I don't know what you're talking about,' she snarled. 'Just please find me something to eat! I'm losing my mind! It's all I can think about.'

'But you're not thinking about bread, or apples, or pastries, are you?'

'Carter, shut up! And get your hands off me!'

'Okay.' He stood back. 'We do what we need to to stop the hunger then we'll talk.'

April's fiery glance raked the cottage room. Those three Misfires were there – two men and a woman. Once they'd been smartly dressed. Now their clothes would suit a whole fright of scarecrows. They'd moved since April saw them last. Instead of sitting against the wall, the Misfires had walked to the door, but it must have been a grindingly slow process. If those things were in motion it must have been no faster than the velocity of a minute hand as it creeps around your watch face. They appeared to be in the process of leaving the room. Meanwhile, April's nerves blazed like she had a crimson furnace inside her head. She wanted to scream, stamp her feet, anything to vent some of that tension that crucified her.

'Take it easy,' Carter repeated. 'We don't know if those lunatics are outside. If they see us, they'll attack.'

Enough! she thought, unable to delay another second. The word food could have been a series of explosions detonating inside of her. She pushed the Misfires aside. One fell against the wall and stayed there. Another slammed back against the floor.

'April, be careful.'

She tore open the door then hurtled along the hallway to

the front door. A second later she was through it and racing along that tunnel of greenery. This time the night was how it should be. Dark. Very dark. Trees were indistinct shapes. There was no weirdly bright moon in the sky. She ran across bare earth, the word *food* pounding inside her head. Food, food, food . . .

Not at any price would she drink from that sordid tidal pool again; such an act of humiliating debasement made her burn with shame. *I'll find proper nourishment and eat like a human being.* That was the last rational thought before her mind cleared again. She groaned. She didn't want to do this. She couldn't believe she was performing this act. But here she was on her hands and knees sucking tepid water from the beach. The pool left as the tide retreated had evaporated to leave a solution rich in salt. It pricked her lips as she drank. That saltiness was the living, pulsating soul of the water. She wanted to ingest more than her body could contain. She swallowed vast draughts of it; sometimes the quantities were so great they spurted out of her mouth again. As her surroundings resolved themselves from the gloom she saw Carter kneel beside the same pool to gorge himself.

Even though there was none of that searing moonlight she could identify the outline of the willows behind her. And here she squatted on a beach of grit, amid pools left by the tide. There were scraps of broken seashells along with the larger exoskeletons of crabs with their articulated legs and pincers. Twenty paces away the river lapped the beach. Beyond that, a vast plain of water stretched toward the horizon. This time she could see artificial lights. There was a string of golden blobs that marked some industrial complex on the mainland. An oily flame burning in the darkness suggested that it might be an oil refinery. Adjacent to that, a vast diffuse glow formed a reddish dome on the horizon. That had to be the million-plus lights of London. Now it seemed an ethereal place to April Connor. A fairy citadel that lay beyond her reach. A Brigadoon glimpsed from afar, yet always unattainable.

Far away came the clump of thunder as she reached down and pulled her remaining sandal from her foot and tossed it toward the river. Even in her present condition with the ripped dress, the mane of sticky hair, the aversion to sunlight, it was downright crazy to walk round with one foot bare, the other clad in a muddy sandal.

She squatted by a little depression in the sand that was no larger than a dinner plate. It held a couple of pints of water covered with a brownish scum. The aroma reached out to her as if it had exhaled a salty breath. She cupped her hand then scooped some of the cloudy water to her lips. Hmmm . . . evaporation had left the small pool even saltier than the others. This was satisfying as homemade soup. She quickly drank half of it with such relish she sighed.

'Carter,' she hissed. 'Carter?'

'Uh.' He couldn't stop himself drinking.

'Leave that. This is better. There's more salt in this one.'

His face wore an expression of gratitude as he scrambled across, knelt down, then like a cat lapping from a bowl put his lips to the precious liquor and drank every last drop in five seconds flat.

'If you select the pools carefully you can find the ones that have evaporated more than the others. Those have more salt.'

'And drink right down to the bottom. It's saltier, but don't disturb the sediment.'

Here they were swapping tips on drinking out of tidal puddles like they were a couple of wine connoisseurs discussing the merits of the latest Merlot.

'Carter,' she said. 'What is it about salt? Why are we addicted to it now?'

'Just the way things are. Look, there's another one.' He dipped his finger into a little pool then licked the digit from knuckle to nail. 'You're right, smaller is saltier. You first.'

She gave him a smile of gratitude. The raging hunger pangs had eased. Cupping her hand, she scooped it to her lips. 'Hmm. Nice.' Then her pleasure gave way to unease. 'Carter?'

'Don't you want it?' He eyed the puddle thirstily.

'What's gone wrong with the world? When I first arrived the moon was so bright it hurt to look at it.'

He couldn't stop himself staring at that petite body of water that was so rich in salt. 'The world hasn't changed, sweetheart. We have.'

'If that's the case, then what have we become?'

He was fascinated by the pool. 'Finished?'

'For now.' She could have drunk it a hundred times over

but now her mind had cleared after the feeding-frenzy she needed answers. Carter was still too fixated on that little treasure trove of salinity to be interested in anything else.

'Why did the sun hurt when it touched us? When we hid under the carpet I couldn't feel my heartbeat, why's that? And when I breathe it's so irregular that it doesn't seem like breathing. It's as if it's respiration through habit rather than necessity. And didn't you—'

'What's that?' He jerked his head up. 'Did someone just walk across the beach back there?'

April looked in the direction Carter was staring. A hundred paces away were a line of dunes.

'We're exposed here,' he told her. 'We should've used the other beach.' Despite his sudden wariness he scooped another palm full of water to his lips.

We're salt junkies, she told herself. That's what we are. We've discovered a new form of addiction.

Then she heard a thud-thud of feet moving quickly across dry earth. She tried to target the sound. A scurry of movement came from bushes at the edge of the island. Rather than seeing individuals there was a suggestion of furtive flitting amongst the vegetation.

'Come on,' he hissed. 'Back to the house.'

'Who is it?'

'Your friends, likely as not.'

'They're not my friends.'

Carter shrugged. 'Even if they were, they aren't now. They'll have been trying to eat anything and everything. Hunger will have pushed them over the edge.'

A blue light struck her; seconds later thunder boomed across the still water. When she recovered from the dazzling blast she saw that a whole legion of shadows flowed through the trees. Still she couldn't identify people. Then she saw glints of eyes. *And who do you think those eyes are looking at?*

'Run!'

This wasn't the time for stealth. The pair on the beach had been seen. April followed Carter across the sands. Those forms moved faster; they streamed through the darkness; nocturnal predators that could think of nothing but the meal that they craved. They began to cry out. Wordless expressions of emotion, as if fear of losing their prey was only matched by the raging hunger pains.

April panted, 'What if we show them how to stop the hunger?'

'Think they'd listen? They will tear you apart. Keep going! Don't stop for anything!'

She placed her faith in the man now. He'd know a way through that chaotic system of paths back to the house. Although what safety it would offer from that hoard of maniacs God alone knew. Nevertheless, she ran as hard as she could as the greenery swallowed them. Constantly, she had to bat aside branches. Rodents scurried from her. One wasn't fast enough; she felt one of her bare feet smash down on to a furry back.

Behind her came an excited 'Ah-ah-ah-ah!' The pack were closing in. She glanced back to see the kid in the denim jacket covered in chains. His face wore such an expression of excitement as he locked his eyes on her it seemed luminous in the dark. The very atoms of his body seemed to resonate with greed. He was nothing more than a conglomeration of hunger pains that craved satisfaction. His mouth gaped open wide. With him, more figures pounded through the bushes. With the 'Ah-ah-ah!' of excitement were screams of terror as if what frightened them most was missing out on sinking their teeth into April Connor's flesh.

Lightning and thunder battered the island. The searing flash of electricity shone through the leaves of the trees and turned her entire world into a sea of green fire. And as they at last charged the door of the cottage the rain began to fall. Carter slammed it into the face of the kid in the denim jacket. All he had to secure it was a single iron bolt. He shot it home.

'It won't keep them out for long,' he shouted.

'What then?'

'Gotta hide. C'mon!'

The Misfires still performed their oh-so-slow-motion dance. In the time April and Carter had been away from the house those near still-life occupants of the house had moved. The ones from the room where April had slept had migrated into the hallway. They stood in single file. One had raised a hand to rest it against a wall that shed its paper in damp strips. Just then, a furious hammering shook the door.

74

'Upstairs,' Carter shouted.

He pushed aside a woman in a nurse's uniform. She slumped against the wall but remained standing. When April pushed by her, their faces almost touched on the narrow staircase. The eyes were still too heavy to open fully; the unfocussed gaze appeared disinterested in her predicament. Her bleached hair stood out in sticky spikes. When April inhaled she identified the woman's smell as nothing more than pond water. That's apt: these creatures that Carter had named Misfires were stagnant. They didn't react to being pushed over. Their faces lacked expression. Even the blood in their veins and the air in their lungs must be stagnant. That stagnation infiltrated their brains, too.

In a blur of movement Carter and April surged on to the pokey landing. A window overlooked the jungle-like garden that was being doused by rain. Even though she couldn't see much a burst of dazzling lightning revealed around a dozen men and women rushing toward the door, desperate for their share of the pair inside.

'Where now?' Just two doors led off into bedrooms that had been emptied of furniture. In each room stood half a dozen Misfires, practising that statue-like pose. At that precise moment the bolt on the door downstairs yielded with a snap.

Carter beckoned her. 'Up there.' Above him was a hatchway to the attic.

'Carter, it's too high.'

'Don't worry. I'll lift you. Put your foot in my hands.' He knitted his fingers in front of his stomach to create a stirrup. Downstairs, the howling was as loud as the thunder as those creatures Carter dubbed the Berserkers invaded the house.

How she did it she didn't know. After stepping into that makeshift stirrup he hoisted her up to the oblong opening in the ceiling. As soon as she found a timber support she dragged herself into the void. On either side of her the tiled roof sloped down. There was barely room to sit up, never mind stand, so she shuffled across the rafters to give Carter space to enter. It took him five seconds to haul himself in, then he slipped the attic hatch cover across the opening.

He whispered, 'Lay down. Keep still. Be quiet as you can . . . very, very quiet.'

The rain drummed against the roof. Every few seconds a

flicker of light would burst through the chinks in the slates followed by a clump of thunder. The shouts from below were muffled now. The clatter of feet on stairs was clear enough though. In her mind blazed vivid images of the Berserkers literally thirsting for her blood, running from room to room searching for them. All they'd find would be those weirdly immobile Misfires.

April looked down at what would be the bedroom ceiling beneath her. Some plaster had fallen from woven strips of wood that formed the wattle. Through the tiny holes she could see seven Misfires in the room below. A couple were women with long hair; they could have been enjoying a party when misfortune had befallen them. There was a chunky guy in motorcycle leathers and other men who were dressed for the office. If anything, they could have been an assembly of shoddy mannequins that had been stored in some backroom for the past decade. As she watched, the door burst open. The kid in the denim jacket entered with a frenzied howl. He grabbed one of the female Misfires by the hair, dragged her head back so it exposed her throat – a curving arch of naked flesh – then he slammed his mouth on to it.

April watched how he chewed. Yet when he jerked his head back to tug away a strip of skin, no blood flowed from the woman's wound. The exposed flesh was grey. The tissue beneath the skin resembled paper rather than human flesh. Once more the youth attacked the throat; this time he sucked at the rip in the skin. A second later he roared with frustration. He pushed the woman aside; she staggered but kept her balance. All through the attack she hadn't even blinked. Her face retained that dull, stagnant countenance that could have been chiselled from granite.

The youth turned his attention to a man with curly black hair who appeared to stare out through the window. His teeth split open the man's cheek as more of the insane poured into the room to attack the Misfires. But these weren't to the Berserkers' taste. No sooner had they torn open the flesh than the mob were howling their displeasure. Whatever the Misfires were, they were also inedible. The crazed fervour for nourishment clouded the judgement of the Berserkers. Instead of taking time to search the house they fled screaming back into the trees.

In the room beneath April Connor, the Misfires gradually regained their composure. True, their clothes were in disarray; their bodies displayed wounds that were a result of frenzied biting, but their expressions betrayed neither pain nor dismay. They merely resumed their silent wait for eternity.

April let out a sigh of relief. She allowed herself to lay down flat across the attic rafters. Carter did the same. As the rain fell on to the roof Carter's hand found hers, then he curled his fingers around it. April didn't pull away.

The thunderstorm didn't last long. But the rain continued all through the night. Before dawn it began to ease. By that time one thought possessed April Connor. 'I've got to go down to the beach again,' she confessed.

'Hungry?'

'Yep. It's beginning to hurt.'

'Me, too.'

'But then it doesn't seem like thirst. It's hunger. But I know if I drink from those shitty pools . . .' She felt suddenly angry. '. . . I know if I drink from them it takes the edge off.'

'If that's what we have to do to beat the hunger then it's the only way.'

'But what have we turned into, Carter? I must have gone insane.'

'We can't all be insane.'

'Then what's happened to us?'

In the gloom, with the rain tapping above them, he paused. 'You know . . .' The gold tips of his teeth glinted. 'When I was little my uncle grew the biggest tomatoes people had ever seen. Some men have football or horseracing or beer to obsess them. My Uncle Tony had tomatoes. He grew them in a greenhouse that filled his back yard. You couldn't have a conversation with him that didn't turn tomato.' He laughed. 'Anyway, one day I learned how he grew the monster tomato. I'd gone with my brother to his house just as a truck pulled up. Two men got out and carried a barrel into the greenhouse. My uncle paid them what looked like a lot of cash and they went away. When he had to answer the phone me and my brother knew there was one thing we must do. We had to see what was in that barrel. Do you know what it was?'

'Go on.'

'We lifted the lid and this barrel was full to the brim with the reddest stuff we'd ever seen in our lives. You've never seen such a thing.' He took a deep breath. 'A barrel full of blood; gallons of crimson.' His laugh was oddly strained. 'Crimson gore. So red it seemed to light up the place.' He smacked his lips. 'That was Uncle Tony's secret. He fed his tomato plants on blood. We were so fascinated by it we didn't hear him come back, just this voice suddenly booming out, "Do you know how many nosey kids it took to fill that barrel?" My brother and I ran so hard . . .' Carter chuckled but managed to smack his lips at the same time. 'Uncle Tony didn't realize he'd scared us so much. Later, he came round with some comics and told us that the blood didn't really come from nosey kids. We pretended we knew all along but we were still shaking.' He smacked his lips again. 'Cows' blood. He bought it from the local abattoir. Lots of gardeners use it. Usually it's a dried blood meal they buy in packs but Uncle Tony wanted his plants to drink it neat. And it worked. Huge tomatoes they were. Huge and round and red.' He sighed. 'Do you know how often I remember that time when we lifted the lid off the barrel and saw the blood inside?'

April couldn't answer. A sense of dread gripped her.

'Let me tell you, sweetheart,' he said bitterly. 'Before I arrived here I hadn't thought about it in years. Now I'm always thinking about it. The image repeats itself. We grip the lid. We lift it off. There it is: the reddest blood you've ever seen. It glows. I can feel the heat of it. And when I breathe in the smell . . .' He was still holding her hand and it suddenly tightened with ferocity. 'That smell.' He licked his lips. 'If I could walk into that greenhouse right now and find all that warm blood . . . You know what I'd do, don't you?'

That night their world changed. The rain still fell with a soft purring sound. Pools of water were everywhere; a stream had even appeared on one of the footpaths to find its way to its gigantic sibling, the Thames.

They left the cottage to the Misfires who wore their bite marks with a numb kind of dignity. Carter walked ahead, his feet splashing through puddles. Already the hunger pangs were intense. What's more, April couldn't shift that image of the blood-filled barrel. She could almost see those gallons of rich liquid. It wouldn't be uniformly scarlet, she told herself. It would be a mosaic of reds. From dark crimson that was almost black to luscious strawberry, then lightening towards a pink of the most delicious hue imaginable.

I'm hungry, but why do I think about blood? I should be picturing roast beef, rump steak, fried bacon. But that lustrous image of glistening blood by the vatful remained glued tight inside her mind.

'We'll have to be quick,' he told her. 'Can you see that grey over the river? The sun's coming back.'

'Damn the sun,' she spat. 'If I don't drink I'm going to start taking bites out of the Misfires, too.'

'You'd get more out of eating dirt. Did you see the look of disgust on the Berserkers' faces?'

'There's got to be—'

'Shhh.' He snatched her back into the bushes. A second later the kid in the denim jacket scrambled by. He was followed by a dozen more men and women. They all groaned as if they suffered a pain that could no longer be endured. Just when April anticipated the creatures would return to the cottage to ravage those people that were more dead than alive, she saw they were racing towards the beach as the tide rolled in. Within seconds they charged into the water. Briefly, there was a tumultuous splashing as they ran through the shallows – then they were gone. The Thames, glistening with all the lustre of black marble, had swallowed them. Not so much as a head or an arm broke the surface.

'Why did they do that?' she gasped.

'I told you. I've seen it before. They reach the point where they get so hungry they just lob themselves into the river.'

'They've killed themselves?'

He shrugged. 'Looks like it.'

Just for a moment she felt the need to talk about what she'd seen. That suicidal dash into the river by the crazed people she'd first encountered on the beach. Only there was something more important.

'Quick,' she told him. 'Before it gets too bright. We've got to make the most of this.'

She went to the beach where she threw herself down at the nearest tidal pool and began to drink.

'Pah!' Carter spat. 'It's just water.'

April grimaced. 'Try another. Remember, stick with the small ones. The salinity is stronger.'

The small ones were just as bad. Clear water that tasted of rain.

'This isn't estuary water.' Carter sounded disgusted. 'The rain's washed it out.'

'There's got to be one that's salty enough!'

In desperation she began drinking at one of the pools on the beach. Clear, sweet water. Not a trace of salt. She drank with a furious single-mindedness in the hope that a saltiness would emerge as she worked her way deeper. But all the flavour she found was that dusty taste of rainwater. The bite in her side itched again. A mad riot of sensation that made her long to rip at the still raw edges of the wound with her fingernails. And all the time hunger pulsed through her.

A moment later she gorged on mud again. Anything to introduce a solid presence in that yawning gulf in her belly. As she ate she found herself recalling Carter's own memory as if it was her own. The day two surprised boys stood in their uncle's greenhouse and lifted the lid on the reddest substance in the world.

Thirteen

The sun didn't show. The storm that had broken the back of the heat wave left its cloud behind to cover the sky. Even so, for April and Carter the light soon reached a screaming intensity. The beach that had been a dull yellow by night now became a fluorescent gold that blinded them as they drank from pools on the beach or gorged on river silt. Most of the time April couldn't bear to lift her head as there was always that tantalizing promise that one of the pools would yield that satisfying salt she craved. Only it never did. Constantly, the light grew brighter and the pain it brought to her skin appeared to force its way through to meet the pain inside her body. That mingling and conjoining of two separate agonies threatened to push her into madness.

So when one pool didn't offer what her body howled for she scrambled on all fours to the next. At that moment all that mattered was food. Gorge on it, savage it, swallow it, munch, gulp, ingest – she must find real food soon. The consequences of going without were unthinkable. Beside her, Carter clawed at the water as if in the hope of finding salinity in the mud at the bottom. As her mind whirled with those second-hand recollections of Carter gazing into the barrel full of blood, and the twin agonies of the light striking her exposed skin, and the pain of starvation, she realized the futility of trying to satisfy her hunger. In the past, saltwater had blunted the pangs. But the rainwater had diluted the estuary water to the point where there was nothing to be gained from gorging on it. The mud didn't help, either. If anything, its bulk only threatened to burst her intestine.

With a supreme effort of will she gathered her senses. 'Carter . . . Carter?'

He plunged his face into a puddle and savaged it like a wolf savaging a lamb.

'Carter, listen to me!' She hauled him from the water. 'Leave that and listen!'

Somehow his sight had turned inwards. She knew that he gazed into that vat of cattle blood again. The memory was transfixed in his mind.

She grabbed his head. 'Listen! This must have happened before. The rain washed the salt away.'

'Uh.'

'When it rained before, what did you do?'

'Nnn-uh . . .'

'You must have done something else to take the hunger away. No, Carter! There's no point in drinking it. It doesn't work anymore. It's been diluted!' Once more she pulled him away from the water so she could shout into his face. 'When it rained before, what did you do?'

He gulped; his eyes slipped into focus as an expression of horror contorted his face. 'It's never happened before.'

'It must have rained.'

He shook his head. 'I arrived at the start of the dry spell.'

His eyes rolled as he mumbled, 'S'never rained. Always hot. Sun . . . it didn't rain. Not once . . .'

'Okay.' She forced herself to think. 'We've got to ride through this. When the tide falls it'll leave saltwater. As soon as the sun comes out the water will begin to evaporate. Salinity will increase. Then we can drink. We'll be okay.'

He grunted. 'Can't wait that long.' Suddenly his head darted toward her arm. She managed to withdraw it before his teeth snapped together.

'Don't bite me. I'm trying to save your life.'

'Why?' His eyes glazed again.

'Because you saved mine.'

'I mean what's the point, we're already dead.'

'Don't say that!' She rose to her feet despite the blinding light falling through the clouds. 'Get under the bushes. We'll wait it out in the shade. It hurts to stay out where it is bright.'

He muttered as if becoming feverish; already his lucidity was escaping him. When she tried to help him stand he darted his mouth at her, trying to bite her arms with those gold-tipped teeth of his.

'You've got to try, Carter. We need each other!'

At last he did stand. He was groaning; the pains were overwhelming; when he opened his eyes there was a desperate searching quality as he scanned his surroundings for something to eat.

'Carter—' she began, but he broke away from her with a scream. Then he fled. Any hope of him dashing back to the house was soon shattered. Arms flailing, he raced down to the water's edge, then waded into the river.

'Carter! Don't do it! Please!'

She saw his bright wake in all that dazzling radiance. The man became a silhouette even thought she shielded her eyes against the glare; a moment later he dipped his entire body underwater and vanished from sight.

April dragged herself up the beach to the place of deepest shadow beneath a willow. The green of the grass and leaves was so bright it seemed to yell at her.

A shouting green, she thought dizzily. Shouting greens, howling light and beautiful singing reds. I want to see into the tomato grower's barrel, too. I've never seen blood like that before. Beautiful, delicious, luxuriant crimson. Red gold.

Red gold. The phrase amused her; she murmured it to herself as she twitched in the grip of delirium. 'Red gold. Red, red gold . . .'

The hunger returned – and the sensation took her. It was as simple and as absolute as that. April even believed she still lay in the shadows, until with a shock she realized that she'd run down the beach and already her feet splashed through the water.

This is how it ends for me, too, she told herself in surprise. The others couldn't stop themselves. Neither could Carter. Now me.

The water reached her waist and as she toppled forward she understood why the others had vanished so quickly; the river bed dropped away at the edge of an underwater cliff. One moment her feet pressed against a solid mass, the next there was only water. And this was water that was possessed by its own life force. The powerful current gripped her and rushed her away into utter blackness.

Fourteen

Trajan had discharged himself from hospital against medical advice, so Ben had to find his home address through a friend of April Connor's. Ben figured that if Trajan and April had just signed for a new apartment then they might be already living together. Just reading the e-mail that contained the address filled Ben with jealousy. Disgusted with himself he thought, I should be focusing on that. I should be angry or frightened for her; instead I'm picturing the apartment that she shared with Trajan and I'm jealous; so why am I behaving like a jilted boyfriend? I was always good friends with April; there was nothing more; no romance. Physical contact was a hug or a kiss on the cheek. Jealousy fixes itself to your bones, then it pollutes your mind. You can't just shrug it off. It's not a migraine that you can zap with painkillers. It stays there and makes you miserable.

'So, what's the answer?' he asked himself as he left his home. 'The answer is action.' He walked past graffiti that must have been added to a wall last night.

VAMPIRE SHARKZ
☺ They're coming to get you ☺

But the graffiti was no longer important to him. He pushed the magazine assignment to the back of his mind. What burned with importance was to find April Connor. For that he had to start with Trajan.

When he arrived the door to the apartment in Bloomsbury was already open. Ben leaned forward to get a glimpse of the gloomy interior. There were faint aromas of cooking spices along with something that could have been disinfectant or antiseptic. Outside, the weekday traffic hummed along still wet streets, yet inside here was a capsule of silence. Leaving a door open even in an upmarket London quarter like Bloomsbury isn't a good idea. Sneak thieves would find an open door to an expensive apartment irresistible. Ben lightly tapped on the door.

'Hello?'

A shape catapulted from the shadows; set in the upper part of it were a pair of eyes that burned with a blue light.

'Have you found her?' A man with the bandaged head lunged at Ben, his hands outstretched as if he planned to strangle him.

'No, I'm—'

'Damn it! Why aren't you people out looking for her? I told you over and over. She hasn't left me. April's been taken against her will.'

'Trajan.' Ben recognized the blond man despite the white bandage around his head. The eyes were wild-looking now; nothing like the blue-eyed disdain shown when he met April and the man down by the river just days ago.

Trajan pressed his hand to the back of his head as the pain of the injury flared again. 'I can't understand why you haven't told the press. If people saw April's picture in the papers then they might—'

84

'Trajan. I don't think you remember me. I'm not from the police. My name is Ben Ashton. I'm a friend of April's. I heard from a mutual friend that she'd—'

'You know where she is?'

'No.'

'I don't need well-wishers right now. I'm waiting for the police.'

With that he blundered back along the passageway to a door that led to the lounge. Ben followed. He was determined not to be shoved back out on to the street without hearing the circumstances of April's disappearance.

'What happened, Trajan? Did you see the man who attacked her? Tell me!'

Ben entered the lounge. The blinds were down, a TV in the corner showed a news channel. Trajan must have been hunched in front of the thing, willing it to report news of the missing woman. Trajan stood in the middle of the room. His eyes were crimped tight shut and his fingers groped through the air as he tried to find a chair by touch alone.

'You should think about going back to the hospital,' Ben told him.

The man shook his head; the pain from that movement alone made him grunt.

'Look,' Ben said. 'I need to ask you some questions. But first lie down for a few moments. Here . . . let me help.'

As Ben took hold of the man's arm to guide him across the room he let out a scream. Trajan whirled on Ben, his eyes snapped open and blazed at something behind him. A second later Trajan smashed Ben back against the wall. And even though they were almost face-to-face, Trajan glared at the wall just above Ben's shoulder, as if his eyes fixed on something through the plasterwork.

'I told you not to touch me,' the man howled. 'Leave me alone! And why did you have to hurt her? What made you do that to her? She'd done nothing to you!'

His entire body quivered; his grasp on Ben's arms possessed a strength generated by terror as much as anger. It lasted only an instant, then confusion flooded Trajan's face. He glanced sideways as if surprised to find himself at home. Ben noticed that a bloody patch leaked through the bandage at the back of his head. He took a deep, shuddering

85

breath before he turned back to Ben. This time his eyes focused on Ben's face.

'You best leave. I'm still not . . .' Trajan grimaced. 'I hurt my head.' He released Ben then stood back, tottering as he did so. This time he didn't resist when Ben led him to the sofa.

'Sit down. I'll get you a drink.'

'Get me a drink? No, you can get me April. That's what I want. April Connor. In this room. Now!' After that outburst he allowed Ben to help him sit down. 'Look. Just go away, okay?'

'I'm staying until I hear what happened. April was my friend.'

Trajan's eyes kept returning to the television, no doubt expecting to see news of April at any moment.

'Trajan, please tell me what you know.'

'What I know isn't worth knowing.' The man grimaced again. 'The police won't act. If anything they think we had an argument and April hit me before leaving. All I know is this. We were walking down by the river a couple of days ago. April met someone she knew.'

'That would have been me.' Ben was mystified. 'Don't you remember me?'

'That's the problem. The doctors tell me it's an effect of the head injury. They say short-term memory needs time to embed itself deep down in here.' He touched his temple. 'If you take a knock on the head it can wipe out memories before the attack took place.' His hands were shaking. 'I remember signing the contract on the new apartment, then a meal; after that we decided to walk along the embankment because the weather was so warm. I remember that perfectly because April pointed out a fox that was walking along the pavement with a pizza in its mouth. It didn't have a care in the world and we marvelled that a wild animal would come into the city to hunt for junk food. Then it gets hazy. April lunged at what I thought was a stranger – but it was you, uh, Mr—?'

'Ben Ashton. Call me Ben.'

'Ben.' He swallowed as if remembering new information made his head ache even more. 'We saw you, and I know she talked to you but I just can't recollect the words. Then we walked again.' His face darkened. 'We were beside the river.

86

I know that. And I know there was a figure; it must have been a man – and this is where it gets all mixed up. There was something about him . . .' He paused, frowning.

'You're sure it was a man?'

'Male alright, but an exaggerated maleness. Something brutish about him. And I know he was doing something . . .' He rubbed his forehead. 'I don't know what. And I can't remember any details about him. All I can recall is his actions were shocking in some way . . . and there was a strangeness about him.'

'Colour of hair? Clothes? Footwear?'

'The police have been through that. All I could tell them was what I've just told you. The man must have attacked me then abducted April . . . but it's all a blank.' Once more his troubled eyes returned to the television that was showing a crane lifting steel beams above the river.

'How's you memory now?'

'I'm being interrogated by Ben Ashton. That good enough for you?'

'You'd left your door open.'

'Deliberate. I'm expecting the police. They're checking her mobile phone and bank card records.' He gave an unhappy shrug. 'See if they've been used since she disappeared.'

'Then you can explain what you said to me a few minutes ago?'

'Look, Mr Ashton, you can see I'm in no mood for questions.'

'When you pushed me against the wall you said, "And why did you have to hurt her? She'd done nothing to you." What did you mean by that?'

He couldn't have been more surprised if Ben had leaned across and jabbed a finger in his eye. 'I pushed you against the wall? No . . . I was unsteady on my feet; I might have brushed by you.'

'You don't remember launching yourself at me? Or asking why I hurt her?'

'Those were my words?' Trajan's eyes oozed both sorrow and pain. 'Oh, God.'

Ben continued. 'Then you shouted this, "I told you not to touch me . . . and why did you have to hurt her . . . she's done nothing to you."'

Trajan bit his lip; for a moment he appeared to be close to remembering, then he pressed the heel of his hand into his forehead. 'No. It's not coming.'

'Those words you used when I came into the room, might they be the ones you spoke when the man attacked you?'

'How can I tell? Everything's been erased.' The bandage appeared to irritate him because he yanked it off. 'The next thing I remember was after I'd found my way into a taxi. Instead of taking me home, as I asked, the driver took me to hospital because blood was squirting out of my scalp. The doctors told me I had concussion. Then they glued the wound to seal it and moved me to the observation ward.'

'You should go back to hospital.'

'No!'

'You really do love her, don't you?'

'April? Of course I love her!' Anger returned to his blue eyes. 'It's crazy that the police think that she bashed me across the skull before running off with another man. Is that what you think?'

Ben shook his head. 'April Connor is nearest thing to an angel you'll ever meet. She's amazing.' The moment he said the words he knew he couldn't maintain eye contact. He turned back to the television; more than anything in the world he longed to see the words: NEWSFLASH: LONDON WOMAN FOUND SAFE.

Trajan had his own thoughts, too. 'You were good friends with April?'

Ben smiled. 'Just good friends. But . . .' He shrugged. 'We were close. Lots of people thought we were in a relationship; even married; you know how people speculate. If you point me at the kitchen I'll make us both a drink.'

The kitchen had that seasoned appearance that only comes with short-term rental properties. None of the cupboard doors fit flush to their frames; where the carpet wasn't worn it was stained. No wonder April and her number-one man had been celebrating the fact they'd signed for a new home. Again came that scalding surge of jealousy. Ben glanced through the door into the lounge as he lifted the kettle. Trajan sat with his elbow supported by the chair arm; the palm of his hand cradled his head as he kept his exhausted eyes on the TV. The man's blond hair was still matted with blood. Stubble covered his jaw. An air of helplessness surrounded him.

Ben had taken an instinctive dislike to him when they first met. The way his blue eyes had stared at Ben as if he was nothing more than a scrap of paper blowing in the wind hadn't helped. But worse – far, far worse – is because Ben knew that April Connor was besotted with the handsome guy with the gold neck chains. And what's worse than that? Ben plugged in the kettle then took two mugs from a shelf. Even worse than knowing that the woman he desired shared that man's bed was the fact that Ben had done nothing to reveal his feelings to her when he had the chance.

As he waited for the kettle to boil he glowered out of the window. Over the rooftops of Bloomsbury rose the classical structure of the British Museum. Contained within it were all those enduring testaments to humanity's achievements – ancient statues, Egyptian mummies, old manuscripts, hoards of gold coins, jewels, all kinds of treasures: all were safely guarded. He, Ben Ashton, had accidentally stumbled upon what he knew was the greatest treasure of his life: a lithe, good-humoured woman by the name of April Connor. Pure gold. And he'd gone to New York and carelessly let her slip through his fingers. Now he'd lost her. Not just to Trajan but perhaps to some tragedy.

In the lounge Trajan groaned with both the pain in his head and the pain of losing April. Ben wanted to not only groan but snarl with anger as he remembered that carefree spell when he'd meet up with April three or four times a week. There were no pressures. They enjoyed meals together or visited pubs with friends. When he thought of her he saw that smile that seemed to permanently light up her face. Each time they met she was overjoyed at seeing him again. It was as if she'd missed him desperately, and all the time he took her lovely smile for granted. That's what he wanted to see now – the whole portfolio of smiles; the pleased-to-see-you smile; the smile as they laughed their way along the streets; the parting smile followed by a kiss on the cheek when they went their separate ways at the evening's end. Dear God. Back then he only had to call her. 'Fancy seeing that new film tonight?' Or: 'I've found this Greek restaurant just off Oxford Street. Feeling hungry?' He only had to ask her to meet him. The reply was always 'Yes!' Those weeks were filled with April's smiling face. He only had to stroll along Charing Cross Road and he'd bump into her as she hurried along, hugging document files to her chest. For three months April was everywhere. Sometimes he didn't have to lift a finger; a tap at the office door and there she would be. 'I was just passing with Jeff and Katrice and I thought I'd stick my nose round the door. Fancy a coffee?' *Yes, a thousand times yes.* Then he had to take that trip to New York. It was going to be little more than a few days. Even when the magazine there asked him to stay on for a while he took it for granted that he'd return to that social whirl with April happily at its centre. Only life back in London moved on. Ties got cut. He lost touch.

'Idiot,' he fumed.

As he crossed the floor to the boiling kettle he noticed Trajan stood in the kitchen doorway. His red-rimmed eyes fixed on him. He said nothing, merely stared like he'd never seen a guy make coffee before.

Ben paused. 'Are you feeling okay?'

Trajan glared. 'That night we met you on the embankment. It wasn't you who followed us and attacked us, was it?'

'You are joking?'

'Christ! You know I'm not bloody joking!' He slammed his fist against the door. 'You had the opportunity. Now with this past you had with April, how do I know you didn't have a motive?'

'The only "past" was friendship . . . platonic, no-sex friendship. Got that?'

Trajan pressed his lips together as a wave of pain surged through him. 'I've got to ask. The police are doing nothing, are they? They think this is just a tiff and she's jumped into bed with another man.' He pressed his hand to his temple.

'Did they give you painkillers?'

'I can't take those.'

'Why not? You clearly need them.'

'What I clearly *need* is to find April because nobody else is looking.'

Ben spoke calmly, 'I will.'

'What?'

'I'll look for her.'

'Why?'

'Damn it, Trajan. She's a mate, a pal, the best bloody friend a man can have.'

'I lost my memory,' he said. 'Same might have happened to her. We should visit the hospitals, ask if anyone's been admitted with amnesia, and we'll get posters copied with her photograph.' The guy was close to collapse. 'Another thing. You were close by. Did you see anyone that looked . . . I can't describe it, but there was something pumped about them. Too big; something out of proportion. You know?'

'Trajan, sit down. I'll bring the coffee through then we can talk.'

'I can talk right here.'

'You look as if you're going to fall down, never mind talk.'

The wounded man tottered back to the sofa.

'Where did you put the painkillers?' Ben asked as he brought in the coffee.

'I'm not having pills. I need to stay focused.'

'You're not focused, pal. You're in agony.'

'I'm fine.'

'You're nowhere near fine. If you take some painkillers they'll relax you.'

'Good God, I don't want to be relaxed. I should be out looking for April.'

'You left the door open in case she just strolled back in, didn't you? Let's face it, that's as unlikely as you searching every street in London single-handed.'

Again Trajan repeated, 'I'm fine.'

'I'm going to get the painkillers. You're going to swallow them. Look, Trajan, if you're relaxed you might start to remember.' He took a deep breath. 'What you said, when you nearly rammed me through the wall, suggests that somewhere deep inside your head is the memory of what happened to you. If we can coax that out it's a start.'

Trajan grimaced. 'Ben. My big sister is just about as bossy as you.' He gave a tired smile. 'Okay, painkillers, hypnotism, torture. I'll submit to anything as long as it brings April back.'

Ben nodded. 'Me too.'

Fifteen

The tide that sweeps up the River Thames is a colossal, fast moving pulse of water comprising billions of gallons. This time, in its cold grip, it carried April Connor. The white heat of hunger wouldn't allow her to consider her situation, or the radical departure from her old life, or even the fundamental questions.

What had happened to her, exactly, when that monstrous figure attacked her on the embankment just a few nights ago? How come she hadn't drowned after he'd thrown her into the river? Why did she shrink from sunlight? Why were there people with those same bite marks marooned on the island? What made them insane with hunger? Why did she have no heartbeat?

If Carter Vaughn had risen out of the depths and grabbed her by the shoulders as she floated there, as inert as a log beneath London Bridge, and uttered the words: 'We are vampires now', she wouldn't have been able to digest the statement. And if at that moment she looked into Carter's face with those soulful eyes that were full of compassion she would have only seen the veins lying just below the skin. Her entire being would have focused on the blood oozing through them. The rest of his flesh and his skeleton would have been nothing compared to the infinitely complex structure of capillaries, veins and arteries – all those beautiful vessels that transmitted the blood through his body.

For the first time in days April felt excitement buzz through her nerves. Here she was floating in the muddy water. If anyone had glanced down from the bridge they would have thought they saw some debris forming a blurred shape just below the surface. They wouldn't have seen an eager face and wide, staring eyes. But the warm-blooded men and women that teemed in those streets just yards from her made their presence felt. She could almost smell the blood in their veins. Smell? No, correction, she could almost *taste* it.

In the Bloomsbury apartment Ben's attention alternated between the television news channel – no mention of April Connor yet – and the evening skyline. All day, showers had swept across the towering buildings. There was an impression in the air that some hostile force gathered just beyond sight over the horizon. The tension infiltrated the streets to tighten the nerves of the population. Every few minutes a police siren would make its howling presence felt. A little while ago Ben had looked out the window to see three youths pounce on another youth. When they knocked him to the ground they started kicking his head. Then, as quickly as it began, it was over. A pair of kids joined the fight. The victim on the ground leapt to his feet as if a spell of invincibility had been cast. He and his friends then began pounding his attackers with their fists. A man passing by with a dog yelled at the teen warriors to cool it. The hefty, black mongrel had lurched forward, its jaws snapping at the kids. As if some force exploded the fighters they all ran off in different directions, darting away between cars. The man who'd intervened bent down to soothe the dog who was still barking. The moment he touched the bristling fur on its back the mutt swung its head round and sank its canines into its owner's hand.

From up here on the fourth floor Ben heard the man cursing. A moment later he disappeared into a side street; he was still haranguing his dog while he nursed the bitten limb beneath his armpit.

Ben turned back to the TV just as a shout came from the bedroom. Trajan had managed to get himself there after taking the powerful painkillers. The guy must have been operating on will power alone; even the pain had helped him stay awake, but once the analgesics worked their narcotic magic he'd simply shut down. For the last six hours he'd slept soundly. But now this . . . Ben expected the man to be hammering at the wall. Instead he found Trajan to still be asleep; however, he fidgeted, and a muttering bubbled out of his throat. As Ben watched the man convulsed on the bed.

'Don't hurt her . . . why'd you bite her?'

93

'Trajan!'

The muttering stopped. The blond head turned on the pillow. A moment later the rhythmic breathing had returned.

Again, conflicting emotions gripped Ben. Here was a guy who was enduring an ordeal. His scalp had been split by what must have been hell of a blow; much worse, the woman he loved had vanished. On top of that he found the police weren't convinced by his story. If anything, they suspected that an infuriated girlfriend had brained him with the rolling pin or whatever, then scooted.

Ben Ashton felt a surge of sympathy for the guy. Yet that green-eyed jealousy demon wouldn't leave him be. Yes, there's the injured victim who's lost his fiancée. But just look at him. He's lying on the king-size bed where he made love to April – the woman that Ben loved. Secretly loved. Insanely loved. Because he'd left it far too late. When he could have revealed his feelings to her he didn't. Too bloody late by far. Ben whirled away to return to the lounge. There he sat with his chin in both hands as he stared at the television. The parents of a missing man, a care-worker by the name of Carter Vaughn, were making an appeal for the public's help in finding him. They held up a photograph of a good-looking, dark-skinned man with distinctive gold-tipped teeth.

'Please,' the mother was saying, 'can anyone out there help find our son?'

At the same time as Ben Ashton watched the parents of Carter Vaughn make their plea, April Connor lay in the river's shallows beneath an overhanging concrete platform. Here she was invisible to people passing along the edge of the river. The buildings across the water were gloomy tombstone shapes in the dusk. She raised herself on one elbow as a passenger ferry droned upstream; the wash from its bows ran out in a curl of white foam that splashed against her chest as it arrived with a hissing noise beneath the canopy. She gazed up at the projecting lip of concrete that extended some ten feet over the edge of the water. Her sensitive nostrils caught the scent of warm bodies close by. Perhaps there was a path which led to a riverside restaurant? There were odours of cooking food. Oddly those didn't interest her. It was the thought of all those men and women that made the hunger blaze inside her. The tide still hadn't risen to its highest point yet and the swell of the river nudged her shoreward as if to say, 'You've made it, April. You're here. Now ... just a little further ... a little more ...'

A sudden swirl of water disturbed the part-enclosed space – with the canopy above and the stone wall of the embankment. She looked to her right as a figure moved out of the shallows and on to the bank of sand that the tide had piled against the wall. The shadowy figure emerged, pulling itself with its arms and dragging its legs behind. To April, it appeared as if something part human, part alligator had dragged its sinuous body from the water on to the hidden beach. It happened again. A second shadowy figure hauled itself on to the sand, belly down, as if its legs no longer worked. When they reached the wall they turned to sit with their backs to the stonework. In the twilight they stared at her; their expressions were impassive but their eyes blazed as if they expected a momentous event to occur soon. One of the figures opened its mouth. She saw yellow glints on the tips of the teeth.

Carter ... At that moment she appeared to be in a state of half-life. She couldn't speak, or even think clearly, but deep down she recognized one of her own kind. The movement came as an automatic response, as a dog salivates at the sight of food, but a second later she emerged from the water, employing that same alligator-like motion. Without standing she dragged herself across the sand to the wall. Without uttering a word, or giving a sign that she'd seen her new companions, she turned herself round and sat with the vertical hardness against her back. She waited as the night slowly fell on London.

Between the end of the afternoon matinee and the evening performance is a wasteland of three hours. There's not enough time to go home; there's only so much shopping can be done and still conserve energy for the evening show. Irving Browning, who played the clown character, Tito, in the stage version of *Laugh, Clown, Laugh*, had an additional problem. The elaborate clown make-up consisted of daubing his face white, then painting oversize lips that rose at each end into a frozen grin. Add to that black wedges drawn on the sides of his eyes, which radiated outwards to create the effect of perpetual astonishment for the audience. All in all, it took an hour to apply the theatrical paint before a show and thirty minutes to remove it afterwards, so there was simply no point in scraping it off his face after the matinee in order to reapply it for the evening performance.

'That's the price an actor pays for their art,' he murmured into the mirror at his clown reflection. He checked the made-up nose. In honour of staying true to the Lon Chaney silent movie, that classic of 1928 where the genius actor played a famous clown who couldn't stop weeping, he rejected the customary red nose in favor of a white nose, which had its origins with the harlequin tradition of Renaissance Italy. Over his elaborate costume, with its diamond pattern of silver and red, he wore an old white lab coat to protect it as he worked in the cellar of the theatre. From clown to Phantom of the Opera. The transformation appealed to the dramatic nature of his soul. Irving Browning whiled away that divide between matinee and evening performance in his own private world, building a circus for his grandson who'd been born four months ago. For Tod's first Christmas he decided to create something that the boy could keep forever. Yesterday he'd finished painting the circus elephants and done more work on the big top. The rigging was giving some trouble as guy ropes couldn't be fixed to the ground like a real tent. Instead his circus tent had a wire hoop sewn into the lining where the roof met the walls, and then a second hoop where the canvas walls would meet the floor. The entire structure would be three feet high by over four feet wide. Plenty of room for lions and their tamers, trapeze artists, the strongman and his girl, plus the red-coated ringmaster, of course. This afternoon he wanted to pay close attention to one of the clowns. Irving had decided to paint the clown to resemble himself; a novel memento of the boy's actor grandfather.

Unlike the sad clown he portrayed in the play Irving Browning was a happy clown. He didn't return to his dressing room in his surreal harlequin make-up to brood darkly on the futility of existence over a bottle of vodka, instead he joked with the other actors to release after-show tensions, and likely as not, he soon had them singing the theme songs from popular TV shows.

This afternoon he had his workshop in the theatre's base-ment to himself. So that left Irving to paint the circus characters to this heart's content. His own smile matched his painted clown smile as he pictured the expression on his grandson's face as he revealed the splendour of the circus on Christmas Day.

That vault beneath the eighteenth-century theatre tended toward stuffiness. Often it smelt of the paints and adhesives he used in constructing the circus; then there might be the whiff of varnish from a new theatrical prop. Always there was the dust smell from old sets stacked away in the corners, and the boxes that contained costumes from bygone productions. This afternoon, however, there was a flow of cold air through the place. In all the months he'd been down here, even in the depths of winter, it never felt as chilly as this. He sniffed the air. It had a whiff of river water. And although the theatre was barely a mile from the Thames, it was still unusual to smell it down here.

'Hello?' His voice echoed away amongst the flats that represented a Scottish castle. He listened hard; he thought he'd heard movement, which had been enough to prompt the hello. 'Enter if you are beautiful and unattached,' he declared in his grand, thespian tones. Usually the staff or cast member would make some suitably light-hearted comment. But after that earlier sound there was only silence. Only . . . Only that gust of cold air had intensified. He shivered then blew into his hands.

'Close the door, dear heart,' he boomed in fruity tones. 'It's cold as the grave down here . . . and Irving Browning isn't getting a day younger, don't cha know?' With that he returned to painting the clown's scarlet smile, but what he heard next startled him so much he jerked the brush and slashed the paint across the figure's throat. 'Silly beggar.' He shouted the words as an act of defiance because the sound rattled his nerves. Dear God, he thought, it sounded like an entire scrapyard had smashed into the place.

He set the brush and figure down and went to investigate. The noise had been a thunderous clang. Clearly a huge chunk of iron had fallen; for the life of him he couldn't imagine what that would be. The scenery flats stored down here were light timber frames with canvas stretched over them. Of course, there was so much stored down here it formed stacks that touched the ceiling so he had to work his way through a maze of canyons, where he could see no more than a few feet ahead at any one time. He glanced at the electric lights set in the ceiling. The force of whatever had fallen had raised so much dust it formed a yellow mist. His nose began to tickle but he resisted wiping it. To do so would smudge his clown make-up, and as a professional that just wasn't the done thing.

He did his best to walk in the direction from where the cold breeze blew, because that, he guessed, must be connected somehow with that metallic crash. The stacks of old scenery meant that it wasn't possible to head directly to it, although he sensed he was heading in the right direction – toward the back of the vault where broken chairs and redundant props were dumped. At that moment a figure emerged from the shadows.

'Ah,' he murmured as he approached an old suit of armor that instead of a helmet sported a plastic human skull. 'How are you, Horatio?' He patted the top of the skull. 'Now, sir, did you hear what I heard?' By now the current of cool, damp air became a torrent. His breath misted white. 'Now . . . what on earth do we have here?'

He peered at the concrete floor. Set there was a massive steel hatchway. The hatch itself had been opened – so it was this that had crashed to the floor. This thing must have weighed three hundred pounds at least. Its pitted underside was streaked with rust stains, and blobs of fungus had formed on it in the damp air of whatever vault or dungeon lay beneath his feet. Irving went to the edge of the hatchway and looked down.

'All is blackness,' he declaimed. 'All is stygian night, but hark . . .' He couldn't resist the theatrical response as he cupped his hand to his ear. From the hole came the sound of rushing water; its echoing nature suggested that it ran through a tunnel. 'A sewer?' He sniffed. 'Or a lost river of old London town?'

Years ago, as a novice actor, when parts were few he'd supplemented his income by acting as a tour guide on the open-topped double-decker buses that plied the capital's streets. As well as reciting the landmarks – Big Ben, Houses of Parliament, Downing Street, Buckingham Palace, and so on – he'd dramatically reveal the hidden aspects of London. 'Beneath the streets,' he would tell the tourists as the bus rumbled along, 'is a mysterious, secret London you never see. There are thousands of miles of tunnels and passageways.

Once there were rivers that ran along its surface, but as demand for building land grew these were buried underground. Beneath Fleet Street lies the River Fleet where boats once sailed. The rivers of Westbourne and Tyburn have been buried, too.' Even back then as a tourist guide he'd made a pantomime gesture of listening. 'They say that in the dead of night you can put your ear down to the pavement and hear the rush of those subterranean waters. And some will claim they even hear the ghostly creak of oars as the phantom boatmen search for a way back home.' If there'd been girls sitting nearby when he made his commentary he'd finish with a ghoulish laugh to try and elicit screams.

Now this conundrum. Here he stood in a clown costume in the theatre basement. The iron hatch yawned open. Below him was complete darkness. A cold breeze blew up into his face. He heard the gush of invisible water. So this really might be one of the hidden rivers of London that rushed through its tunnel toward the Thames.

'But who opened the hatch to yonder cavern?' Irving bent down, expecting to find workmen down there. He guessed checking the 'integrity of the structure' would be the engineer's explanation.

As his eyes adjusted to the darkness he gave a start. Half a dozen faces looked up into his. But he saw, too late, there were no workmen's hard hats. Those faces were strangely bloodless, their lips were blue, dark lines were etched beneath their eyes. He tried to move back but he felt hands grip his ankles. He still moved, but only to topple on to his back. The hands gripped his ankles so ferociously that he yelled in pain. A moment later they hauled him in. He fell through darkness to splash down into a foot of ice-cold water. Gasping, he struggled to his knees. Above him, the opening of the hatch to the warmly lit room beneath the stage could have been his saving, his entrance to heaven. He would be denied admittance to both. The pale shapes flitted with sinuous speed. A second later they pinned him against the tunnel wall. His costume was torn open.

'For God's sake, what are you doing?' he screamed as he felt mouths clamp against his bare wrists, then his stomach, then finally his face. Those half dozen mouths began to chew while their owners grunted in gluttonous ecstasy. Irving

Browning managed to project his scream far away down the tunnel to exit on the banks of the river; there the sound dissipated across the face of the water where it died away without being heard by human ears.

'Okay, Ben, where do we start?' Trajan emerged from the bathroom. He rubbed his face with a towel before dabbing it on the back of his head with a grimace. 'Still leaking,' he grunted as he studied the spot of crimson on the fabric.

'I always do too much research on my articles; it's the curse of living alone.' Outside dusk had fallen. 'Missing person stories are one of the evergreens of journalism. If news is quiet there'll always be a story about someone going out to buy a newspaper and never coming back.'

'It's no laughing matter.'

'I agree, but the hard, uncompromising truth is people vanish. It happens all the time. I wrote up a magazine article a couple of years ago about the body of a woman found in the Serpentine. She lay in the morgue for six months and nobody could identify the body. All the evidence the authorities had was her appearance, her clothes and what was in the pocket of her jacket. That was a key attached to a teddy bear fob and a piece of paper inside a plastic bag. On the paper were the words "My name is Susan Pierman. I have no relatives".'

'So the police had a name.' Trajan was impatient to begin the search. 'They could trace her through that.'

'And so you'd think, but nobody by that name had gone missing in the UK. She may have been from overseas, or it was an assumed name. This Susan Pierman is only one of thousands of people that go missing every year in this country.'

'Come on, there can't be that many?'

'No? Like I say, I'm a writer who lives alone. I do too much research for my own good. Listen, Trajan, we need more information before we start hunting April.'

'We must do something. The police treated me like I was reporting a lost hamster, not a human being.'

Ben sighed. 'That's another brutal fact. Unless it's a child that's missing or there's evidence of forced abduction, missing person cases are low priority. Just last year the Lambeth police division – that covers just a single borough – investigated

100

more than two thousand cases where people had vanished. There are websites that specialize in identifying the remains of bodies found in England. Believe it or not, there are hundreds of cases – people found dead in rivers, canals, supermarkets, city streets, hotels, you name it. Some have been murdered, some killed themselves, others died of natural causes, but the single factor that unifies them is that the police haven't a clue who they were. And day after day the morgues collect more and more corpses from the Thames, or municipal parks or bus stations and nobody can put a name to them.'

Trajan's anger evaporated. He sat on the sofa digesting what Ben had told him. The expression of misery on the man's face touched Ben, and he began asking himself what was his motive for helping to find April. Was it for April's sake? Trajan's? Or did Ben cherish a secret hope that if he found her he could also steal her away from that blond-haired man who sat there grieving for his lost fiancée?

The bottom line was that Ben must do what he could. Whatever April decided after that was up to her; providing they could trace her, that is.

'OK,' Ben said. 'First things first. Nothing unusual happened in the days or weeks running up to the night April went missing and you were attacked?'

'Absolutely nothing.'

'No peculiar phone calls, or letters, or strangers hanging round the apartment block or where she worked?'

'No. And no ransom note made from diced newspaper. Don't you think I've gone through all that with the police?'

'At the moment, Trajan, we've nothing to go on. All we know is what you've told me. You walked beside the Thames. Someone attacked you. When you came round April was gone. There are no witnesses to confirm or deny what—'

'You think I'm lying?'

That sense of violence pervading London crackled in the air of the lounge. It was as if some unseen power tested London's population, trying to goad them into acts of random savagery.

Ben took a deep breath. 'I don't believe you're lying, but you know more than you're telling me.'

'Like what, for God's sake?' Trajan's face flushed.

'You can't remember what happened to you yet, but . . .'

Ben tapped his own temple with his finger. 'It's locked in here. When you were sleeping you started shouting. I checked on you and I distinctly heard you say: "Why did you bite her?"'

'Bite her?' Confusion clouded his eyes.

'Did the individual who attacked you, Trajan, bite April?'

'I don't—' There was a searching quality to his eyes as if he looked into his own mind. 'I wanted to say, "Yes" but I don't know why. I still can't remember what happened.' He gave one of those painful shakes of his head. 'Sorry. All I can recall is something about a figure that was *wrong* in some way. A peculiarity I can't define.'

'How's your head now?' Ben asked.

'Good enough.'

'Then it's time we return to the scene of the crime.'

'Wait. Do you really believe I saw someone bite April?'

'I believe you know something. It's just a case of triggering your memory.'

'I hope to God you're right.'

They infiltrated the city as the darkness took hold. April Connor and her kind had emerged from the waters after their transformation into New-Life, driven by a hunger that overwhelmed all rational thought. They craved food. That need became nothing less than a burning madness. It must be satisfied at all costs.

Beside a railway track that ran through wasteland north of King's Cross, a man who was shooting vermin with a rifle found rats fleeing toward him from a derelict warehouse. There were dozens of them. He couldn't believe his luck as he burst their furry bodies with his gunshots. His luck changed when whatever had scared the rats sped from the doorway and seized him. As he saw the surviving rats flee into the shadows he thought to himself in surprise, *Biting!* The jaws of something no longer human ripped at his skin to release his hot blood.

In Chelsea, an architect dropped his car keys on the pavement just outside his mews home. When he picked them up he happened to glance down a drainage grate set at the edge of the road.

'Hello, how did you get down there?' He looked down into a child's wide eyes that gazed up trustingly into his. 'Did

102

someone put you down there?' asked the architect. He glanced round but there was nobody in sight to offer a hand, so he bent down to see the child better. *What a world! Who'd think of pushing a child down through a manhole into a sewer? The child could have been wandering lost for hours.*

The moment the man's face was close enough to the iron grille two things happened. Firstly, he saw several grey-faced figures below lit by the radiance of a street lamp. Two, the child's arms, that were slender enough to pass through the bars of the grate, reached out; its hands grabbed him by the hair and dragged his face downward to slam against the bars. 'Hey!' Their mouths couldn't reach the architect. Instead, one of the figures below drove a steel spike up between the bars and into his eye. Once they'd yanked it out the man's blood rained down on to the figures below who danced in the ruby cascade; as they danced they licked that liquid nourishment from each other's bodies.

The janitor responsible for locking up the swimming pool in the basement of the hotel yelled into the phone, 'Listen to me. Someone's caught beneath the grid at the bottom of the pool . . . no, I don't know how. All I can see is a pair of arms. They must be drowning down there. Get someone down here now!' He threw aside the phone then ran back to the pool. At this time of night it was deserted so this was the first time in the man's life he would be hailed a hero. He dived in fully clothed and swam down to where a pair of bare arms extended from the dislodged grille. Beneath that was the drainage conduit that would dump the pool's water into the sewers under the hotel. When the manager and the desk clerk made it down to the pool side, they would find the normally crystal-clear waters of the pool turned the colour of rust. Of the janitor there would be no sign.

On a houseboat moored to the riverbank a man searched for his wife who'd stepped out on deck just minutes ago to enjoy the cool night air. He scanned the dark waters. 'Sonia, where are you?' The only answer was the sucking noise the waves made as they lapped against the wharf.

Downriver, towards Tilbury Docks, a stream discharged water into the Thames. On the wall directly above the confluence of waters stood Jez Martine. Zipped into the pocket of his leather coat was the endeavor of his adult life; a home-

103

recorded CD of his songs. Now at fifty years of age he was exhausted. The title song of his album said it all: 'This Man Is Used Up'. Nobody had heard his compositions. The record companies weren't interested. Radio stations didn't even return his complimentary disks, never mind play them. Remember Vincent Van Gogh's self-sacrifice, he told himself, this is the route to immortality. Tonight he would throw himself into the river. When his body was pulled from the water in a day or two, the CD would be found, then the world would mourn the genius that it had lost. Jez Martine heard that death by drowning wasn't only painless, it was a euphoric experience. Oxygen deprivation engenders a sensation of sublime bliss.

Jez stared down into the river. Pale shapes swam there beneath the surface with all the predatory menace of sharks. Yet when something broke the surface it wasn't a shark's fin but a human face with blazing eyes. Those eyes fixed on him, waiting for him to take that lethal step forward. Jez fingered the hard shape of the compact disk in his pocket. Perhaps it might be worth trying the record companies one more time, he told himself, before hurrying away from the river in the direction of home.

London before midnight buzzed with life. Only some of it was the wrong kind of life. It was still hungry. The gang of muggers waited in the park for what should be easy victims – a girl with her companion; a slender guy with gold-tipped teeth. When they were close the five men pounced. The first move would be to beat the guy unconscious then rob the pair of them. It all happened in a blur. The robbers fell one by one, their throats torn, or faces ripped from their skulls. As one of the thugs lay dying the word 'ironic' escaped him. But as he lost consciousness the phrase 'a biter bit' drifted through his mind.

Sixteen

April and Carter gorged on the blood of the would-be robbers. To human eyes the park would be a mass of indistinct shadows but for April the lights of the city beyond the trees illuminated the place in vivid multi-coloured hues. Here in a clearing in the bushes she saw the scene with perfect clarity. Deep inside her, a voice fainter than a whisper of dust falling in a tomb protested that this was a scene of utter horror. Oh no, April told herself, this is a slice of heaven dragged down to earth. For in the clearing lay the source of the most beautiful, nerve-tingling food in creation. The five men who'd made the fatal mistake of pouncing on them lay dead on the ground. Their bodies were a mass of bite marks inflicted during the attack. And now the aftermath of that short battle was a frenzy of feeding.

April inserted a finger into the torn neck of a muscular guy dressed in army surplus fatigues. With that finger she probed the dripping wound until she found what she needed. Oh . . . those lovely ruby drips; she yearned to lick them from his skin, but there was something altogether richer and darker – and far more abundant. She craved more than drops, she lusted after a whole reservoir of the man's lifeblood. That probing digit found the carotid artery deep in the neck. April's hunger gave her the strength to hook it with her finger, then draw it out through the wound; a pink tube that once formed the expressway from heart to brain. She moved with such speed the procedure appeared to be borne of years of practice. But this was her first time . . . her first, glorious, fulfilling, yearned-for time. Through her mind flashed memories of devouring that salty estuary water, but that had only been a substitute for this, the most precious fluid in the world. Her face darted down at the exposed artery; she bit through with an audible *snick!* As the man's heart had stopped beating there

105

was no arterial spurt. *No, this girl's going to have to work hard for her reward.* The very molecules of her body blazed with the ferocious hunger. All that mattered in the universe right now was: *Feed. Feed long and hard.* So this is the beautiful moment of swallowing. She pushed the severed end of the artery into her mouth. Then she sucked hard. The moment of bliss was nothing less than a star exploding in her soul. Those famished molecules all seemed to give a heartfelt 'Ahhh . . .' A unified sigh that magically spread even beyond the borders of her own body. It was as if she nourished a ravenous universe by the act of feeding. She sucked the blood from the man's body with so much power his face began to shrink. As she did so, memories raced through her mind. Of her as a teenager as she sucked on a plastic straw to drain the last of the milkshake out of a cup. This was similar. At first the blood spurted into her mouth from the severed vein in a flood of satisfying salt and flesh flavours. Then as it became depleted in the cadaver's veins she had to draw all the harder until her cheeks ached with the effort. Yet the flood of satisfaction was beyond anything she'd ever experienced before.

Then, finally, as the reservoir of lifeblood was exhausted, and the man's eyes sank into their sockets, she moved on to the next of her victims. This was a kid with a wide-open mouth that displayed rotted teeth; his eyes were wide glassy orbs in the darkness; the expression suggested his own death had come as an unexpected surprise and he still couldn't come to terms with it. She giggled; the bellyful of man-blood intoxicated her. It left her with a warm sense of well-being. The world had become a lovely place lit by delicious rose tints. As she worked on his throat to tease out the carotid artery she glanced across at Carter.

Carter luxuriated in gluttony, too. He'd chewed away the hand of a tattooed street bandit. Now he sucked on the open wrist veins with such bliss on his face, while both of his hands stroked the corpse arm from shoulder to forearm as he coaxed the blood along the veins. April giggled again as she watched him. Carter's milking that arm of blood, she told herself, like he's milking a cow. Maybe she should go along and ask for a taste? Tattoo boy's blood might be meatier than the one she worked on now. But then she gasped with surprise. She hadn't expected this. What an unexpected bonus!

106

The kid she was about to liberate of his precious red-stuff was still alive. Ye, gods, this is pleasure beyond imagination . . . For a second she made kittenish cries of delight as the severed artery spurted blood into her face. The heat of it! Not to mention the sheer force of that jet of crimson hitting her face in a joyous explosion. After licking her lips she pressed her mouth against the wound to feed on that liquid glory. The kid kicked the grass with his heels, gurgled a little, clenched his fists in agony. That's all he could manage.

Once again the image of her as a teen returned. Of the times she sucked on the thick plastic straw of her shake. Slurping, gurgling; an exquisite experience. Now this. It was as if she'd waited her entire life for this moment. And now it was here she'd savour it for as long as she could.

April and Carter walked along the path by the canal. The cloud began to break; a thousand stars shone through. The pair were filled with such happiness that everything appeared wonderful. They pointed out the constellation of Orion reflected in the canal water. An airliner glided overhead, its navigation lights burned brilliantly, causing them to shield their sensitive eyes.

'Imagine all those people on that plane.' Carter whooped. 'They'll all be asleep like this.' He pantomimed a sleeping man with his head to one side. 'Just imagine all those bare necks with those big, *big* pulses going da-dum, da-dum, da-dum.'

She laughed as she put her arm around him. They could have been a pair of lovers returning home after a party that left them exhilarated as much as intoxicated. At that moment they were so energized it seemed as if they were flying rather than walking. Nothing required effort. April laughed as she suddenly twirled round, her arms held out by her side.

Carter leapt on to a wall and crouched there as he made a play of balancing. 'Watch me, momma. I'm gonna surf these bricks all the way to Rio. There the people are so juicy it'll be like eating peaches.' The man was a relentless bundle of energy. He pounded his chest as if he was Tarzan. 'Peaches of the gods!'

April jumped up and grabbed his hands. 'Carter! We've found it, haven't we?'

'We've found happiness.'

'But we've discovered something amazing. This is a miracle.'

'Come fly with me!'

They jumped off the wall hand-in-hand. As they walked with that bouncing stride April rushed the words through her lips with that same energy. 'You know why so-called civilized people hate cannibalism?'

'Tell me, beautiful one.' He beamed those gold-tipped teeth at her.

'It's because it gives you power. When you drink someone's blood or eat their flesh it makes you so strong you feel as if you could lift a building into the air.'

'That's cool. I'm gonna go down to Westminster and throw Big Ben over the moon.'

She laughed as she experienced such rapture she thought she would burst. 'But now we've discovered the truth. We're like Edison, Madam Curie and Oppenheimer rolled into one. Listen, Carter. We'll make the world a better place. Just picture it. If everyone felt like this there'd be no wars. Everybody will be happy. Wait . . .' She grabbed him by the arm as he tight-roped a narrow band of stone at the canal edge. 'Don't you feel it?'

'I feel everything's good.'

'But don't you feel as if you can never die? That you'll live forever?'

'Hmm.' He rubbed his stomach while laughing out loud. 'I feel it.'

'This is the happiest day of my life,' she declared. 'You and me, Carter, we've discovered eternal happiness and immortality.'

'That, my sweetheart, is what I call an achievement.'

April found herself skipping along the night-time path. The city lights were nothing less than a celebratory firework display, and above them the stars shone with their own happy glow.

'We can't keep this to ourselves, you know?' She linked arms with him. 'We've got to share it.'

'Who with?'

'The world.'

'How're we going to do that?'

'I know a guy . . .'

'Hmm, feeling a touch of jealousy here.' He laughed as if every syllable she spoke was the wittiest line in the history of comedy.

'Idiot.' She patted his stomach. 'He's nice though.'

'You're not going to kiss him behind my back, are you?' He tried to mime outrage but burst into giggles.

'Once I thought he would kiss me.' She scrunched her shoulders with pleasure. 'I wouldn't have minded. I had a secret *thing* about him.'

'Oooh, sexy thing?'

'Shh . . .' She giggled again. 'Now, where was I?' She took a deep breath. 'This guy. He's called Ben Ashton, and he's a writer.'

'Wow. Comics? Books? Plays?'

'Stop distracting me, Carter.' She playfully slapped his stomach. 'Ben works for the magazines. Listen, this is what we'll do . . .' Her voice dropped to a whisper as if she didn't want to be overheard, even though the wasteland beside the canal was deserted. 'We'll find Ben Ashton and share our secret with him.'

'You're sure?'

'Sure, I'm sure.' She gave another tipsy laugh. 'Listen, Carter. We've discovered a secret. We can heal the world. Everyone can feel as strong and as happy as we do.'

Carter's face clouded. 'But it isn't always like this. Remember how much it hurt on the island?'

'But that's over. We know how to stop the hunger.'

'Human beings. Hmm . . .' He smacked his lips.

'Ben can write our story for the press.' The thought thrilled her to the bone. 'We'll explain how everyone can live forever.'

'We'll win the Nobel Prize.'

'It's inevitable!' She kissed him on the cheek. 'Just look at us.' Her laughter rang out across the water. 'Haven't you noticed?'

'Noticed what? I'm having such a good time.'

'We're all covered in blood.'

This amused them so much it sent them into a renewed bout of giggles. Then as the starlight shone down they strolled away arm-in-arm into the night in search of Ben Ashton. They had the miracle of New-Life to share with the world.

Seventeen

With the time past midnight, Ben and Trajan took a taxi down to Embankment, that swathe of valuable real estate reclaimed from the Thames a couple of centuries ago. Where there had once been muddy banks, a major road now ran between the water and some of the capital's most prestigious buildings. The summer night was a warm one, and people were heading home either on foot or by car after visiting the restaurants and theatres. Reflected lights shone on the high tide as a gaudy party boat drifted downstream to the accompaniment of a band playing on its stern deck.

After paying the taxi driver Ben followed Trajan to the wall that separated the path from the river. Even in the street lights it was easy to make out the rust-coloured smudge on the back of the man's blond head that marked the position of the wound.

'How are you feeling?' Ben asked.

'Fine. Are we close to where I first met you?' The man appeared tense now, as if unsure he could handle any memories if they should come rushing back at him.

'Just along there near the road sign. I was looking at the river when April came up behind me.' Ben gave a faint smile. 'At first I thought someone was going to chuck me in the water.'

Trajan scanned the roadway. 'It's well lit, and you can see right down toward Cleopatra's Needle. After you left us, did you look back?'

Ben shook his head. 'By that time I was in a hurry to get home.' He also remembered the profound disappointment at realizing that April Connor was moving in with the blond man who had a well-paid career in shipping. He noticed Trajan was staring down at the stone path as he walked alongside the wall. 'See anything?'

'Not yet. I'm looking for my blood. If I see where I spilt it from this . . .' He touched the wound. 'Then I'll know exactly where the attack took place.'

'There was heavy rain last night, Trajan. I doubt if you'll find anything.'

'I've got to try, damn it. What else can I do?'

'You don't remember anything about the attack itself? How you were struck? Or if there was a weapon?'

'I remember figures on the wall – they were odd for some reason.'

'Figures? Before you only mentioned one.'

Trajan blinked. 'Two . . . I'm sure there were two. But only one attacked us.'

'There was a weapon?'

He rubbed his forehead. 'No . . . I don't remember. I just realized later that I was riding in a taxi with blood soaking my hair. Damn . . .'

'No smells? Aftershave? Cooked food? Beer?'

'No! Give it a rest, Ben.'

'A big man? Thin? Plump? Tattoos?'

'Damn it, whatever happened was knocked clean out of my head when he threw me.'

'Threw you?'

A flicker of surprise ran across Trajan's face. 'He never hit me. He picked me up and threw me away like I was a piece of crap.'

'It's coming back, Trajan. You're starting to remember. What did he do to April?'

'I don't know.'

'Bit her?'

'Shut up, Ben. Stop pushing me. Give me a chance to—'

'Forget again. Come on, you lazy bastard.' Fury surged through Ben. 'Think harder. April's life might depend on it.'

'I am thinking, you bloody—'

'Well, think harder. Burst a few brain cells.'

'Shut up.'

'You're safe and sound. April isn't.'

Trajan whirled round and shoved Ben against the river wall. Rage blazed in his eyes, and that aura of violence that hung over London all evening threatened to find its focus right there and then.

111

'See, you're no weakling,' Ben panted. 'You've got muscle; so the guy who put you on the ground must have been strong as a bull.' Ben tried to push the man back but Trajan froze as he stared over Ben's shoulder. 'What's wrong?'

'There's someone in the river.'

'What?'

'There, under the pier.'

'Okay, let go. I want to look.' Ben shrugged himself free then turned his attention to the timber structure that ran out into the water to one of the ferries that had been moored up for the night.

'Someone in the water?' Ben asked as he stared into the shadows. 'Male or female?'

Trajan shrugged. 'Forget it. It's just some kid spraying graffiti.'

Ben moved to his right until the timber bollard that blocked his view was out of the way. There, standing on a beam beneath the pier decking, was the figure of a man. Across the white flank of the ferry boat he was busily painting these words:

VAMPIRE SHARKZ
☺ They're coming to get you ☺

Eighteen

Ben hissed, 'Trajan, cut off his retreat from that end of the pier. I'll catch him from this side.'

The blond man was stunned. 'Catch him? Why do you want to catch some vandal daubing graffiti?'

'Come on, before he vanishes.'

Trajan stayed where he was on the embankment walkway. 'We're searching for April, we don't have time to stop someone painting their name on a boat.'

'Quick, Trajan. As soon as he finishes he'll vanish again.' Ben walked as quietly as he could along the pier as the man, who'd been painting the mysterious slogan 'Vampire Sharkz: They're Coming To Get You', added the twin red spots that served as eyes for the smiley face. As he painted there in the shadows beneath the pier a reddish mist drifted from the aerosol, which he used to create his unlawful art.

Trajan has good night vision, Ben realized. Not many people would notice the man in his black sweater and jeans at work there. Even with street lights the figure was simply another shadow amid many shadows. From what Ben could make out the man stood on one of the beams that supported the jetty structure. Just below him was the surface of the river. The currents were strong and bore branches, bottles, paper cups and other jetsam at a hell of a rate. Moreover, the direction of the flow was upstream, so this was the mighty tidal surge that swept inland. Even as Ben watched he saw that the level of the water crept up towards the man's feet. No doubt the rising tide was an incentive to finish his Vampire Sharkz message quickly before he escaped back to dry land. After all, he only had to slip.

As Ben padded along the pier towards the jetty a hand grabbed his forearm.

'I can't let you do this,' Trajan told him. 'I don't know what that man means to you, but we must find April.'

'Let go of me. He'll get away.'

'No.'

'Damn it, Trajan. See that guy? He's haunted London for the last three months. His graffiti's everywhere.'

'So?'

'Don't you understand? If whoever attacked you makes a habit of it then our painter down there might have seen something.'

Trajan was doubtful. 'You think—'

Ben slipped from the muscular grasp then moved along the jetty. Too late. The second Ben started to climb over the rail the artist moved with the speed of a cat. He shot over the rail on to the platform and sped noiselessly across the boards towards the pier, which would take him back to shore. Then he'd vanish into the streets in the blink of an eye.

Only Trajan was there. The big man blocked the narrow gantry. When the artist saw there was no exit that way he ran back on to the jetty to be confronted by Ben.

In front of Ben was a slightly built guy of around thirty with a crooked nose and dark brown eyes beneath a mass of curly black hair.

The man held up the aerosol, showing he was armed with nothing more lethal than paint. 'Okay, okay.' His words were a gabble. 'My name is Spiro Akinedes. This is my first offence. I'll do as you say.'

'Mr Akinedes,' Ben began. 'We're not the police.'

'No?'

'I just want to talk to you.'

'You own the boat?'

'The one you've just decorated?' Ben shook his head.

'Then you'll let me go?'

'As soon as we've talked.'

'I'm not interested in talking.'

'Then I'm not interested in letting you go.' Ben made his voice tougher. 'And if you don't talk we'll take you to the nearest police station.'

'You wouldn't do that.'

'You're a famous graffiti artist, Mr Akinedes. The police have been looking for you for weeks.'

'What do you want to know?'

Trajan was mystified, but stayed quiet. Ben realized that suggesting this individual might know something about April's disappearance was riotously optimistic to say the least. And yet . . . in the back of Ben's mind was the cryptic conversation with the hermit in his boat on a pole near Tower Bridge. Elmo Kigoma had urged Ben to uncover the meaning of the Vampire Sharkz graffiti then write about it. All this – the graffiti, April's disappearance, the hermit's veiled warnings – suddenly appeared to be linked. It resembled one of those puzzles made up of random shapes that appeared to be on the verge of fitting together to create a recognizable picture. Ben knew he needed to accumulate enough facts and the answer to all these puzzling clues would fit together and make a coherent whole. Even though he'd been commissioned by his editor to find this mystery graffiti artist the story had vanished from Ben's radar. All that interested him was finding April Connor and, by the most slender of possibilities, Spiro Akinedes might know some tiny but vital fact. Meanwhile, the man cast wary glances; standing in one place for too long made him uneasy.

114

Ben asked, 'What's it mean?'

The man turned the aerosol over in his hands, while his brown eyes bulged with fear.

'Ben.' Trajan sighed. 'This gentlemen can't help you. Let him go.'

'He can go,' Ben agreed. 'I just need a moment of his time.' He glanced at the red graffiti on the side of the boat. 'Vampire Sharkz: They're coming to get you. Is that a threat or a promise or a prophecy?'

'It's just a thing I do,' the man replied with a shrug.

'For just a thing that you do you've worked bloody hard at it. How many times have you painted it? A thousand? Two thousand?'

The man's eyes became pained as if he didn't want to be reminded. 'Oh, plenty.'

'Then you have a good reason, Mr Akinedes?'

He gave a grim nod.

'That logo and the smiling faces are all over London.' Ben walked across the jetty boards. 'You don't just paint something like that on an idle whim, do you?'

'Leave him alone, Ben,' Trajan said. 'Can't you see he's scared?'

Ben kept an unwavering eye on the artist. 'Scared? What of? Vampire Sharkz?'

'I need to go now, Mister . . .'

'Call me Ben. So what's troubling you?'

'Shoes!' The word burst from his lips as if to betray him.

The response caught Ben by surprise. 'Shoes? What's wrong with my shoes?'

'You're walking where I've got to work.' Spiro Akinedes spoke as if it was the last thing he wanted, only the words spilled out by themselves. 'Please . . . the soles of shoes are covered with bacteria, viral contamination . . . just so dirty.' He gulped. 'You've got to keep your shoes away from this part here.' He gestured a portion of the decking, then added, 'Show me the bottom of your shoes.'

Ben obliged, lifting one foot then the other.

'Thank you,' the man said with a sigh of relief. 'You can never be sure. You might have stepped in something . . . you know, dog faeces, they can have a worm that . . .' He gestured near his face. 'Feeds on the eyes. Blinding.'

Trajan began, 'Ben, I think the gentlemen's—'

'No, I'm not mad.' In the dim light he abruptly crouched down, shook the aerosol, and began to spray on to the planking; the first letter was a distinctive V. 'If you must know I suffer from OCD. Obsessive Compulsive Disorder. It's related to anxiety disorders – had it since I was a kid. If you're in the grip of OCD you're trapped by repetitive thoughts and bizarre habits. It's not madness. More than two per cent of the population suffer from it.' He worked the aerosol; its atomizer jetted a stream of red on to the timber. V-A-M-P. 'The habits are senseless, distracting; OCD sufferers realize they're locked into irrational behavior patterns, but they find it difficult to break out . . . often they don't . . . usually they accommodate it.' He finished VAMPIRE. 'Symptoms of OCD are obsessional ideas and compulsive behavior – including endless hand washing, arranging household ornaments into special patterns, then checking, and re-checking, for hours on end. Fear of dirt.' The words cascaded from him like a heartfelt confession. By now he'd sprayed VAMPIRE SHARKZ.

Trajan impatiently tapped the handrail. 'Ben, leave him. This is getting us nowhere.'

'Just give me another minute. I'm on to something.'

Spiro Akinedes muttered as he painted. 'OCD has a neurological basis, can respond to medication. OCD can run in tandem with other conditions. Tourette's syndrome. And trichotillomania – this is the urge to pull out hair, eyelashes and body hair.' He glanced up. Ben noticed the man had no eyebrows. 'Pluck, pluck. Please, don't come any closer. It's your shoes. Shoes bother me. They always have. They go tramping through all that dirt; it's a feeding ground for rats; dogs use the streets as a lavatory; not all excrement you see on a pavement is canine; people, too. All shoes are magnets for microbes. Disease of the sole . . . get it?' The joke might have been part defence mechanism, but the man wasn't amused by his own witticism, he merely returned to carefully drawing the smiling faces that flanked the words 'They're coming to get you'.

Ben crouched down to watch the man work, but kept his distance . . . or rather made sure his shoes were far enough away from Spiro's arm as it made long sweeps to aerosol the red circles that would become the ☺.

116

Ben said, 'If you have OCD you repeat the same compulsive actions.'

'Yes. I shouldn't be ashamed, but I am.' The man blushed. 'Since childhood?'

The man nodded as he worked.

Ben rubbed his jaw. 'But this Vampire Sharkz graffiti is new.'

The artist paused for a second before adding the grinning mouth and eyes inside the circle.

Ben continued. 'People with OCD often believe that their rituals protect themselves from danger.'

'Or the people they love.'

Trajan said urgently, 'Hurry up. This is getting you nowhere.'

'On the contrary.' Then he addressed Spiro Akinedes, who compulsively repeated this graffiti across London. 'Who are you protecting with this message?'

'It's not a message. It's a warning. The faces are the protective element. That's what it means to me.'

'So who are you protecting? Yourself?'

Spiro shook his head. 'People look at me and they think I'm a piece of walking crap. They say that what I paint here is meaningless. But the truth is I love people. I love this city. Look at that.' He held up his hand. The fingers and palm were covered in blood red blisters. 'I get blisters because I paint this night and day. It's crucifying me but I've got to do it.'

'But you've not always painted the Vampire Sharkz message.'

'You're right. I used to be preoccupied with shoes. Every morning I'd put on rubber gloves then rub the soles clean with toilet paper. It took ten minutes to do each shoe. I had eight pairs in all. When I finished I locked them in a cupboard lined with clean newspaper. I'd go into another room but I'd be filled with this overwhelming anxiety that I'd missed a speck of dirt. I was terrified that my wife or kids would somehow swallow it and they'd be infected with disease.' He began gulping again as if the idea of dirty soles nearly made him vomit.

'So what happened, Mr Akinedes? Why aren't shoes your main concern now?'

117

'You're an insightful man.' He stopped painting and held out his hand. 'Lift your foot.'

Ben obeyed and the man touched his shoe. 'No, shoes don't bother me like they did. I couldn't have done that six months ago.'

'Instead of shoes it's now Vampire Sharkz graffiti. Why?'

'Because . . .' The man finished the motto. 'Six months ago I stood in my bedroom that overlooks a canal in Teddington. I saw shapes moving through the water like sharks. And just as I can see you they came out of the canal. They just burst out on to the bank in a mass of spray. There were some fishermen standing there. Only those things weren't sharks, they were people. They killed the fishermen by biting their throats and faces. Then I watched them drink the men's blood. After that they returned to the water. They swam like sharks.'

'Vampire Sharkz.'

'That's how I think of them, and if you know anything about OCD you know once a phrase gets stuck in the sufferer's head it stays there.'

Trajan became interested. 'You say there were people in the river that bit the fishermen?'

'Yes, go on, mister. Feel free to mock me. Call me mad.'

Trajan rubbed his face as if he'd woken from a trance. 'Then I must be mad, because I watched a man biting April.' He touched his side. 'Just here, above the hip.' His eyes were troubled and his entire body trembled.

The painter stared at Trajan. 'You've seen them, too?'

Trajan stepped on to the jetty to pore over the graffiti with a sudden fascination. He saw in that slogan the key to April's disappearance.

VAMPIRE SHARKZ
☺ They're coming to get you ☺

Trajan took a deep breath. 'So now you paint this warning all over the city?'

'Nobody else believes me but you.'

'Does anyone else understand the meaning of it?'

'You have to know this fact, mister. Not only do I think it's the right thing to do, my OCD means I can't *stop* painting

118

it. This is my new compulsion. Before, I could almost control my condition because I knew the incessant shoe cleaning was irrational. But this *is* essential. I have to warn everyone.' His voice cracked with emotion. 'It blisters my hands. I'm exhausted, and do you know how much I spend on this stuff?' He brandished the aerosol can. 'I'm selling everything I own to buy more. My family can't take it. Sophie's taken the kids back to her mother.' He rubbed his eyes with the heel of his hand. 'But it's not a disease anymore. This is vital! I don't want anyone else to die, only I can't have painted it enough because your friend was bitten by these monsters; that means I've failed you and I've failed her; if—'

'It's okay,' Ben said gently. 'Now we know what's happening it's not a battle you have to fight by yourself.'

This seemed to relieve the man of his burden. His voice became calmer. 'Vampire Sharkz. It seems crazy but that's what they are. I know they appear to be human but they swim in the rivers and canals. I see them all the time. If you looked in here right now you might see one just under the surface. Fast, like pale sharks zipping through the water.'

Ben eyed the brown swirl of the Thames in the street light. It was closer to the decking as the tide continued to rise. Close enough, in fact, for a hand to dart from the waters and grab him by the ankle.

The man still talked. 'As well as the warning I knew I had to add a symbol of protection. The smiling face is just that. It's a happy human face. That has to count for something, doesn't it? It might help counter the evil that's in that water.' He nodded at the chocolate-brown liquid that swept its bobbing flotsam upstream. 'OCD doesn't fine-tune your obsessions.'

Trajan frowned. 'Are you saying that something that you call a vampire shark attacked my fiancée?'

Spiro said, 'I get obsessive about facts. I know that more people suffer from OCD than schizophrenia. I know it's caused by abnormal neurochemical activity. I can name every street in London. But I don't know the biology of those creatures in the water. But I paint my warning everywhere I can. That's the best I can do.'

Ben nodded. 'Thanks for talking to us, Mr Akinedes.' He held out his hand.

119

The artist shook it, then shook Trajan's with the words, 'I hope you find who you're looking for.'

As the pair left the pier, Trajan said quietly to Ben, 'Does he mean there's some kind of animal in the water?'

Ben eyed the river with distaste. 'That's exactly what he meant, but what the animal is he couldn't explain.'

'But who can?'

'A man said something very similar to Mr Akinedes yesterday. We should head downriver and talk to him.' Ben paused and looked back at the graffiti artist. 'Mr Akinedes. Do you know there's someone else who's been warning about a danger in the river?'

'Then I'm not alone.' The man was relieved. 'There's a chance we can save more people.'

'Do you want to come with us and speak to him?'

'Thanks. But I need to . . .' He hoisted the can into the air like it was the sword of truth. 'There's still some paint left.'

Ben waved a farewell as they headed out towards the road to find a taxi. Okay, the notion that something called a Vampire Shark lurked in the Thames was eccentric, if not downright delusional, but so far they had few clues to April's disappearance. At this moment every lead had to be followed up.

On the pier the man starting spraying the letters in bright red paint. *V-A-M-P.*

He'd just begun drawing the *I* when an arm reached out from the river and swept him into the water with barely a splash.

Nineteen

April pointed down a night-time suburban street. 'Raj's house.'

'Raj's house?' Carter grinned; that glow of intoxication hadn't left him yet. 'Why Raj's house? Who is Raj? I thought we were looking for Ben Ashton?'

April chuckled; the sense of well-being after gorging on the blood of the would-be muggers left her elated; it was a high that wouldn't end. 'Ben moved. I know Raj, he's Ben's editor. I can get the address from him.' Smiling, she rubbed Carter's back. 'Then we call on Ben, tell him what we know, then he writes it for all the world to know! Clever, eh?'

'Wait.' Carter stopped her. 'We haven't thought this through yet, have we?'

'What's there to think? We've discovered something marvelous.'

His grin clouded. 'But it's like we're forgetting something important.'

'Carter. The secret to eternal life and happiness – not just happiness, but pure unadulterated joy, was right there under our noses all along.'

'Just drink blood?'

'Don't you remember that first mouthful of human blood? How beautiful it tasted? It was so *right* on your tongue.'

Carter licked his lips, revealing his gold crowns; he remembered that taste again. That glorious, glorious taste. April found her mouth watering, too.

'When you swallowed the blood you felt the strength rush into your body.' She spoke in hushed tones; this was the voice of someone who'd witnessed a miracle. 'I've never felt so full of life.' She wanted to shout the word. '*Life* . . . it's like electricity inside of me. I feel as if I could lift a house or jump as high as the clouds.'

Despite feeling elated, confusion crept back into Carter's expression. 'But it's not as simple as that, April. You're forgetting something. We aren't the same as we were.'

'No, we're better. Improved. Enhanced.'

'But don't you remember your old life? Would you have wanted to swallow blood from a man's body then?'

'That's before the revelation. We're New-Life now.'

'No.' Carter wrestled with the problem. 'We know we were attacked and ended up in the river. After that we woke up on the island. Changes took place in our bodies. We were hungry all the time.' The word 'hungry' made him swallow. The man's appetite was returning. 'Now we're back in London and we've killed people, April. Surely, that isn't right?'

That evangelical zeal to tell the world about the miracle

made Carter's argument trivial. 'Listen, Carter. One day a creature started walking upright and became a human being. How did those creatures feel when they first started to speak, or chipped at a stone to make the first axe? We are human beings that evolved into a new life form. Come on, we'll find Ben's address then we'll talk to him. He's clever; he'll find answers to all those questions that are bothering you.'

She tugged him by the hand along the darkened street. Carter relented, although his expression suggested he still struggled with some conundrum.

In hushed tones April continued. 'I'll ask Ben to arrange meetings with scientists. Once they see how we've been transformed they'll be convinced.'

A cat on the wall shrank back with a hiss as they passed by. For a split-second April glimpsed her reflection in a car's rear window. Her face was a lifeless grey; black rings etched deep beneath a pair of staring eyes. Lips blue, with more blue patches around the mouth; streaks of blood; a spiky mass of hair frames a deathly face. Even though she clearly saw her mirror image for some reason the truth slipped by her as if she'd glimpsed the face of a stranger. All that filled her now was the glow of certainty; that April Connor was engaged on a quest of global importance. Her mind was clear: find Ben Ashton. Then report the miraculous truth of New-Life to the entire world. Simple.

By the time she pressed the door bell button at Raj's house the first hunger pangs had begun. That's okay, she told herself, I can handle it. I'll eat later. First things first.

She needed to ask Raj for Ben's address. Come to think of it, Raj will be interested to hear about the miracle, too, and he'll want the world exclusive for his magazine. Not that the money's important. What matters is the world learns about this miracle.

When there was no answer at the door she rang again. Through a window beside the door she could see the hallway clock. Almost 2 a.m. Raj'll be asleep, she thought. Give him time to answer. He'll be fascinated by what happened to her.

'No lights, nobody's up,' Carter muttered. He rubbed his hands against his stomach. The aura of well-being had faded now. April became fidgety, too. Her mind kept flitting back to when she sucked the guy's artery. That flood of beautiful blood down her throat. Could do with a little of that now, she told herself.

'Come on, Raj.' This time she knocked on the door. 'Raj?'

'Nobody home.' Carter was losing interest now. 'We could leave it for a while.'

'No. This is important.'

'Hungry?'

'No, not really.' She gulped. 'Maybe just a bit, but it can wait. Carter, we have the most important news to hit humanity in thousands of years. When everyone hears what we've discovered the world's going to be a better place – a million times better!' The final statement came out as a snarl. Her sudden appetite had an urgency about it. 'Oh, come on, Raj!' She hammered on the door. 'Raj!'

Carter ran his fingers through his hair. 'We haven't thought this through. There's something we've missed. This doesn't feel right. We shouldn't go public yet.'

'You're hungry, that's all. Once we've spoken to Ben he'll sort everything out, just you wait and see.' She pounded the door. 'Raj!'

A light blazed through the glass followed by muttering from inside; lock mechanisms clicked. As the door opened a tired voice complained, 'Don't you know what time it is?'

'Raj!'

The brown eyes in Raj's face went huge. 'April. April Connor! The police are looking for you.'

'Raj, let us in; we've got to talk to you.'

'Oh my, what happened to you?'

April gushed, 'Raj, let us in. You must give me Ben's address. My God, I've got a story for him. Ugh, my hair. I'm sorry, I look a real state. This is Carter. Oh, please let us in *now*!'

Raj stared at her. She saw the way he scanned her face, then his gaze traveled down her body. 'Your clothes are all ripped, April. And, my God, what happened to your shoes?'

As if for the first time April noticed she was barefoot. The rip in her dress revealed her bare waist with the bite mark of old. Then Raj regarded her companion with something more than distaste before saying, 'April, my dear, you've been hurt. I'll call an ambulance.'

'No!' It came as a shriek. 'Give me Ben's address. A miracle has happened. He's going to write the story for the press.' Her eyes traveled from Raj's horrified face to his hand that gripped the door frame. She'd never noticed the way his veins showed through the skin before. They could have been glowing with a light all of their own. Just a moment ago she knew what she'd tell the man. She'd recap what happened to her. The attack on the embankment, being thrown into the river, then washed up on the island; she'd laugh and make a joke of it. 'Can you imagine there are desert islands in the Thames? Well, I was your very own Miss Crusoe.' But all that evaporated now. The only thing she focused on was Raj's hand. The pulse throbbed in his wrist. All that blood rushing through. Although she couldn't bring herself to tear her eyes from that limb of so many wonderful veins she realized Carter stared at it, too. What had been hunger pangs in her stomach went stellar. As she'd experienced before that ravenous craving wasn't confined to her gut. It hurtled outward through her body. Even her fingertips hurt with sheer bloody hunger.

'April?' Raj's voice had gone far away. 'April, what's wrong? Are you in pain? Who is this man?'

'Raj,' she panted. 'Let me in.'

'I'm going to phone for the police,' he told her.

'Let me in,' she snarled. 'I'm hungry!'

Carter pushed by her to lunge at the hand that he knew would be crammed with rich, red blood. He snapped those gold-tipped teeth at his victim. Raj was just that bit faster. Carter's teeth clamped on the door frame and ripped away a foot-long splinter.

April saw her next move. It'd take only a moment. Push open the door, pin Raj against the wall then take her time to chew on that delicious wrist of his. She could open a vein then suck the goodness from his body. With all her heart she yearned to feel how she did just an hour ago when she blazed with euphoria; that was a precious time; she wanted to feel that way again when she fell in love with the whole wide world.

April pushed at the door to open it. Silvery links snapped taut in front of her eyes. *A chain? Why a chain?* Already the hunger was so intense she couldn't understand that Raj had automatically slipped on the security chain before opening the door. Now it was the only thing that stood between him and his destruction. Carter beat at the door, too. He wanted in. He craved the editor's blood. Their attempts to break down the door were thwarted when Raj managed to slam it shut. Bolts snapped home.

Raj was shouting, 'Try and keep calm, April. Something's happened to you. I'm calling the police . . .'

'Carter,' she snapped. 'Break a window. We've got to get in there. Carter?'

Her companion had raced from the garden. She saw that he chased after a drunken man – a lovely well-built man – who was tottering along beneath the blaze of street lights. She started running in that direction too, fearful that she might lose her share of nature's riches.

Twenty

At five minutes past two that sultry morning Trajan walked beside Ben as they left the taxi that had carried them from where they'd talked to the graffiti artist.

'If the man was mad,' Trajan said, 'why should we make too much about this Vampire Sharkz business?'

'Mr Akinedes isn't mad. He suffers from Obsessive Compulsion Disorder; that means he completely understands his compulsions are irrational, only he has no power over them.'

They turned off the main road into a park that ran beside the Thames. Nearby, the formidable square structures of Tower Bridge rose into the night sky where they gleamed in the floodlights. Beyond them, the thousands of lights of London still burned brightly even at this hour.

In the gloom Trajan's head appeared as a bobbing smudge of blond as he asked, 'Then did he mean there's a dangerous animal in the river; perhaps something that's escaped from a zoo? Did that attack April?'

125

'Don't have me speculating yet, Trajan. I want to compare Mr Akinedes' story, irrespective of how bizarre it sounds, with what Elmo Kigoma knows.'

'The man in the boat? If he's still here. The last I heard the Mayor had plans to evict him from the park.'

'Oh, he's still here. Elmo's built from tough stuff.'

Elmo Kigoma was, indeed, still in the riverside park but he was no longer alone. Ben groaned at what he saw. 'Damn . . .' There, in the muted gleam of street lights shining from the road, were a group of at least ten figures. They'd clustered around the boat that appeared to float above ground, the pole that supported it rendered invisible by the shadows.

'The guy's got trouble this time.' Ben moved faster.

'Wait!' Trajan caught his arm. 'Wouldn't it be better to call the police?'

Ben fished out his phone. 'If it turns nasty – I mean really nasty – call the cops; but only as a last resort. If they come roaring down here we won't get a chance to talk to Elmo alone. And stay here; you've already cracked your skull once this week.'

After pushing the phone into Trajan's hand he ran toward the aerial boat. By now, the group of men had begun to push at the vessel's pole. They were clearly trying to topple it. The tiny plywood craft swung back and forth as if tossed on a stormy sea. A silhouette of a figure hung on tight to the mast of the boat.

These are stupid odds, Ben told himself as he ran along the path. One against ten? They've been drinking, too, so it's going to be tough reasoning with them.

The men chanted, 'Out the boat! Out the boat!'

'Give someone else a turn, y'old bastard!'

Their laughter was sadistic; they'd worked themselves up an appetite for hurting someone.

'Come down here, y'wanker – y'can kiss my arse.' One of the men bared his backside at the hermit in his boat.

'Dirty little bugger. Where do y'go to the toilet? Bet y'do it over the side.'

'Yeah, right where kids are.'

'Filthy pervert.'

'Get down here . . . gonna get the hiding of your life!'

Ben stopped a few paces from them. 'Excuse me. Gents?'

126

A guy with a tattooed line around his throat with the words 'Cut Here' etched in the skin turned on him. 'Fuck off.'

Ben took a deep breath. 'I need to speak to Mr Kigoma. It's important.'

'Y'hear that?' one of the men slurred. 'These two love-birds want to be alone.' Pure sadism made the thug's laughter harsh.

'It's all right, sir. I'm safe,' Elmo called down. 'Please go home.'

'Yeah, go home,' the men chorused.

'Mr Kigoma. I'm Ben Ashton. We spoke recently.'

The thugs shook the pole, making the boat flip from side-to-side. Ben saw it wouldn't be long before the old man was twitched from his vessel. 'Look, stop that,' Ben said angrily. 'You're going to hurt him.'

The man with the tattooed 'Cut Here' throat calmly punched Ben on the jaw. Ben had no intentions of falling down, but his legs appeared to have no communication with his brain. As they folded under him he slapped down on to the grass with enough force to knock the air from his lungs.

'Down in one! Down in one!' the guy chanted while his buddies cheered his skill.

What had been a numb feeling in Ben's mouth suddenly made way for a whole head full of pain. Any plans he had for standing were forgotten, although he managed to sit as Trajan appeared.

'Do you want it as well?' snarled Ben's attacker. 'Do you?' He swung his fist at Trajan and Ben remembered the guy's head wound only too clearly. A hard punch would kill him.

Trajan side-stepped neatly, then dealt a couple of rapid jabbing punches to the man's stomach that suggested pretty forcefully that he had martial arts training. The tattooed guy didn't fall but he backed away holding his stomach. Ben forced himself to his feet. The odds were still one-sided. They faced a beating. Nevertheless, Ben knew he must stand by Trajan.

The men's faces were ugly with aggression and drink. They shook their fists, and stuck out their chests to make themselves more intimidating.

Ben groaned. 'It looks like you backed the wrong side.'

127

Trajan wasn't a man for running. He held out his arm for Ben to stay back. 'Give me room to work,' he said.

'You can't fight them,' Ben countered.

Meanwhile Elmo Kigoma called down in a panicked voice. 'Look out, they're coming back.'

'Tell us something we don't know,' Trajan said as the thugs closed in.

The hermit's voice rose. 'Look, back there. Dead-bone creatures. Children of Edshu. You must get away from here.'

That did strike home. Ben raised himself on his toes to look over the men's heads. Beyond them, figures loped across the grass from the direction of the river.

'Dear God,' Ben said. 'Here they come . . . Vampire Sharkz.'

'What?' Trajan shot him a startled glance.

As he did so, Ben nodded at the advancing men. 'Watch your backs, boys. You've got company.'

The thugs probably thought Ben meant that someone had circled round behind them. Instead, when they looked, they saw figures of both sexes and all ages race at them with the speed of panthers. The thugs turned to fight them. But the bodies that slammed into theirs moved with inhuman speed and power. The guy with the tattooed neck fell back with a girl of around sixteen ripping his throat with her teeth. A balding man in a torn business suit pounced on a thickset yob and held him down to the ground as he tore away his shirt, then started to gnaw at the beer belly. The thugs' shouts of rage stopped to be replaced by an eerie silence. Then came screams of pain.

High in his boat Elmo Kigoma shouted down at Ben. 'Up here. You won't outrun them!' With those words he dropped a rope ladder over the side.

In his kitchen Raj repeatedly went to the window to peer outside into the darkness, before returning to the corner of the room to drink from a glass of orange juice. He wished he had whisky. That's what he needed right now. A strong liquor. Liquid fire to shock his vocal chords back to life. He'd made two attempts to telephone the police only nothing coherent had left his mouth. Here in the corner where two solid walls met he felt safer. Then his cat burst through the cat-flap. The abruptness of the movement made him jerk the juice from the glass down his pajamas.

Instead of scolding Nipper he merely sighed with relief that it was his pet and not . . . he swallowed . . . not those two *things* that appeared at his door just minutes ago. He knew April Connor. She had one of those smiling faces that was always full of fun. What had happened to her? Beneath a mass of sticky-looking hair had been a grey face that possessed the blue lips of a corpse. Beneath her eyes her skin was etched with black rings. And then there were *those* eyes. Good God, the way they burned with such an overwhelming greed. They didn't even appear human. If eyes communicate something of their owners' thoughts then what April communicated sickened him. He could imagine only too vividly her leaning toward his ear and whispering, 'I want . . .' Only whatever she'd *want* would be so extreme and so perverse, Raj knew he'd have recoiled in horror. Only that scenario didn't have time to take place. Because she and her strange companion had tried to bite a lump out of his hand. If he'd neglected to lock the security chain in place . . . He began to shake again. Meanwhile, the cat dropped the mouse it had caught on to the floor and gazed expectantly up at the man, waiting for his approval.

Raj took a deep breath and decided to give the telephone another try.

The two men scrambled into Elmo Kigoma's boat. There they lay panting in the bottom while the sounds of battle took place below.

Elmo grimaced. 'Why didn't those boys listen to me? Instead they shake the pole and fight the pair of you.' He slapped his forehead as he became angry. 'It's because people don't listen to Elmo. They never do.'

'They're paying the price now,' Ben murmured as he looked down.

'My God,' Trajan breathed as he saw what was happening. 'They're *eating* those poor guys.'

'Not eating,' Elmo corrected. 'Drinking. They're having the blood out of their veins.'

Ben crouched there in the dinghy as it rested on its pole ten feet above the ground. Below him, in the glow of street-lamps, he witnessed the death of the men who'd attacked them. A group of individuals dressed in rags, with unkempt, spiky hair, thrust their faces against the torn bodies of the corpses. Trajan watched, too. They didn't lap the wounds or bite now, the Vampire Sharkz pressed their faces hard to the wounds. Then they drank. It was violent gluttony. These creatures appeared to be starving; now they drank so deeply they grunted as if it physically hurt them to swallow so much blood in one draught. Their entire bodies pulsed with the effort of gorging.

Ben absorbed what he saw: the grey skin of those creatures; their blackened nails; mouths surrounded by blue patches; at least the skin that wasn't smeared with their victim's blood. These things aren't human, he told himself. Okay, they're roughly human in shape but the humanity's vanished from them. These things are something else entirely.

When the creatures finally raised their faces, their expressions were exultant. Feeding had not only satisfied their hunger, it had intoxicated them. Their eyes blazed with alien joy. When one noticed the men looking down at them from the boat it leapt from a crouching position. Ben watched in horror as it appeared to effortlessly glide up toward him. A second later it would catch hold of him and drag him down to that grisly feeding area below with its mangled corpses. Only it was satiated now. Hunger didn't drive it. By its standards the leap was a lazy one. Its fingers almost reached the gunwale before it swiped in Ben's direction. The fingernails raked the hull's flanks before the creature dropped back.

After that, the creatures realized that more prey squatted in the little boat. Fortunately Elmo had raised the rope ladder. Even so, they attempted to climb the telegraph pole that held the boat aloft. Fortunately blood is slippery. And fortunately for the three men the monsters were smeared in the stuff. When they tried to shin up the pole their limbs were too slippy to find a purchase. Soon they wandered back to their victims to suck the remaining blood from their bodies.

Only it wasn't over yet. Trajan muttered, 'Oh my God,' as they watched the next stage in the procedure. One by one the creatures clamped their mouths back on to the wounds of their dead victims. Then they regurgitated. Ben heard the hiss of fluids gushing back from stomachs into throats, then he saw the monsters' bodies convulse as they vomited into the wounds.

Trajan rocked back with his hands over his eyes. 'I

130

remember now. That's what happened to April. They did that to April . . . my poor April . . . Oh God.'

Trajan no longer watched but as the time crept past three and daylight broke on the horizon Ben saw the creatures . . . the Vampire Sharkz as Spiro had called them . . . drag their victims through the park to the river. There they dropped the bodies into the water. Quickly, with a predatory urgency, the things returned to lap every trace of blood from the grass. Then, as sunlight touched the underside of the clouds, they scurried back to the river to vanish into the darkness of its waters.

Twenty-One

Carter and April stood on the bridge watching the cars pass beneath them. Even at this time of night the traffic still surged along the highway as unceasing as the River Thames flowing to the sea.

Carter blinked. 'What happened to us, April?'

'We got distracted, that's all,' she reassured. 'It's this hunger. We're not used to it.'

'But the guy we called on; the one who was going to give us your friend's address . . .' He grimaced. 'I tried to bite him.'

'Never mind, Carter. We're fine now. Don't you feel good? Like you're so strong you could throw those cars like they're just toys?'

'But we knew *exactly* what we were going to do, April. We'd go to the journalist's home. We'd explain our discovery to him.'

'The miracle!' April hugged herself.

'Yeah.' He smiled, yet his eyes were troubled. 'The miracle. The New-Life. It went wrong, didn't it?'

'We have appetites that are above and beyond what anyone has ever experienced before.'

'April, it was more than that. We were so hungry we went crazy; we're no better than Berserkers.'

'We'll control it next time.'

'Will we? If I'd got my hands on him I'd have torn that editor feller apart, and sucked every drop of blood out of him. April, that can't be right, can it?'

'We're fine now. That's all that matters.'

That river of light created by the cars held Carter's gaze. 'Remember the island . . .' He gave a grim laugh. 'You called it the Isle of the Dead?'

'Sure. What of it?' April was upbeat; nothing fazed her.

'We drank from pools of water on the shore.'

'Ugh, don't remind me.' She rubbed his arm. 'Come on, I'm sure we can find Ben Ashton. We'll use the telephone directories.'

'April, listen to what I've got to say.'

'If it makes you happy.' She beamed at him.

'When we were on the island we got hungry, right?'

'Yep.'

'So ravenous we wanted to eat dirt, tree bark, anything? We watched how those Berserkers attacked the Misfires and tried to eat them. But there was something missing, so they couldn't find satisfaction in what they were eating.'

'Sure . . . Can we go now?'

'Just a minute; I haven't made my point yet.' He licked his lips. 'The reason that nothing else satisfied their appetite was because it didn't contain blood. The Misfires are blood-less. That's why they hardly move. They're nine tenths corpse.'

'But you found a way, because you're smart. You showed me how to drink water that had been left behind by the tide. Come on, time to find my writer.'

'Wait, this is important. We drank estuary water left in the beach pools. Because it had been evaporating there was more salt, right?'

'Right!' Her full stomach engendered a sense of glee.

'I read somewhere that seawater with all the salt and minerals and stuff is similar to blood.'

'Our ancestors came from the ocean. We're basically a walking, talking bag full of seawater.'

'So, we managed to find something that was *almost* a

substitute for what we craved. The salty water knocked the edge off our hunger.'

'Absolutely, Carter. Absolutely. Now get moving before the sun comes up.' She walked away.

Carter held out his hands in a desperate gesture, as he tried to make her understand. 'What we were drinking, April, was a substitute for blood.'

'So?' She twirled as she crossed the bridge.

'So why do we have this craving for blood? Why is it so strong that we end up acting crazy?'

'We'll learn to deal with it.'

'Will we? Or are we doomed to repeat the cycle? Where we tear some poor devil apart, suck out his blood, get high on it like we are now . . . and then we make all these plans about sharing it with the world. Only we get so far, then the craving starts again, the hunger drives us into a frenzy, and all that's important is ripping open another victim. April! Wait for me . . . where are you going?'

April started to run. 'It's getting light. We can't be outside when the sun rises.'

'There's a ditch down there that runs into a tunnel.'

'I'm not sleeping in a ditch, Carter.'

'Where, then?'

'I've got somewhere far better. You come with me.' Barefoot she raced along the path, her giddy laughter rang out on the night air.

Raj lifted the phone from its bracket. The cat nibbled delicately at its prey on the kitchen floor so Raj averted his eyes as he dialed. He had a dilemma. Should he call the police or not?

I mean, what is it that I'm reporting? he wondered. If I announce that April Connor, a missing person, turned up at my house they're going to say 'thanks for letting us know', then cross her off the list. If I add that she and her companion tried to bite me, then they'll arrest her for assault. And April isn't a stranger. I've known her years. Okay, she looked strange tonight but you don't report friends to the police, do you? So when Raj dialed, it was Ben Ashton's number he called.

* * *

133

Only when the red glare of the sun burst above the city's skyline did the three men climb down from the boat on its pole. As Elmo Kigoma's boat wasn't even built to float on water it had just weathered a hell of a storm. Albeit a storm of an entirely different kind. Ben noticed rust-coloured smears on the grass that marked where the gang of thugs had bled.

'You first, Ben.' Elmo indicated the rope ladder.

Ben complied. Even so, he shot glances at the riverbank. That's where the creatures had dumped the bodies of the men into the water before joining them in the depths of the Thames. Vampire Sharkz . . . Those were the things the graffiti artist had seen, and had devoted his life to warning the city about. Vampire Sharkz. A bizarre term – yet uncannily apt. As Ben descended the rungs the Vampire Sharkz phrase echoed in his head. When he reached the ground he examined the blood stains on the grass, what there were of them. Either those creatures were fastidious in their tidying up or it had simply been a brutal hunger that compelled them to lick spilt gore from each blade of grass. The end result was that there was little evidence of a battle taking place. If anything, the debris consisted of watches torn from wrists, along with coins, keys and phones that had fallen from the victims' pockets together with a couple of knives. Ben noted that the blades were bent, so they'd been used during the fight. Clearly to little effect. From what he'd witnessed of the battle, the creatures – these Vampire Sharkz – hadn't suffered any visible injury. The orgiastic feeding on the men's blood had been nothing less than a bloody carnival for them.

Ben glanced up as Elmo descended the ladder. The old African moved with athletic ease; the guy's wiry body could have been that of a youth rather than an octogenarian. Above him, Trajan's blond head appeared over the boat's side as he waited for his turn to descend. 'Well, we know what happened to April. One of those things attacked her.'

'You were fortunate that they didn't do to you what they did to those men last night,' Elmo responded.

Ben asked, 'So you weren't bitten?'

'No, just thrown aside like a piece of trash.'

'Then you were lucky.'

'Lucky? I lost my fiancée. How lucky is that?'

As Elmo reached the ground Ben heard his phone. He

checked his pockets but it wasn't there. Then he remembered. 'Trajan, I gave you my phone.'

Trajan picked it up from the bottom of the boat and checked the screen. 'Someone called Raj calling.'

Ben held out his hand as Trajan dropped it down to him. He thumbed the button. 'Hello, Raj, what's wrong?' Raj's voice was breathless in his ear. 'April Connor?' Ben echoed.

Trajan clambered down the ladder. 'April? There's some news?' He jumped to the ground. 'Ben, what is it? Have the police found her?'

Ben concentrated on listening to Raj. The man sounded traumatized. 'Okay,' Ben told him. 'Take it easy. I'll call you later.'

'*Well?*'

It was Elmo who spoke first. 'You should brace yourself for bad news.'

Trajan ran his fingers through his hair. 'Ben, tell me. Now!'

'Okay. But as Elmo says: it's not exactly what you've been wanting to hear.'

'What do you mean?'

'That was a friend of mine. He's had a visit from April.'

'Tonight?'

'About an hour ago.'

'Is she still there?'

'Trajan, listen.'

'Don't prevaricate, Ben. Is she hurt?'

'No, definitely not hurt. At least ...' He took a breath as Trajan groaned in anguish. 'Raj was in a state of shock. He wasn't expressing himself well, but this is what he told me. April turned up at his door at two in the morning with a man.'

'What man?'

'April wanted my address, then she and the guy started acting weird. Raj said the way they looked at him became extremely odd. Then they tried to attack him.'

'Attack?' Elmo Kigoma asked. 'How attack?'

'This is the bad news.' Ben looked Trajan in the eye. 'The pair of them tried to bite Raj.'

'Oh, God ... Where are they now?'

'Raj was lucky enough to have kept the security chain on the door so they didn't reach him. After he managed to lock the door they simply vanished.'

One of the phones on the ground began to chirp. In a sudden burst of anger Trajan stamped it into silence. 'We need to go to where this Raj guy lives and start searching for April.'

Elmo shook his head. 'Don't you see the sun? Those two will be long gone. If they're a product of Edshu, then they're a product of darkness, and belong to darkness.'

Trajan frowned. 'What do you mean?'

'They'll hide away in daylight hours.'

'But we should still search for them.'

Ben shook his head. 'In a city this size? Where do we begin?'

'But we can't stand here doing nothing,' Trajan told them.

In the pause that followed the birds began to sing as the sun rose. As it became brighter there was a second, more chilling dawn chorus. The phones that littered the ground began to ring. Ben realized that even idiots like the ones that attacked him last night had families, too. As wives and parents discovered the men hadn't come home they'd begun to call. Half a dozen phones sounded their individual ring tones: snatches of popular song and comedy catchphrases pumped from the little speakers. '*Answer me, you lazy goon*' and a robotic, '*Oh, master, put your mouth to my sexy, plastic body.*' And an aggressive: '*You what, you what, you what!*' As the ring tones filled the dawn air the phones flashed there in the grass.

'We shouldn't stay here any longer,' Elmo told them. 'I'm done with my boat. The Mayor can have it. There are more pressing matters now.'

Ben blinked as the sun's rays fell on him. 'But where now?'

'You should both get some sleep,' Elmo told them. 'I've my own rituals to observe. Edshu is a tough chap to please. Though I still remember what my family did when I was a boy to encourage the old rascal to move on and do no more harm.'

'Edshu?' Trajan was perplexed.

'I'll explain later,' Ben told him.

'Get some rest first,' Elmo said. 'Now it's daylight it's time to sleep. You must be refreshed before you look for your friend. You'll need all your strength, believe me.'

The unanswered phones still cried out in a way that was strangely forlorn.

136

'I'll go back to my apartment. The police might call if they find her.' Trajan paused. 'Ben, you're welcome to come back if you can sleep on a couch.'

Ben nodded. 'That's fine for me.' He yawned. 'I'll give Raj a call later. We can talk to him then.'

'I go this way.' Elmo indicated a path that led through the trees. 'There is work for me at home. I'll ask the gods and ancestors of my old village to intercede on our behalf.' He gave a grim smile. 'Sometimes Edshu listens to them. Sometimes he tells them to go to hell.' He reached into his shirt pocket. 'Here. This is my card with my telephone number.' His jaw tightened. 'Call me if lives depend on it.'

Ben and Trajan said their farewells to Elmo and walked through the park in the direction of Tower Bridge. Before they'd gone more than ten paces the old African called to them. 'By the way, you should know this fact, gentlemen. If my rituals are successful and Edshu moves on, then his creatures will be of no use to him. So . . .' He clicked his fingers to indicate something vanishing. '. . . if you plan to rescue your friend, you must do it soon.'

Twenty-Two

The moment Trajan stepped through the door into his apartment he noticed it.

'Ben, can you smell that?'

'Something's turned.' Ben flinched. 'Have you left the fridge door open?'

When Trajan turned to Ben his face blazed with triumph. 'She's back home.' He picked up a key with orange string tied around the fob. 'Emergency key. We keep it in the plant pot out on the landing, just in case one of us is locked out.'

That sickly sweet smell triggered alarm bells in Ben's head. 'Remember what Raj told us: April isn't herself.'

137

'But she's back.' Excitement animated him. 'If she's home I can take care of her.' He rushed along the hallway. 'April?'

'Wait, Trajan. Easy does it.'

'April?'

'We don't know what we're getting into. Take it slowly; she might—'

Trajan didn't listen. He burst through the living-room door. 'April, are you, uh . . .'

Ben followed to find the blinds down to cheat the room of the morning sun.

'She's got to be here,' Trajan insisted. 'Only April knew about the key.'

'April might have been here,' Ben allowed. 'There was nothing to stop her leaving again.'

'She wouldn't.'

'Trajan, something happened to her. From what Raj says—'

'She's in shock. That's all.'

Ben saw that the man willed himself to believe his fiancée was alright as he darted across the landing. 'If she's tired she'll have gone to bed.'

This time Ben did grab him to stop his headlong dash into the bedroom. 'Wait. Raj said she was with this guy.' Ben shot a meaningful glance at the closed door.

'Ben? What are you suggesting?'

'Come on, Trajan. Don't be so naive.'

'Let go.'

'If she was with him at two in the morning when she visited Raj's house, then she might not be alone now.'

'I'm going in there, so get your hands off me.'

'Okay,' Ben said. 'But be warned; you might be in for a shock.'

'Understood.' He jerked his arm away, then shoved open the door.

For a moment Ben imagined he saw shadows on the bed coupling in ecstasy. As he passed through the doorway into the room, however, he saw that imagination had played a trick. The bed was empty.

'She was here.' Trajan grimaced at the sickly-sweet odor that hung in the air.

'Or still is,' Ben whispered. 'Try under the bed.'

138

Trajan hesitated for a second as no doubt nightmarish scenarios buzzed through his mind. Then with a renewed determination he dropped to his knees to check the space between the bed frame and the floor. Ben squatted too. The heavy-duty blackout blind kept out the sun, so precious little daylight was available to them. Nevertheless, Ben stared at that shadowed void until his eyes became accustomed to the gloom. And there, in near darkness, curled up on her side like a sleeping child, was April Connor. He could just make out the blue mottle around her lips, and the dark rings beneath her eyes. Even her eyelids had darkness in them, as if the skin had absorbed something of the midnight shadows. Her short hair was spiked with a sticky material. The black dress was filthy, while a large rip revealed her grey skin at the waist. Ben guessed that's where they'd find the bite mark.

'She's breathing,' Trajan confirmed. 'I can hear it.'

'Is she alone?'

Trajan awarded Ben a pain-filled glance, then checked. A moment later he sighed with relief. 'Yes, she is.'

'Good. But there's a chance her friend might be around, too.'

'If he is I'll throw him out into the street.'

'Don't do anything rash. Remember what happened to the gang last night.'

Trajan grunted. 'You mean, you don't want me to end up as breakfast?'

'Something like that.'

They searched the rest of the apartment. Five minutes later Trajan called from the hallway. 'Ben? In here.'

Ben found Trajan staring into the cloakroom beside the front door. It was little bigger than an upright coffin, but sitting there with knees raised and his back to the wall was an olive-skinned guy aged around thirty. He'd unhooked the coats from the pegs then piled them over himself. Only his face was uncovered in that windowless cell. His eyes had sunk into his head and his cheeks were hollow. He wore that same kind of shrunken grimace that Egyptian mummies wore when their lips shriveled back. Here, the guy's lips had shrunk enough to reveal large white teeth that were tipped with gold crowns.

139

'So,' Ben breathed, 'they came here to escape the daylight.'
He glanced at Trajan. 'I'm assuming he's alive, too?'

Trajan reached out as if to check the pulse in the man's
neck. Only he stopped short, reluctant to make contact with
the dead-looking flesh. Ben held the back of his hand under
the stranger's nostrils.

'I can feel him exhale.' Ben shrugged. 'So he appears to
be alive.'

'Appears to be,' Trajan murmured. 'It's time to call the
police.'

'The police? You're kidding.'

'Ben, we need professional help.'

'What the police'll do is take them to some specialized
medical unit.'

'That's what we want, isn't it?'

'The only person with knowledge about this is Elmo
Kigoma. We'll call him.'

Only it wasn't going to be that simple.

Twenty-Three

For Roma it's webcams. For her brothers Juno and Hadrian
it's dirt-bikes. While Roma browsed her favourite webcams
they revved the bikes hard on that hot Wyoming evening as
the scent of clematis crept in to perfume her room. Roma
broke away from the computer and leaned out of the window,
squinting as the sun struck her in the eyes. Her brothers cranked
their bike motors into a frenzy of skull-piercing screaming.

'Hey!' she shouted. 'I went to the dentist this afternoon!
Three fillings! Don't you idiots know the meaning of charity?'

They didn't hear her as they tore away down the track, their
bikes flinging up clouds of dust.

'Good riddance!' Roma yelled after them. 'Keep going
east! Go the long way round through China!' She touched her

lip that was still numb after forty-five minutes in the dentist's chair. The scream of the drill as it tore through tooth enamel still resonated in her ears. In this little town of one hundred and eighty people the drive to the city was usually a treat – a treat that climaxed with pizza and ice cream. Today, the city visit for thirteen-year-old Roma Langelli was anything but a treat. Three fillings, jeez. At least she could spend some time gratifying her webcam fascination. In a tiny town that sat on a dusty American prairie there was precious little to do at the best of times. There wasn't a single store here; school was a fifty-minute bus-ride away, so Roma escaped boredom through the webcams that were her eye on the outside world. With her friends she'd devised games: Weirdest Webcam (a school for ventriloquists in Quebec); Most Boring Webcam: this had lots of competition. After all, most webcams that come streaming into your computer via the internet are simply static views of streets, beaches, industrial plants, or skylines. Of course, the cameras had no human operators. They were like CCTV; simply fixed to walls or posts and left to film all by themselves. This afternoon Sue had sent a link to a webcam that filmed patients in a dentist's chair in New York – *ha, ha, very funny, Sue.* Roma experimentally chewed her lip. The anesthetic was wearing off now so she felt a slight tingle. Also, her tongue encountered gritty bits of amalgam in the bottom of her mouth: filling leftovers. Yuk.

After rinsing her mouth from a water bottle she scrolled through a list of webcams that beamed pictures from around the world. Now for her revenge against Sue for her choice of live dental surgery. Last week Roma discovered a webcam that showed views of stomach-churning intensity; this was guaranteed to gross Sue out. Before e-mailing the link Roma decided to check that the camera was still active, so her friend wouldn't simply be confronted with a blank screen or error message (no fun to be had if Sue didn't suffer at least a teency bit). She moved the on-screen cursor down the webcam list until she found the link marked 'River Fleet Ancillary Branch'. From previous visits to this website she knew that the River Fleet was a river that ran through a tunnel under the streets of London on the other side of the world. And this 'ancillary branch' of the River Fleet was nothing but a great, humongous sewer.

Roma clicked on the camera icon; a second later a box opened up on the computer screen to reveal a view of a genuine London sewer that must be two hundred years old at least. *Jeez, the place is a big watery dungeon.* Mentally, she composed her e-mail:

Hi Sue, Check this place of unrivaled beauty. Heh-heh. Look at it then tell me what you think those stalactites are made of that are hanging from the roof.

She grinned as she watched a picture that in real time revealed what was happening in the London sewer thousands of miles away. The camera must be set on a beam that ran across the throat of the circular tunnel. There were also lights to reveal the curving brick walls that were shades of brown and tangerine. The tunnel rose up a series of brick steps. Tumbling down those was water (and, boy-oh-boy, other stuff) at a depth of what appeared to be knee-high. Unlike most webcams that showed static views of churches or the Grand Canyon or whatever, this actually had a lot going on. Water-levels constantly rose and fell, due to bathroom usage in the buildings above, or storm water surges. Sometimes the water-fall created by the steps was a trickle, sometimes a full-blooded torrent that bubbled and foamed. Then here's the gross stuff. Hanging from the roof were what appeared to be stalactites anything up to two feet long. Only they weren't rigid. Sometimes a breeze blew along the tunnel, then they'd swing pendulum-like. The River Fleet website helpfully explained that these stalactites were composed of a build-up of toilet paper and faeces.

Roma chuckled as she imagined her friend wrinkling her nose while exclaiming, 'Ugh! Poo alert!'

Then came a sight even more gross than those literally shitty tunnel decorations. Rats. Big, hairy, bristly, juicy, yellow-toothed sewer rats. The slimy wet rats scrambled up and down those steps in the places that were free of water. Rat noses would sniff the air savoring those subterranean odors. Sometimes – uck, uck! – the big London sewer rats with their bristly backs would sit on their haunches, hold a morsel, in their front claws then nibble away with such an expression of bliss on their ratty faces.

Wait . . . it gets better (or worse!) than that. This would make Sue squeal out loud. Sometimes rats would climb on to the structure that supported the webcam. Then, without warning, a rat's snout would suddenly loom in to fill the screen. At that moment you could believe a monster rat the size of a bull haunted London's sewers. As the mouth dominated the lens you could even see its bright yellow teeth that would be magnified to the size of gigantic fangs with icky bits of brown stuff stuck to them. Roma found herself laughing as she imagined Sue's shriek of disgust.

More gritty particles surfaced on her tongue. Ugh, dental work. She reached for the bottle of water again as she watched what sewercam revealed. In a hotel someone flushed and a moment later a condom came bobbing along the stream. Her eyes were drawn into the depths of the tunnel where the arching wall vanished into the distance. That dark maw beyond sewercam's lights was hypnotic. The more she stared into the shadows of underground London the more she fancied she could see shapes moving. She'd watched a dozen times before, and it always turned out to be her imagination, or maybe it was simply steam caused by hot bathwater being discharged into the icy, cold sewer.

Only today it was going to be totally different. Roma watched the screen as figures emerged from the shadows. One appeared to be in the lead; its feet splashed down in the sewer water as it ran along the tunnel; its movements were frantic; it was like it fled in panic. When the figure reached the illuminated area, it staggered and had to support itself with the iron handrail set into the brickwork. The webcam supplied vision only, not sound. So even though the figure of a young man in a leather jacket opened his mouth to yell like fury Roma could hear absolutely nothing. He reached the top of the waterfall then descended the steps where the brown fluid tumbled. The guy was exhausted. Blood trickled from his eye, and there was this look on his face. The expression of terror became a force in its own right that leapt from the computer screen to seize hold of Roma's heart and squeeze it so hard she could hardly breathe. Even so, her eyes locked on those images; she couldn't avert them. No matter what happened next.

Then Roma saw why the guy ran. A group of men and women pursued him. But what a surreal bunch they were. One guy was dressed in a business suit, another wore some

143

kind of uniform; a cop or security guard maybe. Then came a woman in a suit in black with white trim; then came a lithe young woman who moved like a cat. Her hair was tousled; her clothes were in rags. The expressions on their faces showed pure glee. They exulted in the pursuit of their yelling victim. Bizarrely, there was even a guy in a clown costume with white clown make-up on his face. How did the people get into the sewer? Why were they chasing the man? Didn't they know the kind of diseases they could catch wading through that crap? Their faces were splashed with matter; their hands slid across the slimy walls as they balanced themselves. Even those shitty stalactites brushed their heads as they chased their victim.

The young guy bounded down the brick steps. Even as she watched his feet skidded out from him and he fell down on to his rear so he sat there amid the gushing water. In that position he faced the webcam lens. Roma estimated he was a dozen feet from it. The man's pursuers reached the top of the waterfall. There they simply leapt off the top to drop the ten feet or so on to him, just like a group of surreal birds of prey. He vanished under the mass of bodies. They shoved each other aside to grab an arm or a leg. She saw the men and women sink their teeth into the man. Briefly he emerged from the scrum of bodies. She clearly saw his expression of agony as the young woman chewed on his throat. There was such an expression of joy on her face.

The foam at the bottom of the waterfall turned crimson. Roma tasted blood in her mouth; for one wild moment she thought she'd somehow magically fallen through the screen into that London sewer and those bloody waters had engulfed her mouth. Then she realized she'd bitten her tongue without noticing. The dental anesthetic still numbed it. In shock she grabbed the water bottle and swilled her mouth. At that moment she took her eyes off the computer screen.

When she looked back she let out a yell of shock. A face had filled the screen as one of the killers loomed in toward the lens. It must be the face of the girl that moved like a cat. Her beautiful almond-shaped eyes stared at her through the glass. Beneath her eyes were deathly blue rings. Her forehead was spattered with her victim's blood. And as the eyes narrowed Roma knew the creature was smiling at her, even

144

though she couldn't see the mouth. The camera wasn't two-way; it was impossible for the woman to know she was being watched. For the rest of her life Roma would insist on that fact. Yet at that moment, as her blood ran cold, she knew that by virtue of some force she would never be able to understand that she-creature gazed through Roma's eyes into her mind. And knew all about her – right down to the last intimate secret of her soul.

Twenty-Four

Elmo Kigoma wasn't coming. The pressure of trying to persuade Elmo to rush over to the apartment hit Trajan hard. He pressed his hand to the head wound as the pain flared up again. 'Get a taxi. I'll pay the fare . . . No, as I was telling you, April Connor is here, and she's with one of those creatures – the same kind that attacked the guys in the park. Please, Mr Kigoma . . . there's something wrong . . . we've tried waking her . . . no, she's breathing. But we can't wake either of them.' Trajan battled with the pain in his head. 'Mr Kigoma, how can we help her? What can we do?'

Ben watched the one-sided conversation with growing impatience.

Trajan continued. 'If you ask me, neither of them are entirely human now. Clearly, we don't know how to help them. We can't call the police for obvious reasons. So, please, Mr Kigoma. You're the only one who can help them. I'll pay whatever you ask. We need an expert . . . no, we need you here now. No, we can't . . .'

Ben reached for the phone. 'Trajan. Let me try.'

'It won't do any good. He's hung up.'

'But why won't he help us?'

Trajan closed his eyes as the headache pounded. 'He told me he has to work. Something to do with . . . conversing with the ancestors and the gods of his homeland, who in turn will appeal to Edshu.' Trajan grimaced. 'Whoever Edshu is.'

'Elmo told me about Edshu. Trajan, you should take a painkiller.'

'I need to stay focused. What's Edshu?'

'A central African deity that's known as the trickster god. His purpose is to cause strife amongst humanity.'

'Some kind of devil?'

'Edshu's more subtle than that. Tell me where the meds are, Trajan and I'll get you something for your head.'

'No.'

Ben's impatience grew. 'Trajan, I know you want to stay awake in case there's any change in April's condition, but you'll be no good to her if you're in so much pain you can't think straight.'

Trajan was angry at what he saw as his own weakness. 'Okay, but keep an eye on her, won't you?'

'Painkillers?'

'By the kitchen sink, you can't miss them.'

'Stay on the couch, I'll get them.' Ben brought the pills from the kitchen with a glass of water. 'What else did Elmo tell you?'

'Basically, he was insisting he shouldn't be disturbed because he had to undertake some ritualistic procedure; that's going to take until late this afternoon to complete.' He swallowed the pair of bright pink pills. 'During the hours of daylight April and the guy in the cloakroom are going to be comatose. But he warned us, too. This ritual he's performing – if it works – has its own dangers.' He began to feel drowsy.

'Go on.'

'Hmm?' He rubbed his forehead. 'Mr Kigoma is of the opinion that if the ritual works we might lose April.'

'And if it doesn't?'

'Then as soon as she wakes, she's likely to attack us . . .' The last word tailed off to a sigh. Trajan had fallen asleep with the glass of water still in his hand. Ben eased it from his fingers then lifted the man's feet on to the couch. The slow rhythm of his respiration induced a drowsiness in Ben; however, he couldn't allow himself to relax.

'Check on the patients,' he told himself. With Trajan sleeping in the lounge he went directly to the cloakroom. Crammed

146

into a sitting position against the wall with the coats piled over him, the stranger was still comatose. Ben hurried to the bedroom. April, the woman he secretly loved, still lay curled under the bed. The way the creatures retreated from the dawn earlier suggested whatever had befallen April made her incredibly sensitive to daylight. The stranger had locked himself in that lightless cell under the coats. April had drawn the bedroom blinds, then crept under the bed like a nocturnal creature that couldn't abide the sun.

Even though his position was uncomfortable Ben knelt there; he found it difficult to take his eyes off her. Her face was relaxed, the eyelids lightly shut. Although she breathed there was an aura of death around her. Her stillness tormented his imagination. What if she never woke up? Then again, Elmo Kigoma had warned that they would be in danger if she did. Ben longed to touch her face, only he couldn't bring himself to make physical contact with that skin. *Will it be corpse-like to the touch? Will the flesh be soft, or possess the hardness of rigor-mortis?*

To expel the unpleasant thoughts he paced the apartment. Trajan still slept. The stranger in the cloakroom hadn't stirred. Ben made toast and forced himself to eat a few slices. Hunger was the last thing on his mind but his body still needed fuel. After that, he made himself a coffee then returned to the bedroom where he sat on a chair by the bed. Was he guarding April? Or was it a vigil? He didn't know. There was simply an instinct to be close to her. Outside vehicles rumbled along the street. Inside, there was silence. His thoughts were slippery now. He recalled images from last night when the men were slaughtered by the creatures. Almost instantly, the scene of bloodletting would be replaced by a yearning to crouch beside April and run his fingers through her hair.

He straightened in the chair. 'Whatever you do,' he murmured, 'don't go to sleep. Stay awake.' By now, it was noon. Outside the sun shone. London went about its usual daily business. Just a short stroll away, Oxford Street would be swarming with shoppers. Cafés would be starting to bustle. After thirty hours without closing his eyes sleep had become an unstoppable force. As he dozed he dreamt he followed April along a city road. She was healthy and beautiful and irrepressibly 'normal' again. In the dream he hurried after her.

He nearly caught up with her when she turned a corner. Although he only lost sight of her for a split-second by the time he'd rounded the corner she was a hundred yards away. He caught up with her again, almost to the point of being able to put his hand on her shoulder, but then there was another of those corners of the damned. A second later she was a hundred yards away, so he had to play catch-up all over again. Next time I'm close I'll call her name. She'll stop when she knows I'm here, he thought. But she was never so close again. The faster he moved the further she receded into the distance, until she was forever rounding the next corner the moment he caught sight of her.

When Ben opened his eyes a dark figure loomed over him. From the shadows above him the face appeared as an oval shadow set with two brilliant eyes. Its mouth opened. Gold glinted. Ben remembered the stranger in the cloakroom with the weirdly drawn back lips and gold-tipped teeth. The man stared at the wall above Ben's head as if he saw something that mesmerized him, then the eyes swept down to meet Ben's. They pulsed with an uncanny glow. Archaic phrases like 'witch fire' and 'ghost lights' spat into his brain as he tensed, ready to protect himself from attack.

Yet the figure stood there as if it was a staff of wood driven into the floor. The creature's jaw dropped open as it drew in a deep lungful of air. 'We can't exist like this. Take us back to the island. I can protect her there.'

Ben stood up. 'Protect who?'

'Her . . . April Connor.'

'Who does she need protecting from?'

'Herself.' The figure drooped as its strength expired. 'The island is our only hope.'

'What happened to you?'

The man either couldn't or wouldn't answer. His eyes drifted back to stare at the wall.

Ben kept his distance but he pressed on with the questions. 'What's your name?' No reply. 'What have you done to April?'

'I didn't hurt her. I saved her. Our only chance is to go back to the island.'

'What island?'

'In the Thames. Downriver.' He gulped as if speaking hurt. 'Toward the estuary. A little island . . .' His speech became

148

dreamy. 'There's a magic there. We could stop the worst . . . we were controlling it.'

'Give me the name of the island.' Again no reply. 'Can you tell me what happened to you?'

The man took a step backwards; his eyes were closing. The body was a husk that lacked even the strength to remain on its feet. As soon as he reached the wall he slowly crumpled as his knees bent. Moments later, he sat with his back to the wall with his head sagging forward until the chin rested on his chest. Ben crouched beside the man, ready to check for a pulse. Only there was an unnerving quality to the skin that persuaded him not to touch it. The dilemma of whether to check for life-signs or not was put on hold the moment he heard the knock on the door. As he moved from the bedroom to the hallway a wall clock revealed he'd slept over four hours. When he pulled open the door the daylight nearly blinded him. For a second all he could see was a silhouette, then he recognized the figure standing there.

'Thank God you've come.'

'That remains to be seen.' Elmo Kigoma stepped inside. 'Because what you do next will be so unpleasant you'll wish to God that I hadn't come at all.'

Twenty-Five

'Thank God you've come.' Trajan spoke the words even as he was waking up on the couch. The rest had recharged his vitality because he added sharply, 'Why didn't you come when I telephoned earlier?'

Elmo Kigoma entered the lounge with an air of quiet dignity. 'Ben Ashton also thanked God for my appearance, but whether you'll still be thanking God in the next few minutes is another matter. Also the ritual I conducted took, by necessity, several hours. You've both slept?'

'Some.' Ben raised the blind to admit the afternoon light.

'Good, because you'll have a long night ahead of you.'

Trajan was on his feet. 'Have you seen April?'

'Ben showed her to me. The stranger, too.'

'What's happened to them?'

'They've been taken.'

'Taken?' Ben shook his head.

'Taken,' Elmo repeated. 'I was born in a village in the Congo where the fields ended the jungle began. Edshu would take people into the jungle for a while. When they came back it would always be at night, and they'd be stricken by a hysterical hunger for human blood.'

'They'd become vampires?'

'Vampire is a term used by your culture, but, broadly, that is what they are.' Elmo gazed out of the window. 'London has a population of millions. This isn't only a feeding ground for Edshu's vampires, it's a breeding ground. Those they kill are also taken away to a secret, hidden place, where the transformation has time to occur.'

'When you were asleep, Trajan, the stranger became conscious. He talked about an island in the river. He wanted to take April back there.'

'Over my dead body,' Trajan said with feeling.

Elmo shook his head. 'You might have to think the unthinkable, gentlemen.'

Trajan paced the room. 'But you're telling us that April has become a vampire?'

'For want of a better term,' Elmo said. 'Vampire is apt. They feed on blood. They shun the daylight.'

Ben frowned. 'And you're saying this trickster god, Edshu, has transformed people in order to attack the living?'

'Edshu is more sophisticated than that. His desire is for mischief. He doesn't want to destroy human beings, no, he'd rather human beings destroy one another. So in my country he would trick tribes into waging war on one another. Edshu could breathe on this city and turn it to dust and its population with it, but that isn't Edshu's way. He would rather plant in your mind the compulsion to destroy the city.'

'Then he's equal to the devil, this Edshu. He despises humanity.'

'Wrong again. The creator gods gave Edshu the task of

150

testing human beings. If they're strong enough to survive the ordeals he inflicts then the gods will continue to protect humanity against the destruction of the species.' Elmo gave a grim smile. 'After all, what god would continue to prop up a failing species? Better to wipe them out and start again from scratch.'

Ben saw Trajan's troubled expression. 'Is Trajan's doubt one of Edshu's weapons, too?'

'Absolutely. For Edshu fear or pride or cowardice or recklessness can be a weapon that he turns against you.' His gaze appeared to casually brush against Ben. 'Jealousy, too. Jealousy is one of the most powerfully destructive emotions.'

Trajan hadn't noticed who that final comment was intended for but Ben felt its sting. *Had his emotions been that transparent to the hermit?*

'Imagine,' Elmo continued. 'If you go into battle with your brother at your side in the full knowledge that your brother will inherit your father's wealth. How hard would you fight to save your brother's life?'

Ben felt a stir of unease that Elmo might ask him there and then to reveal his secret feelings for April so he quickly asked, 'You've completed the ritual?'

'Yes.'

'Did it work?'

'Who knows? Only time will tell.' Elmo regarded the pair of them as they watched him with a desperate trust on their faces. 'My ritual doesn't involve the examination of chicken entrails to foretell the future. I didn't sacrifice goats. I invoke a far greater power. The power of visualization, or if you prefer, imagination. Today I lay on my bed and I imagined a scenario. I pictured my ancestors around a campfire with the gods of my village. There, my father, grandfather and all my uncles argued with the gods to persuade them to undo what Edshu has done because it's unnecessary. I pictured my grandfather, who was a huge lion of a man with copper bands around his neck and a spear that was as tall as a tree, who once drove away demons by tearing a thunderbolt from heaven and hurling it into their faces. I lay on my bed and I pictured my grandfather saying to the gods: "These people in the city are good. They work hard to build lives and protect their families. Life itself is a test for them; they don't need Edshu's mischief. So do away with these vampires. Banish them, send them away, turn them to dust, make them shadows that vanish before the sun." For hour after hour I imagined my ancestors debating with the gods. I pictured them explaining why Edshu should be sent on away, that his test of humanity is not required here.'

'But you can imagine anything you want,' Trajan protested. 'In my mind I can picture April growing wings and flying over the city. You can manipulate those images inside your head to do whatever you want.'

Elmo smiled. 'If you are honest with yourself does that really happen? You might picture the woman flying on golden wings but before you can stop yourself don't you imagine her shedding those wings and falling? Or even flying away into the arms of another man?'

Ben said, 'Okay, but did this scenario you imagined end with the gods agreeing to put an end to Edshu's tricks?'

Elmo spoke carefully. 'At the close of the debate that I visualized in my mind it seemed to me that the gods reacted favorably to my ancestors' argument, and yet . . .' He paused. 'And yet they observed there would be an obstruction to what we desire.'

'An obstruction?'

'A man-made obstruction,' Elmo replied. 'My feeling is that the gods wish to send Edshu on his way, and to rid the city of these vampires. Only there is a human that prevents it.'

'This visualization, as you call it, you're confident it can bring results?' Ben asked.

Elmo smacked his hand against his forehead. 'I'm at fault for not expressing my beliefs clearly enough. I'm to blame that you doubt me. Now . . . sometimes a person will come to me with a problem that dogs their life. What advice can I give them when the answer is inside of them all along? So I suggest that when they retire at night they lie there and imagine they are able to converse with one of their ancestors. Perhaps a grandmother who died twenty years ago. Lie there, I tell my patient; relax, breathe slowly, then picture you are speaking with your dead ancestor. Explain your problem to them. Politely ask how it might be solved. Then allow your imagination to visualize their reply.' He walked to the door. 'Alas, we don't have time for that technique. We must resort to one that is more immediate. You'll need your courage for this, gentlemen. Quickly! Come with me.'

Elmo Kigoma led them into the bedroom. There, the stranger with gold-tipped teeth sat unconscious with his back to the wall. April still slumbered under the bed.

Elmo spoke. 'There are only a few hours of daylight left. We must act quickly.'

'What exactly?' Trajan was troubled.

'It won't be pleasant,' said the man. 'But to have even the smallest chance of saving these people you must put aside feelings of disgust.'

'We're not going to harm April?'

'She'll know nothing but you must undertake the ritual.' Elmo crouched down to regard the woman. 'I'm going to put April on the bed. As I move her don't touch me, and don't touch her. Then you must do exactly as I say.'

Ben's stomach gave a queasy roll. 'Do you need more light?'

'No, the gloom is perfect.'

Trajan's doubt manifested itself again. 'Is this really necessary?'

'Yes. Trust me.'

'I have a friend who's a doctor. He could—'

'Trajan. My beliefs and rituals are perplexing.' Elmo reached under the bed, took hold of April's arms and drew her out to the centre of the bedroom floor. 'All religions are full of perplexing self-contradictions. To many the Bible is a book of peace, yet in the Book of Exodus Jehovah gives this command: "Put every man his sword by his side, and go in and out from gate to gate throughout the camp, and slay every man his brother and every man his companion, and every man his neighbor."'

With hardly any exertion the old African lifted the unconscious woman on to the bed. As he arranged her limbs, as if to lie in state, he spoke in that gentle, sing-song voice: 'In my faith we expect our gods to test us . . . often they test us to destruction. To the gods everything in creation is beautiful and right, even death . . . it's only human beings who judge whether events, objects and people are good or bad.' The man positioned April so she lay flat on her back in the centre of the mattress with her legs straight and her arms by her side.

153

He smoothed down the black dress; there was a rip in the side that revealed raw teeth marks. Her feet were bare. Even with so little light Ben saw she was still breathtakingly beautiful. Her eyes were lightly closed, and the skin around her lips had an eerie colouration as if lightly dusted with a blue powder.

Elmo touched her hair. 'Sticky . . . Dead-bone Woman . . . Edshu, what are your plans for her? You have your strategy, don't you? She's a sticky hair, she's your weapon against man . . .' When he'd placed her in position he took a deep breath. 'Gentlemen. We conduct the ritual now. As I've told you this will not be pleasant. You are going to experience disgust. Revulsion. What I ask you to do won't seem right, but for your sakes, and hers, you must do it.'

Trajan was uneasy. 'This ritual? Wouldn't it be better to perform it on the man?'

Elmo tilted his head to one side. 'You really think this ritual would be better performed with a stranger?'

'Mr Kigoma, you haven't even explained what we have to do to her.'

'I thought that would be obvious.' He beckoned them. 'Come to the bed. There . . . don't touch her yet until I give the command. Now . . . both of you have emotional ties to this woman.'

'I'm going to marry her,' Trajan said.

Ben clenched his fist behind his back. 'I know her very well. For years . . .' The words came out awkwardly.

Elmo smiled. 'You both care about her, I know that. Now, do not touch her, but you, Trajan, sit on the bed to her right. Ben Ashton, sit on the left.' He went to the foot of the bed where he faced them. 'Moments ago, I talked about the power of your mind to imagine. If you are to win her back to this life you must rid your minds of doubt. You must know that she is a vampire of Edshu. Just as that man there is a vampire. And that the vampires now threaten London. If you are in no doubt that you face a real enemy only then can you begin to fight back. Are you with me, gentlemen?' Elmo spoke with a fiery purpose now. 'In a moment I will count to three. On "three" you will each take April by the hand. You will only release when I command it. You are entering a whole world of danger now. You must do as I say, because I know Edshu, and Edshu loves to bring strife to humanity. Gentlemen, imag-

154

ination is aided by stimulus from outside of yourself. If you smell beef roasting how easy is it to picture yourself eating it? This woman is your stimulus. When you touch her hand I want you to feel her skin, feel the contours and the texture, whether it's warm or cold. When you touch her flesh imagine what kind of life she's led over the last three days. Has she been sad? Has she known pleasure? What appetite does she own? What must she do to satisfy it? Do you understand?'

Ben nodded; Trajan murmured his agreement.

'Don't be distracted,' Elmo instructed. 'Allow the feel of that skin to suggest what she has become. On the count of three, gentlemen: one, two, three.'

Ben reached out and curled his fingers about her hand the same moment as Trajan took the other. The hand he now grasped was so small and delicate. Unlike the state of her dress the skin was clean; her fingernails were perfectly shaped with no chips or marks. Whether it was his state of mind, or whether the impulses that ran along his nerves from his fingertips to his brain were blocked in a moment of self-preservation he didn't know. Yet for an entire procession of seconds he felt nothing. He could have been touching an empty glove.

'Gentlemen.' Elmo Kigoma spoke gently. 'Close your eyes. What do you see?'

Nothing ... just blank ... wait! Then the images came. Not a sequence that his mind generated by dint of effort, but nothing less than a lightning strike. And what dark and baleful lightning at that. Ben clenched his jaw as the images blazed.

Twenty-Six

*D*ark ... *dark* ... *dark* ... Ben Ashton sat there in the room and held April's hand. His eyes were closed. He did as Elmo Kigoma told him. When he touched her cold skin he imagined what kind of life she'd lived for the last three days. No images were forced. They roared through his mind. First came darkness. Only this darkness wasn't an absence of light. This darkness was a force to be felt. In his mind's eye he saw the darkness as a power that seized April Connor to hurl her through utter blackness. She fell end over end, as if in slow motion, her arms flung out; these fingers he now touched buffeted by an elemental force.

Water . . . River . . .

Then he saw: images of April underwater. Being swept from the island . . . from willows, a derelict house. In the house lifeless figures wait for eternity. Then she's swept upstream by the tide. The depths of the Thames are black; that blackness flows through the core of her being. It gathers where her heart once beat. Darkness has the power to drive her free of the water. April finds more of her kind there on the shore beneath the concrete overhang. Traffic rumbles, men and women are walking. Above is normality, below on the shore could be the matter of hell itself leaking out to pollute the earth. April slithers up the mud. Alongside her more of Edshu's vampires crawl from the river into the city.

And why are they venturing into the city, these creatures – sticky-hair, dead-bone creatures? These Vampire Sharkz? It is hunger that pushes them. An insane appetite for what is contained in human veins . . .

Ben visualizes April and sees her as she walks along an urban street with her companion; the man with the gold-tipped teeth. Their eyes blaze with eerie lights. The hunger is a force that rages inside not only their bellies but in every atom of their flesh. Every part of their bodies hurt because of that craving for nourishment. When they see the drunk stumbling along beneath the street lights they race to him. In seconds they have ripped away his shirt so they can sink their teeth into bare flesh. Once they have opened the flesh they suck at bloody wounds with such bliss on their faces. The salty taste eases the pain in April's body. And as she gulps it down by the mouthful it becomes nothing less than an explosion of sheer pleasure in her stomach that sends out wave after wave of warming satisfaction through her body to her fingertips and her toes. Between downing those huge draughts of crimson she sighs. They are like the heartfelt sighs of love making. Then more of that violent gorging on blood until their victim is dry; nothing more than a cloth wrung of every last drop of moisture.

Elsewhere in London, Ben sees the vampires feeding, too. From the Serpentine in Hyde Park grey figures emerge from its waters to seize people taking a midnight stroll. They drag their shocked victims back into the water to feed; within minutes the moonlight reveals a scarlet film on the lake. More of Edshu's vampires crawl out of the sewers to claim their prize – a man who'd been stalking his ex-girlfriend didn't notice the open manhole cover in the alley way. Even before he has time to cry out a pair of cold jaws grind their teeth against his face until they break through to the hot goodness beneath. Then the vampires give something in return. They vomit contaminated blood back from their own stomachs into the victim's wound. This brings New-Life. Within hours the victims develop a craving for human blood. So the epidemic spreads. More vampires . . . more victims . . . more death . . . more New-Life . . . demon creatures with an appetite that burns with all the fury of hell . . .

A return to shadows. Although hot air crept into the room Ben held a hand carved from ice. At least that's what the chill that numbed his fingers suggested. Then he heard traffic sounds from the street outside. A horn sounded. For a moment it was all muted as Ben felt those images of vampires, gore and violence run through him; they weren't so much imagined pictures as a deadly radiation that had the power to burn the visions of the undead into his brain.

The voice of Elmo Kigoma appeared to reach out to him from faraway. 'Gentlemen. Take your hands away from April. Don't touch her again unless I tell you to.'

Ben's neck was stiff, while his shoulder ached so much he grimaced when he withdrew his hand from those icy fingers. April still lay on the bed. She hadn't moved. Her expression hadn't altered. Her eyelids were still closed.

'You saw what her eyes saw.' Elmo didn't ask a question; it was a statement of fact.

'You knew what would happen, didn't you?' Ben grimaced again as he rotated his shoulder to ease the tight muscle. 'You made us feel what it was like to be one of those things.'

'And I warned you it wouldn't be pleasant.'

'Trajan, did you experience the same thing? Trajan?'

Trajan had withdrawn his hand from April's. Yet his expression was vacant.

'Trajan.' Ben got up off the bed and walked round to him. 'Hey, Trajan. It's time to snap out of it now.'

The man's eyes were open but they were strangely dull.

'Elmo. There's something wrong with Trajan. Do you think—'

In a burst of movement Trajan leapt from the bed, grabbed hold of Ben by the shoulders and smashed him back against the wall.

'Let go of him!' Elmo tried to drag Trajan away but the man's strength was phenomenal. 'This was the risk,' Elmo panted. 'Trajan sank too deep.'

'Trajan!' Ben struggled to break free. 'Snap out of it.'

Trajan's eyes widened as they locked on to Ben's throat. He opened his mouth, then lunged his face toward the bare skin. Ben whipped his head down, so the open mouth struck his scalp; he felt the sting of the teeth as the crazed man tried to bite.

Elmo spoke calmly. 'Trajan. You're not a vampire. You're a human being. Remember who you are. This isn't your nature.'

With a grunt Ben managed to catch Trajan off balance; he toppled the guy to floor where his head whipped back against the boards. Trajan's face spasmed as the pain tore through him. Ben snatched up a wooden chair by the leg. It felt like a club in his hand, and had all the destructive promise that went with it. In a second he'd raised it above the man's head as he groggily tried to rise to his knees. Trajan reached out a hand to steady his balance and touched the bed where he had made love to April.

Ben realized Elmo was telling him to stand back; not to strike Trajan with the chair.

Trajan touched the back of his head and grimaced as he knelt there on the floor. 'What the hell am I doing down here?'

The image of the chair crashing down on Trajan's blond scalp was an enticing one. Ben even framed a justification for the act. *Trajan's one of the vampires now. Hit him before he can attack us . . .* When the man groaned in pain, however, that expression of human suffering dissolved the temptation to strike him. Ben set the chair down then helped Trajan to his feet.

158

'I'm afraid that fall opened the cut on your head,' Ben told him.

'Uh . . . I just remember waking up on the floor . . . Oh, my God. There was a nightmare. April was in the river. I wanted to save her but she climbed out of the water and then she just ripped into this guy with her teeth.'

'I know,' Ben said with feeling. 'I saw something like it.'

Elmo helped balance Trajan as the man swayed. 'What you both saw wasn't identical – but it's a powerful rendition of when your imagination works together with empathy, and that other element some call sixth sense.'

Trajan gave a low whistle. 'It was so vivid . . . the vampires? For a moment I believed . . .' His words tailed off as he touched his head. 'Damn, that stings.'

Ben said, 'Elmo, that's a powerful mental technique you've got there. It's lucky we were only under for a few minutes.'

Elmo's brown eyes turned to him. 'Why? How long do you think you were seeing those images inside your head?'

'Five minutes . . . maybe ten at the most.'

The African shook his head. 'Both of you were lost in here.' He touched his own temple. 'You were gone for more than two hours.'

Trajan accepted it with merely a nod. The man was still dazed. Ben, however, felt something closer to shock than surprise. *Two hours?* He checked his watch. It was after six o'clock and suddenly dusk wasn't far away. With a glance at the stranger and April, he said, 'Elmo, will those two wake when the sun goes down?'

'Of course.'

'What then?'

'They are vampires that are the creation of Edshu. He's the eternal trickster. They might try to kill you. Their actions are unpredictable. They could act in a way that nobody could anticipate.'

Trajan's expression was a grave. 'All the more reason to figure out what we do next.'

Ben guided Trajan into the living room, and helped him to sit down on the couch.

'While we talk, Trajan, I'm going to do some running repairs on that skull of yours.'

159

'You really are starting to sound like my sister.' He gave a faint smile. 'She's just as bossy as you are.'

Elmo said, 'You both must eat; take plenty of strong coffee, too. You're going to face an ordeal tonight.'

'The stakes are high, then?' Trajan asked.

Elmo Kigoma nodded. 'A matter of life and death high enough for you?'

Ben grabbed a box of tissues from a coffee table then began dabbing Trajan's scalp wound. 'When the man through there started talking he said the only way to save April was to return to an island. But which island exactly, I don't know; other than it was downriver toward the estuary. Trajan, keep the tissue pressed to your head.' He turned to Elmo. 'So what do you think? Do we try and find the island?'

Elmo's nodded. 'Start with the internet; it'll give you access to charts of the Thames.'

'But will it do any good taking April to this island, even if we can find it?'

'For now,' Elmo said, 'it's the only clue you have. When they wake it might be possible to ask them for its where-abouts.'

'That is if they don't kill us,' Ben said.

'If they don't kill you,' Elmo agreed. 'And that is possible, without a shadow of doubt.'

Twenty-Seven

Trajan mechanically chewed the sandwich as he stared at the laptop's screen. 'I wouldn't have believed it – the River Thames is full of islands.'

'So how do we find the one that the guy wants to return to?'

Elmo said, 'It's the nature of these creatures that they are removed from humanity when they undergo the transition from mortal to vampire.'

'So we're looking for an island that's not inhabited?' Trajan nodded as he studied the computer screen. 'That rules out the Isle of Sheppey and Canvey Island. There are thousands of people living there. What we have left are a lot of obscure islands.' He began to recite a litany of strange names. 'Isle of Grain, Eel Pie Island, Headpile Eyot, Pigeonhill Eyot, Firework Ait and Deadwater Ait. Whatever they are.'

Ben looked over Trajan's shoulder. 'Eyot and Ait are medieval names for island. You can disregard everything upstream of London. The guy was clear enough; the island's located down in the estuary.'

'Some of these islands are nature reserves. They're not much more than a couple of acres of marshland. It's going to be like looking for a needle –' he grunted with frustration – 'on the dark side of the moon.'

'You don't have long, gentlemen,' Elmo told them.

Ben caught the mood of frustration, too. 'Tell us something we don't know.'

'What you don't know,' Elmo continued in that calm voice, 'is that if you delay too long then you're going to have to make choices.'

'What kind of choices?'

'Soon April and her companion are going to wake. You're going to have to choose between keeping them prisoner here during the hours of darkness, when they are awake and dangerous. Or you can take them to the island in the hope that you can save them. Or . . .' He shrugged. 'Or you can kill them, then destroy their bodies.'

'I don't care anything about the guy,' Ben said. 'But there's no way we'll harm April.'

'Nevertheless, those are the options.'

'You really think the key to this is to find the island?' Trajan asked.

'So far, that's your only option if you wish to make April well again.'

Ben nodded at the computer. 'Okay, Trajan. Keep searching.'

Trajan pushed the keyboard away from him. 'No good. How can we identify a particular island from what the guy told you? I mean, how big is it? Are there any distinguishing features?'

'Elmo –' Ben turned to the old man – 'is there any way of waking the guy in the other room?'

161

'You would need to wait until the sun is much lower.'

Trajan slammed his hand down on the table. 'But we can't wait that long.'

'But he was conscious enough to walk and to speak to me.'

'He cares for the woman,' Elmo told them. 'It was a supreme effort of will on his part.'

'Look, if he woke up once, he can wake up again!' Ben raced through into the bedroom. April lay on the bed as still as death. The stranger sat on the floor with his back to the wall. His eyes were closed and his head hung forward until the chin rested on his chest.

Everything became a blur; Ben knew that all that mattered now was to wake the man. Earlier this inert piece of crap had talked about the magic of the island, wherever it was.

'Hey!' Ben crouched down. 'Wake up! Come on, you've got to talk to me.' Ben roughly shook the man. There wasn't so much as a glimmer of consciousness. 'Wake up.' Ben didn't relish touching the man's bare flesh; nevertheless, he roughly shoved his head back against the wall, then he slapped his face. He slapped hard and repeatedly while he shouted, 'Wake up! Talk to me! Come on! Wake up!' Ben's palm stung but he didn't raise so much as a grunt from the vampire. 'Snap out of it.' This time he bunched his fist to deliver a blow against the man's cheekbone.

'Okay, that's enough.' Trajan gripped his wrist, preventing the punch.

'I've got to rouse him, then we'll get some answers.'

'It's not working, Ben. He's unconscious.'

'Bring a candle. We'll use the flame.'

Elmo ghosted into the room. 'You might derive satisfaction from burning his flesh but I doubt if you'll wake him. He'll open his eyes when the sun goes down.'

'Then it might be too late.' Ben's anger intensified. 'You told us that they might kill us. And if that ritual of yours works then Edshu might simply yank the plug and walk away. What happens to these, then?'

'By rights they should have died either through blood loss during the original attack, or drowned when they were thrown into the river.' Elmo gave a painful shrug. 'If they *should* be dead, then when Edshu releases them, what then?'

Trajan asked, 'So, what can we do?'

'The man spoke about an island,' Elmo replied. 'That could be where you find the means to rescue April.' He held up a finger. 'And yet . . . remember Edshu is the trickster. He may be the architect of a deceit. He might wish to lure you to the island for his own malicious purpose. You understand?'

Trajan took a deep breath. 'The island it is then. We'll just have to weather everything Edshu throws at us. You with me, Ben?'

'You don't have to ask. But how do we find it?'

'You heard Mr Kigoma. In a couple of hours April and this fellow are going to wake up.' He gave a grim smile. 'Once they're awake they can show us the way, can't they?'

'How?' Ben asked as he followed Trajan into the lounge.

'I'm going to get hold of a boat and we'll take the pair of them downstream. With luck, they'll recognize the island.'

'Trajan, instead of acting as navigators they're going to rip us apart.'

'No, they won't.'

'You saw what happened to those men in the park. So how are you going to persuade April and the guy to behave like they're out for nothing more than an evening river cruise?'

'That,' Trajan told him, 'is something we haven't figured yet. But we will.'

'And how are you going to find a boat at such short notice?'

Trajan picked up the phone and began to press the keys. 'My family's company ships medical aid to the people who need it. A lot of what we do is funded by trust and favors rather than money. Say a little prayer for me, Ben, because I'm going to test that good-will to breaking point.' He took a deep breath and picked up the phone. 'Hello, Jeff. Do you still have that boat in Chelsea harbour?'

As Trajan spoke on the phone Elmo murmured to Ben, 'Edshu will test Trajan and yourself in the coming hours. This will be your time of crisis. This is when both of you and April will be in extreme peril. Listen to these words, Ben.' The man's dark eyes were hypnotic. 'You will face danger; you will be attacked from quarters you can't begin to imagine. But this is the crucial fact, the threat won't always come from outside. Sometimes the danger will come from here.' Elmo Kigoma pointed a finger at Ben's heart.

Twenty-Eight

An unconscious human is a difficult object to move. Immensely difficult. It has to be moved in one piece. When you want it to be rigid it's flexible. When you need to move it round a tight corner it doesn't bend like you want it to. And all the time you have to be careful you don't drop the inert person. So you end up struggling to move something that seems as heavy as a slab of concrete, yet more fragile than an antique vase.

These thoughts repeated themselves in a seemingly endless cycle as Ben worked with Trajan and Elmo to shift the guy with the gaunt face and gold-tipped teeth down into the basement garage of the apartment block. The stranger had a slender build; his body appeared emaciated; you could encircle his upperarm with your fingers, yet he was an object that was near immovable. Not for the first time Ben said, frustrated, 'Damn it, he must have bones of solid granite.' Then he added mentally, *or is Edshu testing us again?*

The most logical way of moving the man was for Trajan and Ben to take an arm each; hold it over their own shoulders and carry him horizontally, like they were helping a friend home after a whisky too many. Only to carry him like this meant that the vampire's head rolled from side-to-side. When the creature's face slapped against Ben's jaw he recoiled so much that he dropped him.

Trajan didn't complain at Ben's squeamishness. 'When I touch him,' he said, 'I see those images again . . . the same as when we held April's hand . . . feeding on blood . . .' He shook his head. 'We've got to figure out another way to do this.'

Trajan found a sleeping bag that he unzipped and laid out flat on the hallway floor. What came next wasn't easy. However, they managed to roll the guy on to the opened sleeping bag. Then Elmo and Ben took a corner each at either side of the man's head. Trajan took the two corners by the feet. Lifting it was torture. Ben's shoulder ached; shooting pains blasted through his elbows. But sweating and panting they made it to the landing. Constantly, there was the threat of a neighbour stepping out of their own front door to discover what appeared to be the aftermath of murder.

'There's a lift to the garage,' Trajan panted, 'at the end of the landing.'

The only one of the three who appeared to be handling the burden without complaint, or even undue exertion, was the eighty-six-year-old African. He gripped the fabric of the sleeping bag in both hands and sunk all he had into carrying the dead-to-the-world figure.

Sleeping like a baby. The thought nearly produced a bark of lunatic laughter in Ben. The guy hadn't even murmured during all the manhandling to get him on the sleeping bag, then some pretty savage buffeting against the door frame to haul him out of the apartment. As they hoisted their cargo by closed front doors Ben smelt cooking as people prepared their evening meals; he heard snatches of conversation from those homes, together with a burst of music or applause from televisions. Sweet heaven, he thought with a sudden passion, here we are doing this! They're inside getting ready for a pleasant evening. Ignorance really is bliss.

And that's how we survive, isn't it? he thought. It's not what we know that keeps us functioning: it's what we *don't*. How would the steak on your plate taste if you knew the journey from calf to supermarket? Would you sleep at all if you walked through a cemetery where the soil suddenly became as transparent as glass – that and coffin wood, too – so you found yourself looking down through a material that was clear as air to hundreds of corpses in various stages of rot beneath your feet?

How do you close your eyes at night when you've gazed into a face that's shaped from pure horror rather than flesh, and those gaping eye-sockets filled with a glistening slime stare up into yours? And the buried man is not just peeping from his grave at you out of curiosity. No! You know only too well that dead brain harbours malicious thoughts. 'That's alright, Oh Living One, take a really good look at me. Do

165

you see my rib cage through the holes in my shirt? Do you see the maggot squirming in my heart? Have your eyes devoured the appearance of my face? A face that slides away from my head as corruption loosens its grip upon the bone? Can you imagine what it would be like to smell the inside of this casket? How cold would it feel against your fingers to shake me by the hand? Would you remain sane if you embraced me? Keep watching me, Oh Living One. Feast your eyes. BECAUSE WHAT I AM NOW YOU WILL BECOME!'

There's mocking laughter coming from the dead in their graves. The laughter is cruel but so knowing. All the men and women in the graveyard lived their lives believing that somehow death wouldn't find them. But it does, you know, doesn't it?

And those people in the apartments grilling steaks, easing corks from wine bottles, have persuaded themselves death will *never ever* happen to them. Wrong. Wrong! Wrong! Why not hammer on the doors and show them what we're carrying! 'See the man that looks like a corpse. This is a vampire! Don't believe me, huh? Just you sit beside it here and wait for the sun to go down . . .'

'Ben –' the sound of Kigoma's voice struck him like a blow – 'remember what I told you. Edshu has the power to attack in many different ways. Keep your guard up.'

Ben's heart hammered. For a moment there he'd almost lost his mind. It had been like falling asleep. His grip on reality had nearly slipped away with such an oily ease; it was like his thoughts had become lubricated. The image of that transparent cemetery with corpses floating there underground had been so brutally vivid. Ben took a deep breath. *Dear God, this is going to be harder than I thought.*

As they waited for the lift that would take them to the subterranean garage a door opened and a middle-aged woman looked out. 'Hello, Trajan. Keeping busy?'

Smoothly, as if dematerializing, Elmo Kigoma slipped away along the hallway until he was out of sight of the woman. The woman stared at them in surprise; her drop earrings even flicked against her neck as she turned her head so quickly to look at the sleeping bag they'd dragged to the lift doors.

Ben glanced down expecting to see the man lying on the fabric; however, Trajan had the presence of mind to flick the material over the body. What was on view was a lumpy sausage shape covered by the sleeping bag.

Trajan smiled. 'Hello, Rita. We're just getting rid of the heating boiler. These things weigh a ton.'

Rita was confused but still smiled back. 'They do, don't they?'

Even though she was clearly suspicious she appeared reluctant to accuse Trajan outright of moving what resembled a corpse wrapped in the sleeping bag.

Trajan smiled again. 'We'd better get going. Have a nice evening, Rita.'

'Oh, thank you.' She bobbed her head and the drop earrings jiggled. 'Cheerio.' With that she stepped back inside and closed the door.

Ben murmured, 'I'd bet good money she didn't believe your boiler story.'

Trajan began to perspire. 'I agree . . . Come on, lift, where the hell are you?' An illuminated arrow flashed to show it was climbing slowly – far too slowly – towards them.

Ben's heart pounded. The thing covered by the sleeping bag flap might as well have screamed: Dead Man Inside! The elongated shape, with those suggestive bulges of torso and head, was so damned obvious. With agonizing sluggishness the lift ascended. Behind the closed steel doors its mechanism clicked. The wretched thing was going to take its time; it must feed on a diet of sadistic pleasure as well as electricity. Ben experienced that surge of paranoia that always surfaces the moment your car doesn't start, when the key doesn't fit the clock, or the ATM flashes up 'Insufficient funds' when you know you've just been paid.

Behind him, the door handle turned. Ben called, 'She's coming back. She wants a second look.' He glanced back at the lift doors, willing them to open, but knowing full well the lift wasn't going to arrive in time.

The apartment door apartment opened. As it did so Elmo glided forward. A revelation came to Ben. *Dear God, he's going to slug her.*

Instead, Elmo spoke politely. 'I'm sorry to disturb, madam. I preach at the Church of the Transient Apostle in Westminster; I wonder if I could interest you in attending one of our services?'

167

'Uh? No, thank you. I'm Methodist actually.' At that moment she didn't know whether to look at this striking man who'd manifested himself at her door, or the pair with their suspicious bundle. She recovered her composure to add, 'I'm not interested, thank you.' She wasn't ready to yield her ground yet, and began to edge by the man.

'I understand, madam. Before I go, may I ask you for a small donation for the upkeep of the church? Last week vandals damaged our stained-glass windows.'

'I'll say goodnight to you.' She attempted to step past him.

'Only when I called earlier your husband asked me to come back tonight. Didn't he mention it to you, madam?'

This distracted her. 'My husband?' Frowning, she called back into the apartment. 'Richard? Richard, there's a gentleman here who says . . .'

Fortunately, Ben didn't have to watch how Elmo's deception played out. The steel doors slid open; a moment later they'd dragged their morbid burden into the lift. Trajan punched the button marked 'Basement'.

As the doors closed Trajan sighed, 'One down, one to go.'

With it being early evening the cars that ferried people home from work had already been parked up. When the lift doors opened to that concrete catacomb there was only one vehicle in motion as a girl headed out in her pink Mini. She never even noticed the pair dragging the heavy object in a sleeping bag. Once the car had vanished up the ramp to street-level they resumed their labors.

Trajan nodded toward the corner of the basement. 'Red Renault. The back seat reclines . . . there's a blanket in there. Once this is under it we'll go back for April.'

Muscles straining, they bore the dead weight to the car.

'Okay,' Trajan grunted. 'They say space wagons are as dull as buses, but at least they've got room . . . for whatever it is you're carrying.' He opened the hatchback, pushed the rear seat flat, then together they hefted the man into the luggage area. After that they dragged the sleeping bag free, then covered him with a blanket. By now their skin was slick with sweat. A pain speared Ben's side where a muscle had been over-stretched.

When Trajan locked the car he simply panted, 'Next passenger.'

'And we get to do this all over again when we take them down to the boat?'

'Yep. But we can drive up right alongside. It's only at Chelsea harbor.' He caught his breath. 'Shouldn't take long to get there.'

'Pray that it doesn't. It's going to be dark in a couple of hours.'

'Probably less than that. After you.'

Elmo Kigoma was waiting for them upstairs. His pose as some kind of urban missionary had been enough to drive Trajan's neighbor indoors.

'You must hurry, gentlemen,' he urged them. 'The sun will be setting soon.'

'We hear you.' Ben was still breathless. 'But we're doing okay.'

'Okay? Gentlemen, okay isn't good enough. To survive this you must work miracles.'

April Connor knew she lay on her bed at home. Every so often street sounds reached her; car horns, or motorbikes. They swam into her senses and back out again. Even though she was in dreamy state she told herself, I'll wake soon. I know this time Carter and I will tell everyone about what happened to us. I know we can make the world a better place. For a moment she tried to open her eyes but there was still no strength inside of her. It was as if her energy had been extracted. It wasn't lost. Some force beyond her comprehension guarded that physical energy for her. What's more, they cultivated it. That New-Life energy was being improved. Soon it would be returned to her body and she'd awake refreshed and strong and determined to continue her quest to deliver the good news to everybody. She'd tell them this: You, too, can live forever! You can feel elated and stronger than you've ever felt before. All you need do is submit to a moment of pain.

April's lungs expanded in her chest. She was aware of her respiration. It grew stronger. It wouldn't be long before she woke.

The setting sun filled the buildings with blood. At least that was Ben's impression when he took a moment to peep through

169

the kitchen blind. London's tall buildings reflected the light of a low sun that turned ruddy and bloated as it dipped between the office blocks. Ben's gaze was drawn to the millions of window panes that caught the scarlet rays of the sun. Elmo Kigoma told them that those vampires had the power to infect mortal people and transform them into vampires, too. But Ben realized it went beyond that. The vampiric force possessed remorseless power. Not only did the vampires infect humanity, they had the potential to infect the very fabric of the city. At that moment London gorged itself on the blood-red light of the sun. Meanwhile, the mighty River Thames was the artery that ran through its heart. What manner of life lurked in that arterial flow?

Ben knew that once darkness fell those vampiric creatures that hid themselves away during the hours of daylight would invade this community of seven million souls.

Elmo appeared at his side. 'It won't be long now, Ben.'

Ben turned to the African. The statement bristled with several meanings. More than one of those was darkly ominous. 'How—?'

Trajan appeared at the doorway. 'Quick. April's waking up.'

Ben followed Trajan into the room. 'She's not moved?'

'I don't think so.'

'What then?

For a split-second Trajan appeared awkward. 'I touched her.' Then he added in a way that challenged them to criticize he announced, 'I kissed her. She's my fiancée.'

'It's understandable,' Elmo said, 'but it's not wise. If she'd woken she might have struck.'

'So why do you believe she's waking up?' Ben pressed the question.

'Earlier, she was like a block of ice. Now her skin's hot.'

Elmo touched her hand with his fingertip. 'Her face is flushed, too. We shouldn't delay moving her to the boat.'

This time carrying April on the sleeping bag went smoothly. The lift was waiting on their floor. Rita, the neighbour, didn't show her face. It was only when the three lifted the unconscious April from the lift into the basement garage that they realized their world was changing.

Twenty-Nine

'Is it my imagination,' Trajan said as they gripped the corners of the sleeping bag and carried April toward the car, 'or is there something wrong with the lights?'

A gloom crept into the basement with its low concrete ceiling and smells of fuel and exhaust fumes. In the shadows, the pipes that emerged from the floor to run up the walls into the guts of the apartment block assumed the menacing aspect of serpents that possessed the girth of tree trunks. Elmo glanced up at the strip lights; instead of a brilliant white they were now yellow.

As an intense quiet crept into the vault Elmo broke the silence. 'The vampire isn't Edshu's only weapon. Anything that makes humanity weaker he will exploit. I can warn you, gentlemen: expect trickery.'

The lights dimmed from yellow to orange. There were no windows down here and the only other light was a bloody glow from the sun that oozed down the vehicle ramp. They gently set April down on her makeshift stretcher.

'Remember what I told you.' Elmo rubbed the strained muscles of his forearm. 'It is Edshu's mission to test humanity to breaking point. Rest assured that he is watching you, just as my ancestors and the gods of my village watch.'

Ben clicked his tongue in exasperation. 'But why are your gods and ancestral spirits interested in what is happening here?'

'Ben Ashton, I thought you were the one of the few who understood what I was trying to do when I kept my vigil in the boat. You understood my message; now you express utter ignorance.' The man's eyes flashed with anger. 'Our bodies live in the physical world. Our minds live in a Sea of Thought. All our gods and all our ancestors inhabit that universal ocean. And when your body dies your mind will continue to reside in the Sea of Thought. If you, Ben, care about what happens to your fellow countrymen here in this city, do you also care whether a man, woman or child is sick in Pakistan, China or Brazil? I know that you do. You are a compassionate man, Ben. But you are not unique in your compassion.

'My ancestors and my gods might not live in this world of concrete and metal and electricity but where they reside in the Sea of Thought they still care about the well-being of not just you; not just Trajan; not just the stranger in the car; not just April Connor – they care about the people of this city and this world. They don't want them to suffer misery, or feel the pain of a broken bone, or torn flesh.' He lunged forward to grip Ben by the jaw. The man's slender fingers were stronger than Ben could have imagined. He even heard the teeth in his gums creak under the pressure. Elmo's face came within inches of Ben's. 'Do not become the idiot now. Not after you've come so far. Don't you understand, both of you? The life of London and her people hang in the balance now. You have become its champions. By an accident of fate you are being tested. If you fail the test, then the city dies with you.' At that moment a throbbing noise started. Even though it was low the rhythm was quick; a suggestion of urgency. 'And if you don't believe me, leave these vampires lying here and go out into the city and walk its streets. Because I guarantee that by midnight you will see your capital city begin to die before your very eyes!' Elmo pushed Ben from him; his eyes radiating nothing less than fury.

The beating sound, almost like drumming, grew louder, more intrusive. At the same moment the overhead lights dimmed until they were the colour of rust.

Trajan tilted his head. 'The noise is coming from the pipes.'

Ben reached out to touch one of the outlets to the sewer below ground. It vibrated so much it made his skin tingle. 'You're right. But what the hell's doing it?'

Elmo nodded at the inert form of April on the sleeping bag at their feet. 'Her kind know what you're doing. They're making known their displeasure.' Even as he spoke the violent drumming intensified. It seemed as if entire legions below ground beat at the pipes. By now the lights had dimmed to mere spots of red light.

'You must hurry, gentlemen. These two will wake soon. When they do you've got to be ready.'

172

After Trajan unlocked the car they lifted April into the back and laid her down beside her companion. Both were still. But both were hot to the touch; their chests rose and fell as if they were deliberately hyperventilating before taking part in some act of incredible endurance. At the far side of the garage a manhole cover was set in the floor; a dark square of iron against pale concrete. The drumming sounded louder, then Ben saw why. The iron cover to the drain was slowly being raised. Beneath it, he glimpsed a pair of naked arms that were held outstretched as they pushed against the iron trap door.

'Faster, gentlemen.' Elmo stared at the manhole cover. 'They are here.'

Ben and Trajan covered the pair in the back with the blanket.

'Get inside, Mr Kigoma,' Trajan shouted.

Elmo Kigoma didn't move. His eyes were fixed on the manhole cover as a second pair of arms joined the first to push the metal panel upward.

'Elmo!' Ben shouted. 'Get in the car.' He held the door open for the man, but he wasn't coming.

Elmo's voice reached him above the frenzied pounding noise. 'I picture my ancestors. I imagine my grandfather leading them. He has copper bands around his neck. In one hand is a shield of zebra hide. In the other hand a spear. My grandfather is a warrior. He is not afraid. He has pledged to protect the innocent; he is our ally. He returns from the Sea of Thought to help us.'

Elmo's eyes were glassy as he watched four naked arms push the manhole cover open. In a moment it would topple back; then whatever was concealed underground could rush out at them.

Elmo continued. 'My grandfather is swift as a panther; he has copper bands around his neck. He carries a shield, and a spear that is a thunderbolt.'

By this time Ben had begun to gauge the possibility of physically dragging the man into the car. But as he stood by the vehicle he glanced across the garage at the opening trap door. Just for a moment, as Elmo intoned about seeing his warrior grandfather, Ben thought he saw a shadowy figure dart at the trap door. A moment later the manhole cover slammed shut. Whatever was in the pit below was sealed back inside. For now.

Just for a second the sound paused. There was a sense of stunned disbelief on the part of the unseen drummers, then the sound rushed back with a vengeance.

Elmo slid gracefully into the front passenger seat of the car. Trajan bounced down into the driver's seat; Ben climbed into the back. The rear seats had been laid flat to accommodate the corpse-like cargo, so he had to perch alongside them and simply hold the grab handle above the window as Trajan reversed out of the parking space.

Elmo Kigoma regarded the manhole cover that sealed the entrance to the sewer. 'In life my grandfather was a strong man. In my imagination he's stronger than ever.'

As the car surged toward the ramp that would take them to street level Ben said, 'I know what you did. You visualized that your grandfather came here. Then you pictured him pushing the manhole cover shut and stopping the vampires leaving the sewer.'

'See,' Elmo said with satisfaction. 'You are learning. If you continue to learn about the power of imagination then it might yet save our lives.'

The city streets were darkening now the sun had all but sunk out of sight. Trajan powered the car along the maze of roads. They were busy with traffic and pedestrians alike but now the rush-hour was over they were at least passable.

'You're right, Mr Kigoma,' Trajan said as he sped through a junction. 'The tricks have started. See the traffic lights?'

Both the red and green lamps burned, throwing the traffic into chaos. Even from here they could see into the entrance of a tube station where the passenger barriers had spontaneously locked everyone out so crowds began to back out on to the streets to make the congestion even worse. Everywhere people were having trouble with their phones. Ben saw perplexed faces as they looked at the screens while they thumbed the keys.

Ben grunted. 'Tell me I'm wrong, but I think the ghost just got into the machine.'

With the sinking of the sun the dusk seemed to creep out of the ground. Most traffic lights appeared to be failing. Meanwhile, the police did what they could to keep vehicles flowing. The saving grace was the time of evening when the roads were at their quietest. As Trajan piloted the car round clumps of buses Ben asked, almost in jest, 'Elmo? Does it help if I imagine the streets are clear of cars?'

Elmo glanced back. 'Everything positive and life-affirming you can imagine helps.' Then he nodded at the two slumbering forms beneath the blanket that reminded Ben so much of corpses. 'Imagine those two will continue to sleep. It wouldn't do if they woke up now.'

Ben shifted uncomfortably as the covered shoulder of the comatose vampire pressed against his hip. 'I'll do my best.'

Trajan steered round a mail van that had bumped against a truck where all the lights blazed green and drivers shouted curses at each other. 'Should I picture a successful outcome, too?'

'The more of us that do, the better.'

'But you're telling me Ben here's better at it than I am?' Trajan asked.

'We all have unique strengths,' Elmo told him. 'But the power of thought is a remarkable thing in all of us. In everything men and women make, we use our minds to generate an image of its appearance. What happens next is purely the labour to turn a dream into an object that we can reach out and touch.'

They cut down a side street. More people had trouble with the telephones. A man pounded his fist on to the screen of an ATM as the machine refused to return his card or deliver the cash. On another corner two women ripped at one another's hair after their cars had collided at a set of faulty traffic lights.

Ben said, 'It's more than the inconvenience of power failure and temperamental electronics; this is creating animosity. Strangers are falling out with one another.'

'And so the pressure of anger grows,' Elmo said.

'So this is Edshu's doing?'

Elmo nodded. 'First he divides the population; they fight one another before he launches the next onslaught. Now his vampires are out there, waiting. When the city is in disarray that will be the best time for them to attack.'

They drove into Chelsea with its expensive real estate. That wasn't immune either. Lights flickered in offices. An ATM pumped banknotes into the street. Water gushed from a grate to flood the road. Trajan resolutely ploughed through it. 'Not far now,' he told them.

175

Ben found it hard to take his eyes away from the two forms beneath the blanket. It may have been the motion of the car, but he thought he saw their limbs begin to twitch.

'More speed would be appreciated,' Ben said. 'I have a feeling they're starting to wake.' Outside the sky had become a deep blue. On the horizon smears of red marked the position of the sun's descent.

'Just another couple of minutes until we're there.' Trajan switched on the radio. After a couple of false starts when music surged through the speakers he hit one of the talk radio channels. A bemused male voice was announcing:

> '. . . more news coming in. Forget using the Northern and Piccadilly lines as well. There's a power outage that might take hours to restore. We're also hearing problems with signals on the Docklands Light Railway. Elsewhere, escalators have slowed to a snail's pace at underground stations, while disruption to the capital's traffic lights have brought chaos to the streets. Even here in the station we're experiencing voltage surges that are blowing fuses all over the building. Stay with me, your friend in town, Lightning Ray Elmsall, keeping you abreast and up-to-date wherever—'

Trajan switched off the radio. Ahead, the main road had been blocked by a truck lying on its side. He cut off on to another route that ran beside the river. By now the Thames had turned the colour of lead, while here and there glints of copper shone on its surface.

Trajan let out a sigh that came from the depths of his soul as much as his lungs. 'There's our boat,' he told them. 'And the guy on the motorbike is here to deliver the keys.'

Trajan spoke to the motorcyclist who held the keys in his hand. For a moment Ben wondered if the man would ask awkward questions – why do you want the boat? What's that in the back of your car? However, he was simply a hired courier, requiring a signature on a clipboard before handing the keys over. Within seconds of delivering, the courier jumped on to his bike and roared away into the dusk.

Trajan loped back to the car. 'It's only a dozen yards to the gangplank,' he told them. 'There isn't an easier way, I'm afraid, so it's a case of carrying them on board.'

176

Ben was grateful to quit the car as a deep bleakness flooded the street. What's more, the stretch of road between a warehouse and the river was deserted. This time their job of moving the pair should be easier . . . as long as they didn't wake up.

Thirty

Trajan had wealthy friends. Ben smelt the leather upholstery of the millionaire's launch as he helped carry the stranger on board. The craft was a sleek vision of luxury in ivory. It was more than eighty feet long and boasted a lounge upholstered in leather in that same soft shade of ivory. Some of the furnishings were still wrapped in plastic, while electrical goods stood in boxes on the floor waiting to be installed.

They carried the man on using the hammock arrangement with the sleeping bag. Trajan grunted. 'It's still being fitted out but I've been promised she's sailable.'

'And fast, I hope.' Ben helped set the stranger down on the richly carpeted floor of the salon lounge.

'Twin diesel motors; a top speed of thirty knots; she'll do the job.' Trajan rubbed his strained elbows. 'Ever sailed a motor yacht like this before?

'I've rowed a dinghy on a park lake, that's all.'

'You're going to learn fast. I need you to man the pilot-house and steer the boat as I cast off the lines.'

'You trust me enough not to wreck it?'

'I trust you with my life, Ben. Come on, once we have April and Mr Kigoma on board we need to move fast.'

But even as they headed out on to the deck Elmo Kigoma leapt on board, with April over his shoulder.

'Elmo, we can give you a—'

'Move!' Elmo shouted. 'They're here!'

Ben looked at the deserted street.

'No, not on shore,' Elmo called out. 'In the water! Trajan, you must get the boat moving or they'll swarm all over us.'

Ben tried to help the man carry the unconscious woman.

'No! I can manage. You help Trajan.'

Trajan raced to the pilothouse at rear of the boat. 'Ben, follow me. I'll start the motors and put her into forward at slow speed, then I'll untie the lines. As soon as she starts to move head to the centre of the river and keep the nose pointing downstream.'

'Trajan. This thing's a hell of a size. I don't know if I can—'

'You'll be fine. It's like steering a car. Just don't touch the throttle controls. As soon as we're free of the mooring I'll take over. Okay?'

In near darkness they ran to the stern deck where the pilothouse was located. By now the lights in the high-rise buildings should be blazing but they were in darkness. Was this Edshu's doing? Had the trickster god from Elmo's homeland killed the electricity supply? From across the water it seemed as if a hundred different sirens wailed as ambulances and police cars raced to a multitude of emergencies that the power failure had caused. Before entering the pilothouse Ben glanced over the railing into the river. The moment he did so the surface exploded into gouts of spray as shapes broke the surface. In that swirl of movement and water he saw threshing limbs. Faces broke the surface; they possessed blazing eyes that stared at him with a ravenous intensity.

Trajan had seen, too. 'Mr Kigoma was right. If we don't get away in the next twenty seconds they'll be on board!'

He rushed into the pilothouse. Meanwhile, Ben stood there, transfixed by that vortex created by the vampires as they writhed in the water. They appeared to be in a state that combined ecstasy and agony. He sensed their hunger. And he knew why they fixed him with their searing eyes.

'Ben! I need you now. Take the wheel!'

Ben snapped out of it. Engines hummed as the propellers chopped at the water. Although they'd be going nowhere until Trajan untied the mooring lines. Ben ran into the wheelhouse to be confronted with banks of monitors and electronic equipment.

178

'Ben, when she starts to move steer away from the bank. Keep midstream. I'll be right back.' The engines' purr sent vibrations through the boat's wheel. He felt the vessel tug at the lines as if it craved its release from dry land. Through the windows he could see Trajan in the gloom. The blond head bobbed as he ran to the prow to untie the lines there; seconds later he was back amidships to release a line. One remained at the stern.

Then they climbed the steps that ran up the harbour wall. Ben watched as a dozen men and women moved like panthers. Water dripped from their matted hair; their soaked clothes were torn; some only had a few strands of material hanging from their grey bodies. Again, he sensed that vampiric hunger. It drove them at ferocious speeds. And at that moment Ben had no doubt at all the creatures knew that two of their own kind were on board. Elmo Kigoma had warned Ben and Trajan that they would be the focus of the trickster god's attention now. From whatever lair these creatures spent the daylight hours they would be converging on the boat. Above the hum of motors he heard the thump of fists striking the hull. Meanwhile, the vampires that had scaled the steps began to lope toward the boat.

'Trajan!' Ben yelled. 'We've got company!' He glanced round the pilothouse for a weapon of some sort, but even the furniture was bolted to the floor. 'Hurry up!'

The grey forms flitted along the harbour pathway towards the boat. Five more seconds. Then they'd simply leap on board. And still Trajan worked at the loop of orange rope around the mooring point on deck. The prow of the boat began to move away from the harbour wall; only the motion was so slow it was agonizing to watch.

Ben shouted, 'Hurry!' At that point it could have been aimed at Trajan or the boat – or both.

A second later Trajan moved along the deck carrying the unhitched rope. Instead of hanging slack it was taut. Ben realized that one of the vampires in the water had been able to reach up and grip it. Now it wouldn't let go. On the harbour wall the creatures were only a dozen paces from leaping on to the deck. A glance at those powerful arms told Ben that he wouldn't be able to manhandle them over the side. Trajan still appeared to be having trouble with the rope as he struggled to tug it free from the hands of the monster in the water. The boat continued its unhurried departure from the harbour.

Ben called to Trajan. 'Have you untied it?'

'Yes, but—'

The affirmative was all he wanted to hear. Ben gripped the helm wheel in one hand, while he gripped a large chrome lever that extended from the controls with the other. Although he'd only seen this done on TV he knew that this must be the throttle lever. He rammed it forward as far as it would go. The power units down in the engine room were no weaklings. The bellow of the motor battered his skull. For a moment the boat appeared to stand on its tail as it surged away from the dock. At the same moment the vampires leapt from dry land to the deck.

A howl of pure joy erupted from Ben's mouth as the boat jetted toward the centre of the river. As the water raced by, waves exploded against the prow to send drops of water fifty feet into the air where they gleamed like diamonds in the moonlight.

'We did it, Trajan!' Ben screamed. 'We bloody did it!'

When he glanced round Trajan had vanished. The silver wake formed a shining trail back across dark waters to the harbour. Worse, when he looked through the windows toward the front of the boat he saw three pairs of arms clinging to the guardrail. Most of the vampires hadn't made the leap aboard, but three of their kind had jumped far enough to catch the rail. Now they hung down the port side. He saw three grey faces appear over the rail. Their eyes, which burnt with an uncanny fire, locked on to him through the window. He recognized the satisfaction in their expression. *We've got him*, their faces seemed to say. *There's nothing he can do to save himself.* Ben searched the banks of the river. On Cheyne Walk cars still ran freely. Their headlights illuminated part of the banking there. Then he saw a block of darkness at the edge of the river. With the motors pounding at full revs he steered the boat toward that black oblong on the water. The three vampires that clung to the rail were now hoisting themselves up the side of the boat. In seconds they would climb fully on board.

Ben prayed that he'd mastered the steering enough to get this right. He charged at the block of darkness on the river.

Only at the last moment did the shape resolve itself into the outline of the huge dredger that scooped mud from the Thames. He swung the nose of the craft round, then deliberately raked the port side of his vessel down the massive steel flanks of the dredger. Pieces of that beautiful ivory hull were sheered away with a piercing, grinding noise. Electric blue sparks filled the air as the two surfaces chafed against each other as the boat sped alongside. Then the dredger was gone. Along with a streak of ivory paint left by the motor yacht's contact with the dredger was an almighty smear of glistening red. Two of the vampires had vanished. A pair of hands and a head remained at just the other side of the rail, but when Ben leaned forward to take a closer look he saw that the entire body beneath the creatures' armpits had been torn away. For a moment the face of what had once been a man turned toward the pilothouse. With nothing less than hatred the eyes continued to blaze at Ben. Then a wave buffeted the boat. The tremor shook what was left of the creature free; it dropped into the water to be buried by the foaming wake.

As soon as Ben was satisfied nothing remained of the vampires that had clung to the rail he pulled back the throttle lever. The motors dropped from a bellow to a hum. Within moments the boat had slowed until it did little more than drift in the current. To one side the huge Gothic bulk of the Houses of Parliament slipped by.

Ben scrambled out on to the stern deck; now it was so dark he had to rely on lights from cars plying the roads that flanked the river. At that moment he was sick with not only dread at what might turn out to be the loss of Trajan, but a guilty excitement as well. What if Trajan had been dragged overboard by one of those creatures as the man tried to wrest the rope from it? With Trajan gone April would be his responsibility. If he could free her from this vampiric curse then what would stop him from declaring his true feelings to her; that he loved her, and he was prepared to devote his life to her? Trajan's death wasn't his fault. Neither guilt nor blame would attach to him. As he stepped across the smooth surface of the deck a kind of dreaminess stole over him as he pictured himself helping April through her recovery. He'd stroll with her in the park as she convalesced; when she was tired she'd link arms with him. He could almost imagine the light pressure of her arm against his.

181

'Ben . . .'

He looked down over the rail. Trajan clung to the mooring rope. His face was a mask of exhaustion as he grimly hung on for dear life. Beneath him the black waters became smooth, almost unctuous, as he clung on.

'Ben,' he grunted. 'I didn't expect you to hit the throttle like that.'

Ben continued to stare down. The man's feet were just inches from the water. Just beneath the surface grey faces peered up with wide eyes as their prey dangled.

'I can't hang on much longer . . . if you give me your hand. I should be able to . . . uh . . .' A hand broke the surface of the river to grip Trajan's ankle.

Ben watched the long fingers that were the colour of raw fish. Each finger terminated in a deathly blue nail.

'Ben!'

Just one tug and Trajan would fall back into the river where dozens of vampires swarmed like predatory sharks. His death would be almost instant. With Trajan's disappearance there would be nobody in the way. April would become the love of Ben's life. He pictured the passion they'd share. A tingle spread through his veins. He could imagine hugging her as she whispered his name into his ear.

A new image invaded the one of him sliding beneath the bed sheets with a naked April; this one was of Elmo Kigoma intoning, 'Ben, Edshu's greatest pleasure is turning friend against friend.'

'Got you! Kick your legs! Kick it in the face!' Ben sucked the air into his lungs as he dragged Trajan clear of the creature below. The vampire still hung on to Trajan's ankle. Ben's adrenalin-fuelled lift raised not only the human but the monster from the water. He saw the figure of a girl of about twenty. Her breasts gleamed in the moonlight, while her mouth yawned wide in readiness to bite Trajan's limb.

'Kick!' Ben yelled.

Trajan, as he dangled there, kicked as hard as he could. The toe of his shoe struck the creature in the side of the head. With a howl it released its grip and fell into the water. By now the creatures in the river used one another as floating platforms in order to climb up the stern of the boat. Already, he saw fingertips brushing the bottom of the guard rails as they tried to get a grip so they could haul themselves on board.

Ben gritted his teeth while he dragged Trajan on to the deck. As soon as he was satisfied the man was back over the rail, and in relative safety, Ben set to work. By now, vampires had begun to climb up the hull. He let fly with almighty kicks that smashed fingers as they gripped the rail. The creatures screamed as they tumbled back into the water.

'Ben, get us out of here,' Trajan shouted. 'We're drifting into a jetty.'

Ben hurled a punch into the face of something that had once been a middle-aged man. With a grunt it tumbled back into the Thames. Using his last reserves of strength he kicked the hands of a pair of vampires that climbed up the other side of the rail. When their broken fingers could no longer hold them, they, too, slipped back into the swarm of vampires that churned the water around the boat. There must have been dozens now. Ben knew he couldn't fight them all. Exhausted, he staggered back into the pilothouse. Once more he hit the throttle. Only this time he managed to find reverse. The boat slid backwards as the big propellers chopped the river like whirling knife blades. A second later it wasn't just liquid they chopped as the propellers hacked through limbs and torsos. When he accelerated the boat forward again he left the remains of a dozen shattered bodies twitching in the waters. More vampire bodies slammed against the vessel's prow as he sped away from the bank into the gathering darkness, and toward their destiny.

Thirty-One

Ben had no qualms in handing over the piloting of the motor yacht to Trajan. The man skillfully guided the boat downstream despite him still panting with exhaustion, and the fact that he'd only narrowly avoided being torn apart by the vampires just minutes ago.

I nearly let them take him, Ben thought to himself, as he watched the blond man at the wheel. There was an opportunity to get rid of you. It would have left the way open for me to get close to April again.

Ben gripped the back of the chair almost to steady himself mentally rather than physically. Because with the mental image of Trajan falling victim to those creatures he realized he felt no guilt at the thought of his rival for April being destroyed. Even at this moment he could grab Trajan and topple him over the rail into the river. Nobody would suspect Ben because nobody knew about that secret longing for April. For a while he was so wrapped up in this electrifying revelation that he didn't realize that Trajan called to him above the thunder of motors.

'Pray we don't hit any debris or any boats . . . The moon's bright but it's still hard to see objects in the water. Ben, keep a look out through the windows at your side. Shout if you see anything in the water. Okay?'

'Okay.'

'The tide's turned so we've a current of around four knots pushing us downstream anyway. I'm hitting thirty knots now so we should be out of the city in thirty minutes.' He shot him a grim smile. 'We're breaking the speed limit, so just hope the river police are busy somewhere else tonight.'

The massive boat skimmed across the water. In the moonlight Old Father Thames resembled mercury. One moment it was black, the next a metallic silver. With the failure of the electricity supply the buildings that flanked the banks were huge monolithic oblongs; tombstone shapes that blotted out the starry sky. Cars still crawled along the streets. Every so often he glimpsed a face onshore that turned to watch the boat, and sometimes he suspected that it was not a human face. London's landmarks were nothing more than indistinct ghosts of their former selves under the flood of darkness. He glimpsed the dark finger of Cleopatra's Needle pointing skyward. Each bridge they passed beneath could have been an entrance to hell itself as they cut out the moonlight and left Trajan's steering to become an act of faith in the total blackout. Then the boat would surge into moonlight again to allow glimpses of the London Eye and the glittering colossus of Canary Wharf.

He glanced back at their wake, which formed a V shape of white foam that rushed out to the riverbanks. The Thames itself wriggled through London in elongated S shapes; so, despite their speed, sometimes their progress was almost thwarted when the water channel double-backed on itself as it did now at the Isle of Dogs with its mass of warehouses and the glittering pools of the West India Docks. The blackout extended even out here. Some power that Ben couldn't begin to comprehend had strangled London of her electricity supply. When Ben glanced back again to watch their wake he saw the silhouette of two figures in the doorway to the aft deck. Trajan kept his eyes forward on the night-time river, so he hadn't noticed the intruders. From the bank the stray lights from a vehicle illuminated their faces with a sudden brilliance that made Ben catch his breath.

'April!'

This made Trajan turn his head. 'April, thank God you're alright!'

And yet Ben noticed a change. 'April, what's wrong?'

Somehow her face appeared to blaze with its own inner-light. Her eyes held a flame of ineffable power. The smile on her face held his own gaze. She was the picture of warmth, joy and tenderness. At that moment he couldn't see past that to notice the sticky spikes of her hair, or the fact her dress had become little more than a filthy rag that clung to her body. Dimly, he was aware that a hole had been torn at the waist to reveal an area of naked flesh the size of his open hand. The wounds caused by teeth that had violated her skin. At that moment the negative aspects of her appearance were obliterated by her uncanny beauty. He saw himself grasping her, and hugging her, while he released all those secret feelings he harboured. The urge became overwhelming. He could put his arms round her and confess everything. How much she meant to him. Leave Trajan. He, Ben Ashton, would prove he loved her.

'Trajan,' she called. 'Something marvelous has happened to me. I need Ben to tell the world about it.'

The second figure shook his head. 'First we must go back to the island. Then we can talk.'

'No, Trajan, please turn the boat round!'

'First, the island,' he insisted. 'Once we've regained control of ourselves, then we can discuss this.'

185

Trajan was torn between looking ahead as he piloted the boat and wanting to look back at April. 'What happened to you, April? Have you been hurt?'

'No, something wonderful happened, Trajan. Oh, God, please let me share it with you. It's New-Life. It is going to change the world. Stop the boat. We can talk about it right now.'

A third figure slipped like a ghost into the pilothouse. Ben recognized the slim figure of Elmo Kigoma. 'Gentlemen, these are vampires. You must take care.'

April looked hurt. 'Why do you say we're vampires? That's not true! Ben, look at me. See how healthy I am.'

Elmo said, 'They possess self-control at the moment. It won't last. As soon as they become hungry they'll become dangerous.'

'That's rubbish.' April's eyes flashed. 'We wouldn't harm you!'

The stranger spoke. 'The man's right. Our only hope is to return to the island. I could control this thing there. We weren't crazy.' The man's gold-tipped teeth glinted as he spoke. 'I can show you where it is. It's down in the estuary, opposite one of the big oil refineries. Look for a low-lying mound toward the south shore; there's a mass of willows and a ruined house. It's the only building on the island.'

'Don't listen to him, Trajan. Yes, we went through a rough time at first. But we know what to do now. We can control this thing.'

'Yes! By feeding on people, wringing every last drop of blood from their bodies!' The stranger became agitated. 'This man understands us.' He nodded toward Elmo. 'I can tell from his face. He's seen our kind before.'

'You must do what you can to remain calm,' Elmo told him. 'What's your name?'

'I'm Carter Vaughn. This is April Connor.'

'We know her,' Ben said.

Elmo continued. 'Carter Vaughn. You have a name and identity. Remember it. Strive to hold on to your memories. What's your mother's name?'

Carter had become edgy. 'Why's that important?'

'Your memory belongs to you. It is the anchor of your personality. Can you remember your mother's name?'

186

'Yes, of course, it's . . .' He bit his lip as his eyes roved the ceiling of the pilothouse as if he'd find it written there. Meanwhile, Ben noticed that April's smile had widened into a leer; her eyes fixed on him with a fiery intensity.

'April,' Ben said. 'Do you remember your mother's name?'

'Ben. You're the most brilliant writer in the world. Write my story for the newspapers. You know people in television, too. They can make a film about what happened to us. We discovered New-Life. It's going to change the world. Nobody will be ill again. And it fills you with such . . .' She took a deep breath that seemed to sizzle with sheer eroticism. 'It fills you with such happiness.'

'The island,' Carter grunted. 'Take us back there.'

'I'm trying,' Trajan answered. 'But the estuary's vast. You've got to help me.'

'I will, sir. I will, sir.' Carter began to perspire. 'If I can, I will.' He closed his eyes for a second. When he opened them he gasped, 'My mother's name is Pearl. Pearl Vaughn, aged fifty-two. Lives in Lambert Road. Takes medication for blood pressure. Likes to watch . . . likes to watch . . .' His eyes rolled before he took another breath to steady himself. 'Watches documentaries about ancient history. Works as a cleaner in a school, but she loves programs about ancient civilizations . . .'

'Carter?'

Elmo held up his hand. 'Trajan, let Carter speak. If he's remembering he's keeping a hold on his rational mind.'

'Ancient cities,' Carter murmured. 'She knew that the Romans built the first London. Roman galleys sailed the Thames. Centurions, legionnaires. My mother's name is Pearl. She told me to be proud of my colour. We aren't strangers in a foreign town because London was founded by Romans from Italy. And people from all over the world built the rest of it. She said if you took everything contributed by the Poles, French, Russians, Chinese, Africans, West Indians; the Huguenot, Hindu, Muslim and Jew; if you could magic everything away that they gave to London you'd have nothing but a swamp again. No city, no—'

'Shut up!' April slashed one arm at Carter, knocking him down as if he'd been nothing more substantial than a reed.

187

'Turn the boat around. This is a miracle! Don't throw it away! The world is dying; it needs a second chance!'

'Don't listen to her!' Elmo Kigoma held out his hands. 'What she's talking about is infecting everyone with the curse. She wants everyone to become a vampire.'

She lunged forward, trying to claw her way to the controls. Elmo gripped her in his wiry arms. 'Listen, child. I know you still have some humanity inside of you. Fight this thing.'

'No, this is New-Life. Don't you people understand? This is the good news that the world has been waiting for. This is the end of death.' She pushed forward until she could grab Trajan's arm. 'Listen to me. Turn around. Bring scientists and doctors, I'll make them understand!' With a formidable strength she shoved Trajan aside despite Elmo's best attempts to hold her. Trajan immediately lost control of the boat, causing it to swing violently to one side. It seemed at that moment it would capsize.

'Keep her back!' Trajan fought for the wheel.

Carter sprang to his feet. With both hands he gripped April's wrist and pulled it back.

Elmo turned to April. 'Child, come with me. You can talk to me about the miracle. Just leave Trajan to steer the boat.' He spoke soothingly. 'Tell me what happened to you. I am interested, believe me. No, don't hurt Trajan. Please try to remain calm.'

Carter and Elmo managed to move her a couple of paces back from Trajan at the wheel. Without having to kill the speed he quickly got the boat under control.

By now Elmo and Carter held April between them by her arms. As her chest rose and fell from the exertion of the struggle her eyes fixed on Ben with such an expression of longing his heart began to pound.

'What is it?' Elmo asked her. 'Do you want to tell me what happened to you?'

She shook her head.

'What, then?'

'Hungry,' she hissed. 'I need it.' She groaned. 'Carter, it's starting again. I'm hurting. Please get me some food.'

Carter renewed his grip on her as she began to struggle. 'It's taken hold of her; she won't be able to control herself now.'

'What's wrong with her?' Ben asked.

Carter shot him a grim look. 'She wants your blood. She longs to fill her belly with it.' He grimaced. 'And so do I.'

The throb of motors seemed over-powering in the confines of the pilothouse. Ben saw how Carter's eyes gleamed as his lips drew back to expose the teeth with the gold tips. In the river water, heads broke the surface. From the banks men and women slithered down the mud into the Thames with the menace of crocodiles in pursuit of prey. Vampires gathering for the kill.

'Remember who you are,' Elmo urged. 'Carter Vaughn. What is your profession?'

Carter's eyes clouded, dampening the fires that blazed there. 'I'm . . . a community worker.'

'You save people?'

'Rehabilitation. Addicts. Young offenders.' He took a deep breath as his eyes focused. 'Oh, God.'

'You're back with us,' Ben told him. 'Now stay with us!'

'Ben's right,' Trajan called back from the wheel. 'We need you to get us to the island.'

Carter shook his head. 'I won't be able to hold it together much longer.' He grunted. 'I'm feeling it, too. It's more than hunger, it burns. You feel as if you're on fire.'

April struggled. 'Carter, I've got to eat. Let me eat for pity's sake.' Her words rose into a scream. 'I can't stand this pain. It's killing me. Let go of me!'

Carter maintained his grip on her arm. 'April, listen to me. There's been no miracle. This New-Life that seemed so important to us – it's an illusion. We're not superhuman; we're monsters. Don't you understand?'

'You bastard! Let go of me!'

'We're monsters, nothing but disgusting monsters. We only make ourselves feel good by destroying other people's lives. This man is right. We are vampires. We need human blood to make us well again.'

'Give me . . .' She grunted. 'Give me some . . .' She fixed Ben with that incandescent glare of hers. 'C'mere, Ben . . . c'mere. You'll kiss me, won't you?'

By now Elmo and Carter had to struggle to prevent her breaking free. As well as grasping the writhing woman, Carter struggled with himself. His expression fluctuated between

189

concern and a greedy leer. And yet through sheer will power Carter maintained his self-control. 'You've got to move this boat faster. I'm hungry now . . . all I can think about is . . .' He gritted his teeth.

'We need you to show us the way,' Trajan told him. 'You're not like the others. You know who you are and what you're doing.'

Sweat beaded on Carter's forehead. 'Believe me, it won't last. It's like holding on to a rope that's covered in grease. I'm trying hard but it's running away through my fingers. I can feel it . . . uh . . . it's starting to hurt.'

Elmo called out, 'We can't hold them both. Ben, help me get April into the next cabin. We'll lock her in there.'

'What about Carter?'

'I'll help as long as I can,' Carter replied. 'Only I can't promise you'll be safe. I might hurt you . . . I won't be able to stop myself. I don't want to but . . .' He licked his lips. 'When this starts . . . It's like acid in your veins. You burn so much you . . . uh . . . eat . . . it's blood you want. All that red . . . I can taste it. I want—'

'Hurry, Ben. Take hold of April's arm. Carter, stay here. Keep repeating your name, your mother's name, anything that reminds you of your identity.' Elmo nodded to Ben, indicating he should take April's arm. It had begun to flail. 'Now isn't the time to be gentle. Hurry!'

April lunged toward Ben. Just an inch from the bare skin of his face he heard her teeth snap shut as she tried to bite him. The air from her lungs was the same as when you open an oven door; the heat scorched him, making him flinch.

'Hold on tight,' Elmo warned.

Carter howled. 'Hurry. I can't hold on much longer!'

A step led down to the door of the salon. As the boat bucked over waves Ben and Elmo bundled April through the door. She cursed them as she tried to struggle free. 'I'm going to hurt you,' she screamed. 'If you don't let go of me, you'll wish you'd never been born!'

'If we let go of you,' Elmo said, 'that's when we *will* regret being born.' Then to Ben, 'Lock the doors to the deck and put the key in your pocket.'

As Ben ran across the heaving floor Elmo forced April down until she lay on a sofa. Even so, she tried to turn her head back to bite his forearms. When the doors were locked Elmo nodded at the door to the pilothouse. 'Take the key from that door . . . no, don't go yet. See how those curtains are tied back? Take two of the velvet cords with you. Good . . . in a moment I will release April. Be ready to close the door after me when I come through. Understand?'

Ben grabbed the plush velvet tie-backs from the curtains, then when he reached the door he shouted, 'Okay, ready when you are!'

Elmo moved like a cat. In seconds he was through the door to the pilothouse. Ben slammed the door shut after him, turned the key. A second after that April's face slammed against the glass in the door. He saw how the eye pressed there to glare her fury at them as she pounded the panel with her fists.

'Toughened glass,' Trajan told them. 'It'll hold.'

'Hurry.' Carter's voice was a howl of agony now. 'I can't hold on. I can feel it slipping away . . . *me* slipping away. Something else is taking over. Uh . . .'

Elmo took one of the velvet cords from Ben. 'Carter. Listen to me. I'm going to restrain you with this. It's for our safety. Do you understand?'

'Yes.' He grunted the word through clenched teeth. 'Do it . . . C'mon, faster!'

Trajan coaxed the man. 'Keep it together, buddy. We need you now. You've got to take us to the island.'

'I'm trying . . .' Carter panted. 'God knows . . .'

'Remember who you are,' Elmo said as he tied the cord around his wrist. 'Know your name. Think about your days at school. Who were your best friends?'

'Mathew . . . Josh . . . his family had dogs, lots of dogs . . .'

As Carter grunted the mantra of past friends, Elmo worked fast. At either side of the doorway, which opened on to the rear deck, were cleats that fastened lines to where a sun awning would be extended to provide shade on hot days. Elmo tied one of Carter's arms to the right cleat, then the other arm to the left. Within moments the vampire was held there in the open doorway in a crucifixion pose, arms stretched out by the cords. Behind him was the aft deck with the wake stretching out behind the boat.

Odysseus tied to the mast, Ben thought. Only instead of Sirens trying to entice him it's the blood in our veins.

He glanced back at the door to the salon. April still gnashed her teeth while she slammed her fists at the glass panels. Smears appeared there as she broke the skin across her knuckles. She didn't feel a thing. All that mattered to her now was hunger.

'We must be close,' Trajan shouted as he scanned the way in front of them.

For the first time in what must be thirty minutes Ben looked out at the moonlit scene. The banks of the river had receded into the distance now. The boat bucked across waves that had more in common with those of the ocean than inland waters. Then again the Thames this far downstream had the appearance of open sea. Vehicle lights on dry land appeared to be a vast distance away. A wave exploded against the prow in a surge of spray; the nose lifted before smacking down to the surface again.

'I'm not slowing down,' Trajan shouted over the engines' roar. 'She's just going to have to take the punishment.' Then he glanced at Carter. The man's eyes rolled in his head as he stood there as if nailed to a cross. 'Carter. Can you give me any help?'

'Only if you can give me some of your blood.' His face took on the aspect of a drunken leer. 'Just a bit . . . just a taste.'

Elmo shook him by the arm. 'The island. Do you know if we're close?'

Carter aimed a bite at the man's hand. Only Elmo saw it coming and withdrew quickly.

Ben spoke softly. 'Carter. We need you. Hang on. Can you see it yet?'

With an effort he forced himself to look through the windows. After a struggle he managed to whisper. 'You're too far away from the south shore. Get closer. When you can see the big oil refinery you're close.' A moment later that look of hunger roared back into his eyes again. 'Give me just a little to keep me going . . . just a taste.'

Trajan leaned forward. 'I can see the vapour burn-off.'

'There's more than one refinery in the estuary,' Ben told him.

'We've no choice. We're going to have to search this stretch of river first.'

As April pounded the door and Carter lunged against the

192

restraining cords, trying to snap at them like some rabid dog, Trajan powered the vessel toward the oily flame rising into the sky.

Thirty-Two

April Connor howled her rage at the locked door. *How can they do this to me? Don't they know what I've discovered? This miracle will change everyone's life! I've brought them the promise of heaven on earth!* And with those thoughts came a hunger that seared every atom of her being. *Why did the old man talk about vampires? His accusation's disgusting. I'm not a vampire. I'm New-Life. A miracle of evolution.*

She pounded at the glass panels. 'I want to help the world! I'm going to make it a better place! I know the secret!'

Beyond the unbreakable glass Ben stood with his back to the cabin wall. He stared at her as if she howled incomprehensible gibberish at him. But to her the words had a beautiful clarity. So why couldn't he understand?

'Ben, let me out. I'm not talking about cannibalism. This can be measured in a rational way. All we need do is calculate how much blood we can share between us. If you ingest human blood it empowers you. Blood is the elixir of life. Ben, you have to bring scientists and doctors together to debate this. We need to share the good news through you; you're my key to the media.' Her voice was clear, lucid, as bright as a newly cast bell. She had become a prophet for New-Life.

As the boat sped toward the south shore Ben found he couldn't take his eyes from April. Her eyes bulged as she screamed. Although she seemed to be making some effort to frame words not so much as one syllable was understandable. At that moment, he didn't see her as April Connor, the woman he'd privately cherished for months. Instead, he saw a monster that raged and howled for human blood. Elmo Kigoma had described her as a vampire. That's exactly what she was.

Meanwhile, Carter Vaughn writhed as the ropes held his arms out by his sides. There was an expression close to martyrdom on his face as he panted out directions. 'Not so close to the bank. About a mile off shore. A low island . . . covered in willow.' He fought against the craving that wracked his body; a losing battle for sure.

Elmo caught Ben's eye. 'It won't be long now. But there's a new crisis coming. You will have to make decisions that will affect more lives than yours.'

Meanwhile, April's wordless screech attained a banshee intensity.

With her bare feet April kicked at the locked door. Why on earth couldn't she make Ben understand what she said? He merely stared at her with a mixture of bafflement and disgust. What had gone so wrong with him to make him look at her like that?

The hunger blazed through her. More than once she found herself rolling on the floor in agony. Dear God, if only she could eat; if she could fill this searing void inside her body she'd be able to think clearly again. Desperately, she tried to hang on to her vision of helping humanity. Again and again she tried to visualize herself sitting beside Ben at the computer as they worked on her extraordinary story together. The miracle of how a vicious attack evolved into the most wonderful discovery of modern times.

For a moment she mouthed her story as if dictating to Ben. 'I was walking beside the River Thames with my fiancé when we were attacked. Who was our attacker? Oh, just some thug. It's what happened after that's important. I was washed up on an island that must possess miraculous properties . . .' *But it wasn't like that was it, April? The change didn't begin with your arrival on the island. The man who attacked you tore open your dress. Then he bit through the skin on your waist . . .*

She opened her eyes. Somehow she'd stumbled on to bare boards. In surprise she looked round. Above her, the moon shone as bright as a blow torch. The wind blew her hair. She saw a window to the salon was open wide. *My God, I climbed through it without realizing. I'd been thinking about what happened to me. The man who bit me sucked blood from me into his body then regurgitated it into the wound.*

The image came with shocking suddenness. She scrambled on to her feet then stood there on deck, clinging to the rail that ran along the flank of the boat. Open water stretched into the distance. And constantly the moon that was brighter than the sun blasted its silver light down on the world. She tried to think about her mission to make the planet a better place. But her entire mind, body and soul focused on one thing. *Hunger.* It burned inside of her. The hunger began to consume her own flesh from within. If she didn't eat soon she would die. And when she did picture food she imagined a vast wound in a living body that pumped an endless stream of crimson into her mouth.

With her last grasp on sanity gone she raced to the stern of the boat. Carter had been strung across the doorway with his wrists tied to the frame. His head rolled from side-to-side as he howled with hunger. Beyond Carter were three living vessels filled to the brim with pure nourishment. Saliva ran from her lips as she pushed by Carter into the little pilothouse where Trajan steered the boat. With a howl of glee at having so much food for herself she leapt on the three men.

Elmo Kigoma warded off the bite directed at Ben. April's teeth crunched through Elmo's skin on the back of his hand, ripping away a shred to expose raw flesh beneath. Ben pushed her back by the shoulders as she sucked the scrap of skin into her mouth to squeeze the traces of blood out on to her tongue. Her howl gave way to a moan of pleasure.

Even though the pain of the bite must have been considerable Elmo Kigoma merely grimaced. 'You've got to hold her, Ben. Don't let her bite you.'

Ben tried but her strength was uncanny. She pushed him back so hard he cannoned into Trajan. In turn, Trajan bounced against the craft's wheel; then he fell back to the floor clutching his chest. Ben struggled to keep the boat on course with one hand, while holding back April who fought him like a wild animal. Her entire body became a blurred flurry of movement. Her mouth darted at his face. Behind her, Elmo had hold of her hair, impeding her but not stopping her. And,

195

behind the old African, Carter had succumbed to his vampire nature. He struggled against his bonds. If he should break free . . .

Trajan had been badly winded. Between gasps he shouted, 'Ben! I saw the island . . . directly in front of the boat . . . try and hold a course toward it . . .'

'I can't do both!' He meant he couldn't steer as well as hold back this raging typhoon of a creature, even with Elmo's help. Nevertheless, he glanced out through the window and saw a moonlit island to his right. Little more than a few acres in the vastness of the Thames estuary, it appeared alive with willow trees that shifted restlessly in the breeze as if they anticipated dangerous times ahead.

Fingernails raked his cheek forcing him to exert more strength to try and push April away from him. The vampire's strength was formidable. He couldn't hold her back much longer. How close were they to the island? It couldn't be far now. He risked a glance back. From the willows that formed a swarming mass of shadows he glimpsed the roof of a house.

'Carter,' he called, 'is that the island?'

Carter howled, 'Let me go!' His eyes rolled as saliva trickled from the corner of his mouth. The velvet cords had begun to fray. How long before they snapped? The pair of vampires would tear the mortal men apart in seconds.

As April opened her mouth and jutted her face forward an object slipped between them. Ben realized that Elmo had managed to remove his belt and had dragged the leather strap into April's mouth like a bridle. Insanely, eyes blazing, she tried to gnaw through it. Elmo tugged her back with the looped belt.

Trajan struggled to his feet. 'Knock off the power!' he directed. 'You're heading straight for it!'

Ben turned away from Elmo battling with the crazed woman to see the island directly in front of him. One moment the boat skimmed across the water, plumes of spray jetting up into the air, the next a series of collisions threw Ben back against the wall. Beneath the keel came a deafening scraping sound. When he managed to look out of the window again he saw the mass of trees. Then there came a tremendous jolt. Instead of water being hurled up by the prow suddenly there was a geyser of yellow material that could only be sand. The nose of the boat flipped up until it seemed as if the boat stood on its stern then it crashed back down on to solid ground.

Thirty-Three

The silence following after the boat crashed ashore was profound; for Ben it possessed a menacing resonance all of its own. Even April and Carter were stunned by the impact. At the third attempt Ben managed to scramble to his feet. Beyond the windows lay a beach of sand that was a mixture of greys and yellows in the moonlight. Willow trees formed black, beastlike shapes at this time of night. As the breeze passed through them they wriggled as if they were primeval animals that shook their backs as they began to wake.

In the doorway, Carter struggled to break the velvet cords that held his arms out straight in that crucifixion pose. His jaws worked as if he tried to chew lumps out of the very air around him. He'd lost all self-control now; his eyes had become two fiery orbs of pure insanity. Ben turned his attention to April who'd fallen to her knees. Elmo Kigoma still managed to keep the leather belt in her mouth so it held her jaws apart. Trajan had recovered enough to help restrain her threshing limbs. Even so, the men were weakening. Exhaustion obliterated all expression on their faces. Soon April would break free.

Ben pulled a penknife from his pocket. 'Hold her still!'

Trajan recoiled in shock. 'No, Ben. We can hold her.'

'You can't.' He eased out the small blade that was sharp as a razor.

Trajan's stared at the glittering blade. 'What are you going to do?'

'Give her what she wants.'

Trajan turned to Elmo as if expecting the man to stop Ben.

197

Instead, he merely refreshed his grip on that sticky hair of April's in order to hold her head still. Ben turned his arm so he could choose a place on his bare forearm. Do it quickly, he told himself, before you change your mind.

Human skin is tougher than it looks. He pressed the edge of the blade into his arm as firmly as he could. Then he made a sawing motion. The keen steel edge generated a prickling sensation as if a dozen needles had been forced into his flesh. At last the mouth of the wound opened to release a rush of blood.

'Don't go too deep,' Elmo told him. 'That's enough.'

'Hold her tight.' Ben moved to where they held April in the kneeling position in the centre of the cabin. By now she'd stopped struggling. Her eyes had become vast shining disks as she stared at the blood running from the inch long cut. Ben stood so that his arm was directly above her.

'Don't let go of her, but take away the belt.'

When the belt was removed she tried to rise to her feet. With a supreme effort Trajan and Elmo managed to keep her kneeling. As the blood coursed down Ben's forearm in a thick rivulet of crimson he allowed his arm to dangle so his fingertips hung just inches above her face. The bloody tide sped down his wrist then followed the line of his extended fingers. A moment later his life-blood trickled from his fingertips as she opened her mouth wide to receive the nourishment. Ben could tell she wanted to clamp her mouth to the wound but the men held her down to prevent her drawing off more than he could safely give her.

In the doorway, Carter howled with envy as he watched the woman feed.

'Just permit her enough so she regains her sanity,' Elmo told him. 'Don't give so much you become ill yourself.'

With gasps of ecstasy April caught the ruby drops in her mouth. When she had close on a mouthful she swallowed with such an expression of gratitude. The contorted face relaxed into a smile of bliss. With the second mouthful her body became almost limp. Hunger yielded to satisfaction.

'That's enough, Ben,' Trajan said.

'Please,' April begged. 'Just another mouthful.'

'Ben, no.'

With an effort Ben remained standing. 'I need to give her just enough to stop the craving. We need her to be able to function.' Then he added grimly, 'It's either this or she'll take what she needs from us anyway.'

With her face upturned her mouth became a cup that soon filled to the brim with what could have been a dark, red wine. This time when she closed her lips to swallow Ben moved back and clamped his hand over the wound.

'April? Do you understand me?' Elmo gently shook her by the arm. 'We're going to let go now. You know you mustn't attack us.'

She sighed. 'I'm fine. I won't hurt you.' Even so, her glance at Ben's bloody hand was one of infinite regret. How she craved to lick his fingers clean.

Trajan released his hold on April with a grunt as he rubbed his aching shoulder. 'Ben,' he said, 'there's a first aid kit on the shelf behind you. Bandage the wound before you do anything else. Oh, one more thing. I need your knife.'

Ben gave him a quizzical look.

Trajan nodded at the man who raged against his bonds. 'Carter needs some, too.'

As Ben handed Trajan the knife, April looked out of the pilothouse window. 'Be quick,' she warned. 'They're starting to come out of the water.'

Trajan and Ben emerged on deck, each with a bandage around their forearms. Elmo, Carter and April followed. For now the two vampires were functioning as human beings. Although Ben saw that the blood they'd drunk had failed to give them complete satiety. Their eyes still flashed with hunger. The little blood that the two humans had been able to spare wouldn't keep these creatures satisfied for long.

The boat had hit ground at low tide. Although the vessel leaned at an angle and most of the paint had been stripped away by its abrasive contact with the beach, at least it was intact. A mile or so across the moonlit water Ben could make out the oil refinery on the mainland. Yellow flames rose from the chimneys that burnt off excess vapours. As for the island, it didn't extend much more than a few acres. Most of it appeared to be covered by willow trees that rustled and shook; a herd of monstrous beasts that scented the arrival of fresh prey. Ben's imagination had reached a point where everything had become laced with danger.

199

'April's right,' Trajan agreed. 'Here they come.'

Emerging from the night-time river were dozens of crawling figures. While they'd been in the water the description Vampire Sharkz was apt. But now that they dragged themselves across the shore on their bellies, they adopted the same ominous manner as alligators. Their legs were limp as they pulled themselves forward with their arms. Most wore the remnants of clothes but a few were completely naked; their clothes had simply decayed from them. One factor they all shared was the way their heads were raised so they could watch the human beings on the boat with predatory eyes.

'One thing's for sure,' Ben said. 'We can't stay here.'

Trajan turned to Carter. 'How do you feel?'

'I can't thank you enough. My mind's clear again. You don't know what it's like when the hunger hits.'

'You said that when you were on the island you could maintain control of yourself. How?'

'We drank from the salt pools on the beach,' April said. 'After the estuary water began to evaporate the mineral content and salinity must have made it resemble blood. Certainly close enough to keep ourselves under control.'

Ben glanced at the things emerging from the river; one by one they rose slowly to their feet. 'Why are those things different to you? They've become mindless eating machines.'

'I found that drinking from the salt pools took the edge off the craving,' Carter said. 'It must have been a crucial state of transition from human to . . .' He shrugged. 'Whatever we are now. I think they were damaged through lack of food. They became mindless monsters – Berserkers, I call them. April and me escaped the worst of it.'

'Will it work again?' Trajan asked. 'If you drink the water from the pools?'

'It might.' April didn't sound hopeful.

'And it was only a short-fix,' Carter added.

Elmo spoke. 'We must find a permanent cure for their condition.'

'How?'

Elmo's hooded eyes regarded the creatures advancing up the shore toward them. 'The answer is here on this island.'

Ben gripped Elmo's arm. 'Tell us what it is.'

'That's just it. I don't know. It's for you to find out. I'm not being deliberately obstructive but you, Ben, must enter that Sea of Thought.'

'You can't be serious. You mean it's down to me to find the solution?'

'Yes.'

April tugged Trajan's sleeve. 'You can't stay here. They'll kill you.'

'Worse,' Carter grunted. 'If they catch you, you'll become one of them.'

In the moonlight, the figures appeared as silhouettes as the last ones rose from the sands to their feet. From each shadowy form a pair of eyes shone like splinters of glass. A baleful hunger blazed there.

'Come on.' Carter dropped from the deck on to the shore. 'It's you three they want. And April and me aren't safe, either. Those things will tear anything apart if they think there's even a drop of blood inside.'

The group ran across the sand toward the willows. At least Carter knew the way; in seconds he'd found a path that led through the thicket of trees.

Ben thought furiously. *What did Elmo mean? Why must it be me who finds the cure for April's condition? Where do I begin to look? There are only trees here.*

Then a revelation struck him. He caught the African by the elbow. 'Elmo,' he panted. 'You knew something like this would happen, didn't you?'

'I've been warning of the dangers that humanity faces all my life.'

'No, it's more than that. When we first met, when you were still in that boat, you knew I'd be confronted with this, didn't you?'

A breeze whispered through the branches. Above them, the moon beamed its light on to Elmo's face as his gaze met Ben's. 'I saw something,' he agreed. 'Destiny. Fate. Inevitability. Whatever the description you apply, I saw in my mind's eye.' He touched his temple. 'You were to fight in a great battle. The city of London depends on you. You are its protecting warrior.'

'No. You can't expect that from me. What the hell do I know about fighting those monsters?'

'Nevertheless . . .'

'You've picked the wrong man.'

'The gods of my village and my ancestors think differently.'

'You're mistaken. Do you know what I do for a living?' Ben's voice rose in anger. 'I write articles for a magazine. Frivolous bits of text that editors use to fill the spaces between advertisements. I'm no more a warrior than any other guy who sits at a computer from nine till five!'

The others continued through the trees. Carter paused to call back. 'Come on. It's too dangerous to stay here.'

That was the moment when a figure leapt out of the bushes on to Carter's back. The vampire launched its frenzied attack; its mouth open wide as it tried to rip Carter's face from his head. Ben darted forward. He saw what would once have been a woman of around thirty. She wore the remains of a tight red dress. Her eyes blazed down at Carter with sheer ferocity as she struggled to sink her teeth into him.

When Ben reached the pair he didn't stop running. He leapt as if jumping into a swimming pool with legs outstretched, his feet in front of him. It knocked the woman backwards into the undergrowth. With a roar of frustration she sprang to her feet. Even though Ben's footprint revealed itself on the bare skin of her upper chest she wasn't fazed; didn't even show any sign of hurt. Her jaws opened again in readiness for biting whatever flesh came close. The mad light in her eyes increased its intensity. A Berserker. Carter's name for this breed of vampire said it all. This ferocious creature is berserk through and through and through . . .

Carter wouldn't be on his feet fast enough to outrun the creature, so Ben searched the ground for something he could use as a weapon. The only thing that came close was a fallen tree branch that was nearly as long as he was tall. In a second he'd scooped it up as the vampire launched itself from the ground in a muscular leap. As it flew at Carter, its jaws wide, Ben drove the end of the branch into that gaping mouth. The branch was as thick as a wrist, yet he aimed it with such accuracy it passed between the creature's teeth to slam into the back of its throat. With all his strength he followed the attack through by pushing so hard that the creature fell backwards. He didn't let up the pressure. He positioned himself so he rammed the branch down with enough force into the vampire's

202

mouth to stop it from rising. There it lay on its back; the end of the branch filled its mouth. The Berserker erupted into nothing less than a maelstrom of furies: it writhed, bare legs kicked, arms reached up to try and claw at his hands as they gripped the branch, and all the time it roared out its rage at him.

Damn, the thing was strong. Even from that position, with Ben bearing down on the tree limb with all his body weight, the monster lifted its head from the earth. Its upper lip curled back as it sank its teeth into the dry wood. Another moment and it would break free. His heart pounded in his chest as perspiration blurred his eyes.

Then Carter was at his side. The man gripped the branch and helped force the Berserker back down to earth.

Ben panted, 'Give it everything you've got! One, two, three – push!'

Together they exerted as much force as they could. The branch creaked as the downward pressure grew. The creature that had once been a woman choked in agony as the blunt end of the branch broke the flesh at the back of its throat, then sank through the muscle to burst through the skull at the back.

'It's still alive!' Ben shouted. 'Keep pushing!'

They continued to force the branch through the mouth, through the back of the head, and into the soil. They only stopped when it couldn't penetrate the ground any deeper. But by then it must have embedded itself more than two feet deep. Now the vampire was effectively pinned to the earth. Even though it was still alive – kicking its legs, flailing its arms, jerking its hips – it couldn't rise.

'Good work, Carter,' Ben said as he patted the man on the back.

Man? This thing is a vampire. In another ten minutes that wild look might return to its eye and it'll try and kill me.

At that moment, however, Carter grinned back. The gold tips of his teeth shone in the moonlight. 'Come on, Ben, this place will soon be swarming with those things.'

When they rejoined the others they quickly made their way through the trees in the direction of a ruined house.

Elmo ran alongside Ben. 'I saw what you did to the vampire.'

'It wasn't pretty. But needs must.'

'You told me you were no warrior, Ben Ashton. Are you still so certain?'

Thirty-Four

They ran toward a house that had been abandoned years ago. The garden had merged with the forest. In the chaotic growth that had once been the front lawn were the remains of lobster pots and a rowing boat. The door of the house gaped open with all the grim promise of an entrance to a tomb. Ben's mind whirled. Clearly Elmo Kigoma expected a mighty deed from him, and to fight evil just as Elmo's warrior ancestors had done. Ben still didn't know how. Okay, so he'd managed to pin down one of the vampires using a tree branch. But there were dozens of the creatures – those Berserkers – swarming all over the island. He couldn't stake down every single one of them, could he? So how was he expected to save not only their lives but the entire population of London?

As they raced through a tunnel of greenery toward the door of the house Carter called back, 'Inside there are men and women. They won't harm you.' At the door he paused to beckon them through. 'Hurry! They're here!'

Ben glanced back. Pale shapes swam through the shadows with all the menace of hungry sharks. The vampires moved so smoothly and so rapidly it reinforced the notion that those creatures somehow glided through the night air rather than ran. But that illusion of grace soon evaporated when a pair of creature burst through the undergrowth in an explosion of leaves.

For a moment the group stood gasping for breath in the hallway as Carter slammed the broken door shut in the vampires' faces. 'Help me!'

All four ran to the door to hold it shut as a barrage of fists pounded at the timbers. Then the Berserkers began to push. Hinges creaked. A panel split with the sound of a pistol shot.

Elmo said desperately, 'We need to barricade the entrance.'

'It won't give you long,' Carter shouted above the hammering. 'They'll find a way in!'

April cried, 'The downstairs windows are boarded. They'll hold for a while!'

'Keep holding the door closed,' Carter told them. 'I'll bring whatever I can to build the barricade.' Moments later he hauled a dresser from the kitchen. It was little more than a wreck that sprouted blobs of orange fungi but as a piece of furniture it was a heavyweight. With April's help he tipped it against the door. 'That's the best we've got.'

Trajan pointed. 'They're inside the house!'

Ben saw the figures of men and women standing on the staircase.

'Those are Misfires,' April explained.

'Misfires?'

'The ones that never made the change from human to vampire completely. Don't worry, they're harmless.' That's when the revelation struck. Her eyes widened in horror. 'Not like me. Trajan, I'm one of those monsters, aren't I?' She gulped and a frantic searching expression came into her eyes. 'Oh, my God. I've done terrible things. I've attacked people and drank their blood. The worst thing is I know I'm going to do it again.' She clenched her fists. 'And soon. I can feel the hunger. Trajan, you can't be near me when it comes over me. I'll hurt you.'

Ben watched Trajan smile fondly at her as he lightly stroked her cheek. 'We're fighting this together now. I'm not going to give up on you.'

That hungry, searching expression faded as she smiled back at him. The tenderness in her smile sank a knife into Ben's soul. That secret hope of being with April as a couple shriveled in on itself and died.

Ben glanced at Elmo. The old man's dark, soulful eyes met his. Elmo knew what had just gone through Ben's mind. And the rhythm of the pounding on the door quickened. The vampires wanted in. They were hungry. They wanted blood. Craved blood. It energized them with this berserk power; an

205

incredible strength that would allow them to claw through solid stone given time. From the back of the house more fists beat the boards covering the windows.

Carter had become edgy. His appetite was returning, too. Nevertheless, he took a deep breath and said, 'We should think about retreating upstairs.'

He indicated the way up the staircase with its strange, immobile cargo of those things he termed Misfires. Ben appreciated the description. With all the clamouring outside the Misfires hadn't moved; they didn't even appear to notice that the house had new occupants. Four men and three women stood on the steps where they faced the front door. They could have been a still from a film. Their skin possessed a bluish tint, their hair glistened with the same sticky substance as April's. Little more than scraps of mildewed cloth, all that remained of their clothes, hung from those motionless bodies. A spider had even spun a web from the ear of a young woman to her shoulder. Ben avoided touching the sentinels as he passed by them to the upper floor. Their faces could have been cast from resin. A total absence of expression. Eyes part open, apparently seeing nothing. Once he reached the upper landing he followed the others into what had been a bedroom. There, lank shreds of wallpaper hung from the walls, while five women and a man in a business suit guarded nothing in particular. Again that statue-like immobility. Carter peered out through a gap in the planks that had been nailed across the window. Ben joined him. Outside, in the moonlight, vampires surged through the trees to join the other creatures that were now tugging at the boards on the windows downstairs. The pounding on the door became faster. A dark heartbeat that seemed to be propelling the entire world toward a crisis of nightmarish proportions. From down below came a crash.

April raced through the door with the words, 'They're inside!'

'Keep moving higher,' Carter told them.

'What's the point?' Ben roared. 'They're going to get us in the end!'

Elmo's calm eyes regarded him. 'The point is to give you enough time to reach your decision.'

'But *what* decision?'

206

'You're close. I can tell. Remember what I told you about the Sea of Thought?'

'To hell with the Sea of Thought!' But beyond that Ben didn't have time to reply. Carter and April urged them through into the little passageway that led from the stairs to the bedrooms. Carter jumped up to punch open the loft hatch. That done, he lifted himself up into it. Then he reached down to haul up April.

From the direction of the hallway came the clumping of feet. Trajan ran toward the top of the stairs to meet the foe.

Ben was faster. 'I'll hold them back. You stay with April!'

'No, I'm going to—'

'Trajan! Do you love April?'

Ben looked Trajan in the eye as the man nodded. 'I know you do,' Ben told him. 'I wish you didn't honestly love her, but I can see you do.'

'What do you mean?'

'Just get yourself into the attic!'

Trajan relented. He followed Elmo up into the void beneath the roof.

From the top of the stairs Ben could see the vampires tearing up toward them. The creatures swept the Misfires aside as if they were nothing but cardboard cut outs. A bulky figure stood beside Ben; this Misfire wore a bus driver's uniform. Even as the vampires climbed toward him the Misfires didn't flinch. Ben put his hand between the bus driver's shoulder blades and pushed. The thickset figure tumbled downstairs like a falling log. He struck more of the Misfires on the way down until something like a flesh and bone avalanche crashed down the steps sweeping the vampires back down to the ground floor. They howled with frustration. Ben saw how the maniacs raved and bit one another in the melee. Only it would be short lived. Once they'd untangled themselves they'd race up towards their intended victims once more.

Ben knew he had no weapons left to continue the fight there so he ran back along the corridor to the hatchway. From the opening in the ceiling a mass of arms hung down waiting to grab his hands and haul him up to what would be a precarious safe-haven. Probably, only a fleeting one, too. The vampires would soon batter their way in. What was up there to fight them with? Cobwebs and dust?

207

Ben held up his arms. Trajan took one hand; Carter the other. Together they easily hauled him up into the tiny attic. The boards between the rafters were crumbling, which afforded views into the bedrooms below. Even though it was gloomier here Ben saw the way April pressed her hands to her stomach. The hunger pains were building. She wouldn't be able to hold on much longer. As for Carter, he relied on sheer will power to talk rationally. Yet that edginess had crept back into him; his eyes wore a hungry, searching look. Meanwhile, Trajan had shut the trap door; there he crouched on it, no doubt hoping his own body weight would prevent the vampires pushing it open from below. Some hope. Some poor, bloody hope.

Ben moved on his hands and knees with the sloping roof just above his head. Cobwebs dragged against his face, splinters from the rafters dug into his palms.

Beneath him, the vampires invaded the bedrooms. Through tiny holes in the plaster board he watched them attack the Misfires. But as soon as the vampires bit into them they knew there was nothing to satisfy their appetites in those dry veins. In contempt they shoved the immobile figures aside.

Then, as one, the vampires looked up. It didn't matter whether or not they could see the humans in the attic – they *knew* they were there. Ben saw the blaze of insane delight on the monsters' faces. And as one they thrust their hands upward. Instantly their outstretched fingers smashed through the ceiling boards in puffs of white powder. Trajan beckoned April from where he still held the trapdoor closed. She went to him. Although Ben noticed a different expression on her face. She'd reached that unstable borderland between sanity and madness. Soon the hunger would tip her mind over into unreason. But, equally, Ben saw that Trajan understood that. Trajan's love for the woman wouldn't stop him holding her until the end came.

Elmo appeared beside Ben as if he'd simply materialized there. And when he started speaking the vampires' attack became somehow distant, as if Ben and this ancient African visionary had stepped outside of the rules of time and space. At that moment it seemed as if Elmo Kigoma and Ben were sealed in a bubble of peace.

'Ben Ashton,' Elmo said gently. 'A few hours ago I told

208

you that my way of helping you and the people of London was to imagine a debate between my ancestors and my gods. I imagined my grandfather and his forefathers asked my gods to put right the damage Edshu had caused, then to eject Edshu from this world . . .' His soulful brown eyes were hypnotic. 'I explained that I saw my ancestors argue with the gods that the people of London, and of this earth, were sorely tested enough by life itself. It wasn't necessary for Edshu to test them.'

'Yes, I remember. You told me that the gods reacted favorably to what your ancestors said. But . . .'

'But what?' Elmo Kigoma smiled in his wise, caring way.

'But there was a man-made obstruction to the gods agreeing to what was asked.' All of a sudden Ben shivered. 'And I know what that obstruction was.'

'Really?'

'My selfishness. I loved April Connor.'

Movement. Yet slow movement. Some force retarded time's flow. Black mist seeped into the attic. April had opened her mouth. It would happen gradually but soon her teeth would crunch through Trajan's throat.

Ben continued. 'My ego was so strong I refused to accept that she could genuinely love Trajan. But how can my loving April and wanting her to leave Trajan for me cause all this?'

'Remember what I said about you assuming the role of warrior. Isn't a warrior someone who is tested to destruction?'

'You mean I've become the test specimen? Your gods are going to watch how I deal with this attack on us? And on London itself?'

'Why not?'

'But why should your gods from your village thousands of miles away be concerned about what happens here?'

A hand moved through the holes in the ceiling boards to seize Elmo's ankle. April's jaws had almost reached Trajan's throat. A dozen Berserker hands broke through between the rafters. But once more the motion slowed to a stop. This was the universe holding its breath; something, somewhere, had granted a pause in the headlong flow of life and death. A pause that would last only a moment.

Elmo's grave eyes fixed on Ben's. 'Why should my gods be interested in your well-being and that of London? Come,

come, Ben. Deep down you already know. What's crucial here is that *all* gods and *all* ancestors, yours included, still live on in this place my people call the Sea of Thought. These beliefs I hold to be true. What happens now is up to you.'

Ben nodded; icy shivers trickled down his back as he began to understand. 'You told me about visualizing solutions to problems?'

'Yes.'

Ben closed his eyes for a moment. 'If I have been given the role of defending warrior I'm picturing the only thing that's in my power to stop this and to defeat Edshu.'

'What pictures do your imagination paint, Ben?'

'First look down at the vampires. What's happening to them?'

'They are dying.'

Ben gazed down through the holes that had been smashed in the ceiling boards. What had once been ferocious creatures had begun to shrivel. As their flesh fell from their faces they stumbled away. A tall vampire that gripped Trajan by the ankle simply shed its entire muscle structure to reveal a skeleton before it stumbled back to fall to the floor where it shattered.

Ben looked at April. As Trajan hugged her she smiled at him. That expression of hunger had gone. Carter studied his fingers as if seeing some transformation there.

Carter suddenly laughed. 'My God. I feel like *me* again.'

April touched her hair. 'That stickiness has gone.' She laughed, too. 'We're alright.'

In the rooms below all that remained of the vampires was a chaotic jumble of ribcages, skulls, thigh bones and scraps of clothing.

Ben told them, 'The tide's rising. If we don't get back to the boat it'll be carried away and we'll be stranded here.'

They left the house to return through the trees to the shore. The moon still shone down on the willows and the river. Carter loped off ahead of them back to their only means of escape from the island. Ben walked with Elmo some way behind Trajan and April who held hands.

'Elmo, I've some questions,' Ben said.

'Ask away.'

'Have the vampires really gone?'

'Yes.'

'Will Edshu return?'

'Of course.' He smiled. 'But not for a long time yet.'

'April and Carter are well?'

'They are in perfect health.'

'What will happen to me?'

'What will happen to you?' As Elmo echoed the words his smile died. 'What did you see when you visualized the defeat of those creatures?'

'I imagined the destruction of the vampires. And I imagined a happy ending, just like this, where we return to the boat and leave.'

'And what else did you see?'

'I knew it wouldn't be as simple as that. I had to offer more to the gods than simply admitting that I'd never win April away from Trajan.'

Elmo's face became grave. 'You offered yourself in return for our lives?'

Ben felt a stir of anger. 'Isn't that what a warrior is supposed to do?'

'My friend, there might have been another way!'

'I ran the images through my head, and I realized the payment for this miracle was to sacrifice myself.'

'I'm sorry, Ben.'

'Don't be. I offered myself of my own free will. Isn't self-sacrifice the most powerful sacrifice of all?'

They reached the fringe of trees at the edge of the shore. Carter had already climbed on to the boat that was being floated free by the tide.

'Hurry,' Trajan called back to them. 'You've got to be on board before the current catches hold.' In seconds he and April had scrambled on to the deck. In the moonlight they appeared impossibly distant figures.

'You too, Elmo,' Ben told him. 'I guess the propellers were torn off when it came aground but the River Thames has a strong tidal surge. It'll carry you back into the middle of London. You'll be back in time for breakfast.'

'Ben, I'll stay.'

'No. That wasn't part of the deal I made with the guys on the other side. Besides, I must be getting more popular the

211

older I get. I'm the only one they want.' He held out his hand and Elmo shook it. 'Elmo, just one more thing. What will happen to me now?' Before he could answer Ben shook his head. 'Don't tell me. That's for me to find out, right?' He nodded at the boat. 'Time to go, Elmo.'

The ivory vessel had begun to swing out into the flow of the river. Elmo sprinted down the beach as if he was still in the first flush of youth. In moments he'd waded deep enough to swim the few strokes to the boat where the three on board helped him on to the deck. Then Trajan, April and Carter waved to Ben, and shouted for him to join them before the boat drifted away on the flood tide. As Ben watched it glide away he stood in the moonlight with a hand resting against a willow trunk.

The three figures on the boat still waved frantically, while Elmo remained motionless. I'll wave back, Ben told himself as a calmness he'd never known before stole over him. He tried to raise his other hand to wave a farewell. Only it was frozen by his side.

He stayed there without moving until the boat had floated out of sight on the river that reached into London's heart. On the horizon he saw a glow as the city's lights returned.

This is it, he told himself, it's over. Even if they try to come back to me tomorrow I know they'll never find the island again. All along it existed in another time and another place. At that moment, standing beside him, he saw Elmo Kigoma, or some version of him, only one that was more ancient, ethereal, phantom-like, with eyes that were luminous orbs in the light of the moon. And whether the following words came from him, Ben Ashton, or from the African visionary, or even from some universal spirit that dwelt within them both, he could not say.

'*Even though the island will remain for you, along with its trees, the skies, the sun and the moon, it sinks even now back into the Sea of Thought. There it will remain until the next time humanity faces destruction. For now, you are the world's champion, so remain here in peace.*'

There was a spell of silence and darkness, and a sublime tranquility, then he found himself standing as still as a statue in what had been the living room of the old house. Moonlight fell in needle-thin rays through slats in the boarded windows.

The remains of the vampires had vanished. In the room with him, however, were more of his kind – those silent, immobile men and women – standing as if they posed for a portrait by some unseen and unknowable artist. Or maybe waiting for their own new life to begin one fine day in the world of some distant future.

In any event, he told himself, this is where I must stay. And for the first time in years I'm no longer alone.

Epilogue

Thirteen-year-old Roma Langelli had changed since she witnessed the attack. When she'd sat at her computer, watching images from the webcam located in a sewer beneath London's streets, Roma had watched in horror as the youth had blundered through the tunnel, his feet splashing the water, as uncanny figures had pursued him to his death.

Roma's thing about webcams never left her. In fact, her interest became an obsession. Now she spends every free moment in her room. The vastness of Wyoming's plains beyond her bedroom window might have been nothing but a landscape painted on the glass panes. It was what she saw through the window of her computer screen that was important now. Night and day it revealed views of the entire world via the millions of webcams fixed to walls in offices, bars, shopping malls, zoos, city streets, airports, mountainsides – you name it. Tonight her brothers played their guitars in the next room but she gazed at the screen with such avidity that those howling Fenders might have been nothing more than a breeze whispering through a meadow. The webcam she'd accessed showed a view along Broadway in New York. The street blazed with light, yellow cabs buzzed too and fro; the pavements were awash with men and women. The camera must have been set around ten feet from the ground so the store fronts were clearly visible. New York is a clean city these days; vandals and graffiti artists have been forced out into the suburbs by intensive policing. So Roma was surprised to see the writing on the wall:

VAMPIRE SHARKZ
☺ They're coming to get you ☺